NEW HISTORICAL VOICE CONTEST WINNER!

"A Stolen Time is a romance with some true grit . . . an amazing debut!"
—Pamela Britton, bestselling author of Seduced

◆

AN OLD ACQUAINTANCE

Janet smothered a smile. With thick black hair hanging down to his shoulders, the man who'd just been fighting looked like a shaggy dog. Now the blood was gone, she could see he had a dark complexion, a strong nose and jaw, eyes the color of . . . a . . . she felt the blood drain from her face and a roaring in her ears. He was . . . oh, damnation!

This was the vile lawman who'd shot her. Her hand grabbed her throat; God, she couldn't breathe! She took a step back. Her horse was at the livery, she could—

"Miss, are you all right?"

She stopped, halted in place by the concern in his eyes. Her heart hammered so loudly he'd surely hear it. But he couldn't. Her brain started to work—he'd said *Miss*. He didn't know her.

And if she didn't make a fool of herself, he'd never guess.

A STOLEN TIME

◆

SHARI BOULLION

LEISURE BOOKS **NEW YORK CITY**

A LEISURE BOOK®

July 2003

Published by

Dorchester Publishing Co., Inc.
276 Fifth Avenue
New York, NY 10001

ISBN 0-8439-5229-6

Visit us on the web at www.dorchesterpub.com.

A STOLEN
TIME

Prologue

Northern California
Spring 1861

"Watch that beard, girl." The leader of the Garret gang shifted in his saddle and frowned at Janet.

"Yes, Pa." Janet Garret cautiously wiped the cold rain from her bushy blond beard and pulled her hat lower to shield her face. Beneath her, the mare stamped impatiently, and Janet stroked its wet neck with sympathy. Why couldn't Pa pick sunny days for roadwork? How'd he like to have *his* beard falling off?

Last year her beard had dropped like a dead muskrat on the boardwalk right outside the bank they were robbing. Pa had grumbled for days about how close they'd come to having the youngest Garret revealed as a female. Her brother, Clint, had teased her unmercifully until she'd had to smack him good. Gave him a black eye, she remembered with satisfaction.

She turned to Clint to badger him, then sat back in the saddle. Pa didn't like chatter before an ambush,

1

although 'twas hard to hold her tongue when she was excited.

Taking a deep breath of snow-scented air, she tried to settle down. Spring had arrived late this year in the northern California mountains. Beneath imposing pines, the last stubborn pockets of snow were slowly melting under the relentless rain. A gust of wind shook icy showers from the trees and Janet shivered. Hellfire! If they sat here much longer, her hands would go numb, and then she'd probably drop her gun and blow the wrong person out of the saddle.

Then through the muffling rain came a jingle of harness, and her hands tightened on the reins. Anticipation and fear churned in her stomach as she sucked in a breath.

Her father straightened in the saddle. " 'Bout time. Damned pack trains are getting slower every year. Janet, Clint, weapons out."

Clint grinned and drew his pistol.

Janet slid her Colt out of the holster and moved her horse into the center of the road, behind her massive father.

Tall and lean, Clint took up his usual position beside her, pulling his face into a tough scowl. She suppressed the urge to taunt him by telling him how sweet he looked.

The splatter of hooves and the creaking of leather harnesses announced the approach of the mule train. Down from the mountain gold mines, the pack animals would be carrying the first sacks of gold ore of the year. The loot would be ample, and Pa had promised them a trip to San Francisco to celebrate.

Her pa pulled his shotgun from the saddle holster and readied himself. A shudder ran through Janet at the sight of the huge double-barrels. "Only a fool draws on a shotgun," Pa would say, willing to sacrifice the extra shots of a revolver for the intimidation of the shotgun.

Head down, trudging wearily, the first mule appeared over the hill, then the next, and on and on. About ten or so animals, she calculated, burdened heavily. Pa had learned that the man who usually rode shotgun had busted a leg, so they had only one man to contend with.

A burly mule skinner rode the lead mule. He jerked erect at the sight of the three mounted outlaws. "Whoa!"

"Don't try anything funny, mister," Pa shouted. He aimed the shotgun squarely at the mule skinner, whose mud-streaked face turned white. "Give us four sacks of dust and you can keep your life."

"Don't shoot, dammit. You'll get your gold." The skinner spat out his wad, then slid slowly off the mule. "Just gimmie time ta unload it."

Janet grimaced as the man moved like molasses toward the mules. She hated the risk involved in road holdups, especially now that the gang was reduced to three. She'd tried to talk Pa into a quick store robbery, but to no avail. He loved gold.

As the mule skinner inched down the line, Pa squinted into the gray mist over the rise. "We won't be able to see anyone coming till they're here," he muttered. "I'll stand watch. You two go'n help. Make sure we get gold, and not flour or ore or somethin'."

Flour. Like she was an idiot! Janet slid from her horse, then followed the mule skinner. Next to the man's bulk, she felt like a midget. Clint holstered his gun and grabbed the reins of the Garrets' two pack-horses, tied at the edge of the road.

Walking slowly, the mule skinner fumbled to untie a pack.

"I'll get this'un," Janet growled in her lowest, har-shest voice, to make up for her lack of height.

Clint handed Janet the reins of a packhorse. She pulled out her knife to cut the lashings holding the sacks in place. The mule skinner moved to the next mule with her brother. Clint began on that one. Not volunteering to help, the skinner made his way back to the front of the train and leaned against his mule.

Cursing the tough, wet rope securing the bags, Ja-net pulled it tighter.

Dumb mules. If the stupid animals moved faster, they wouldn't have to load the plunder onto their horses; they could have just rode off leading the mules. She heard splashing coming from behind her. Clint must have managed to load his horse and was headed back to help her.

"Come on, you blasted rope," she swore, and finally the knife cut through. The gold sacks dropped to the ground, splattering mud everywhere. The animal shied back, jostling the other mules, setting off an an-noyed braying.

"Shut up, dammit!" She hauled the sacks out of the mud and heaved them onto the packhorse, securing them with a quick tie.

Suddenly, a pistol blasted, then the distinctive roar of Pa's shotgun sounded. The horrendous echoes rolled through the mountains.

"Pa!" Pulling out her revolver, she ran forward, then drew up short.

Cussing in a low voice, Pa leaned heavily on his

saddle horn, glaring at the mule skinner, who was facedown in the mud. A pistol lay beside the downed man, a curl of smoke trickling from the barrel.

Had the skinner hit anyone? Janet's gaze darted around. Clint was unhurt. Pa? She moved toward him. "Pa, are you all right?"

The mountain echoes died. "I—" In the sudden silence, her father's shotgun hit the wet road with a splash. His jacket gaped open, his shirt stained bright red.

"Dear God!" She grabbed his arm to check the wound.

He shoved her hands away. "Get the packhorses." His voice sounded rusty, like it hadn't been used in years.

"But—"

"Dammit, girl, grab the gold so this trip won't be fer nothin'!"

Her heart thudded like a blacksmith's hammer, but years of control proved her equal to the task. She snatched the reins of the packhorse, yanked him over to her horse and mounted.

Clint came alongside with the other packhorse. "Let's ride."

As they spurred their horses up the rise, Janet heard galloping horses behind them, then, a minute later, shouting, and her heart sank.

Once they had cleared the rise, the trio rode partway down the road and then turned off onto a small deer trail they'd scouted the day before. While Janet and Pa waited impatiently, Clint took a branch and scraped and filled in the deep muddy hoofprints. When he finished, just the brush marks could be seen.

Only an expert tracker would notice the signs of their leaving the road.

The deep pine needles on the ground muffled the sound of the horses' hooves as they made their way through the forest. Over the clank of the bridles and the creak of the saddles, Janet heard her father's harsh breathing. "Pa, are you all right?"

After a moment, he replied, "I got to stop."

Clint looked around, his face white in the thin winter light. "All right, Pa. Hold on just a few more feet. There's a clearing ahead."

They emerged into a small glade and pulled their horses to a halt. Like a felled oak, Pa toppled from the saddle. The heartrending groan he gave when he landed terrified Janet. Her pa never moaned, never winced, never admitted to being hurt.

"Oh, no; oh, no . . . please, Pa" She threw herself from the saddle, scrambled to his side and dropped to her knees beside him. Blood saturated his favorite fleece-lined jacket. With fingers gone numb, she fumbled for the buttons of his jacket.

"Clint! Fetch a shirt and water from my saddlebags."

She glanced up to see her brother standing stockstill. "Now, dammit!"

Giving up on the buttons, she ripped the jacket and shirt open. "Noooo," she moaned under her breath. Too much blood, too big a hole, too near the heart. How had he been able to ride at all?.

"Oh, Pa." Clint's face tightened at the sight. He dropped an old shirt and the waterbag into her lap. "I tied the horses. We can't stay long, sis."

"We need to stop the bleeding," she said urgently, talons of grief already ripping at her. Pa turned his head and coughed, a gurgling, horrible sound. Frothy blood bubbled over his lips and down the gray beard, and she knew her father was losing the battle for survival.

"Janet." She could barely hear him, her giant father whose idea of a whisper was a loud shout. He glared at her, angry at his own weakness. "I'm not gonna make it, girl."

"You will, Pa!" Determinedly, she jammed the old shirt hard against his chest. "You can't quit on me!"

The makeshift dressing turned red under her fingers, his blood spilling hot across her cold fingers.

"Clint," the old man growled, then coughed again, weaker this time.

"Yes, Pa." Janet's brother sank to his knees and took his father's hand. He cleared his throat twice before asking, "What can I do?"

"Take Janet and—" His voice hitched. When his eyes searched mistily upward, Janet leaned forward. "Janet, yes. Child, promise me you'll go straight."

"But, Pa!"

"No buts! Promised your ma afore . . . she died . . . cut you loose . . . see you off outlaw trail." He wet his lips. "Couldn't do it. But now . . . you're a woman. You don't belong . . . you should marry, have children."

Her jaw dropped open. Marry! The blood loss must have fuzzed his brain. But he was gritting his teeth, awaiting her answer. He was losing more blood, hurting himself.

"Sure, Pa, I'll do whatever you say," she promised hastily.

Next to her, Clint choked out, "But we're a team, a—"

7

She shot him a glare.

"All right, you bastards, reach for them clouds above!" The deep shout blasted through the clearing like thunder.

Janet jerked her head around. Her haunting nightmare of capture took on the terrifying form and figure of two men.

Two big men. They stalked out of the darkening forest, pistols already out and aimed. The first, a slim man with brown hair and a brown hat, sidled off to her left.

The next man, like a harbinger of death, was dressed all in black, holding a Colt Dragoon as if the weapon were an extension of his arm. Janet couldn't pull her eyes from the ominous star on his shoulder. A marshal.

He glanced at her frozen brother, then moved to stand next to her. The lines in his darkly tanned face showed experience, a bad thing in a lawman. A trim black mustache emphasized stubborn lips and a hard chin; not someone who would back away from a fight. His broad shoulders and lean, muscular build discouraged any thought of jumping him.

Face averted, she pulled her hat lower, grateful for the black grease, mud and massive beard that were part of her disguise.

With eyes the gray of a winter sky and an expressionless face, he stared down at her father. "So, Garret, looks like you caught one. The mule skinner nail you?"

"He did, the lucky bastard." Pa gave a hissing laugh, then lifted his chin, brows drawn together. "Be truthful, lawman. I'm dead, aren't I?"

8

He showed no fear at all, and Janet felt pride intermingle with grief.

The marshal's strong jaw tightened; then he nodded. "You are. Appears like the bullet hit your lung."

Janet's grip tightened on the bloody bandage until her knuckles whitened. So cold this lawman was, cold and hard as the mountain ice pack.

"G-give me a minute with my children."

The man in black's gaze met Janet's for a moment, his eyes piercing and painful. Biting her lip hard, she stifled the sobs rising in her throat. She felt betraying tears shining in her eyes and blinked. Men didn't cry, outlaws didn't cry, she wouldn't cry.

Rubbing his trim black mustache, the marshal glanced at Clint, then sighed. "Hell . . . all right. Toss your guns over there." He motioned with his pistol toward the edge of the clearing.

Feeling like she was ripping away her arm, Janet threw her revolver. Clint's pistol landed beside hers, far too far away.

"A few minutes only." The marshal stepped away from them and the brown-haired man joined him. While she pressed the cloth against her father's chest, Janet listened with one ear to the two men arguing. Seemed to her the younger one disagreed with the lawman's decision—

"Are you mad as a loon? Let's hog-tie them while we got the chance."

"Their pa's dying."

"Better him than us."

"I can't deny a man the right to say good-bye to his children."

"And I always thought I was the softhearted fool. You take the prize." The brown-haired one kicked at the mud, then stood scowling, his fingers tense on the butt of his pistol.

For Janet, time seemed to stand still. The insolent wind threw rain in her face until she knew her tears could flow without notice, but she forced them back. Pa didn't want her to cry, and his eyes were fastened on her face like a halter to life.

Her breath came in hard, tearing shudders as she watched the life empty from him in a relentless stream. She wanted to scream, to make time stop, to go back to yesterday, when they were laughing around the campfire. His blood was like fire flowing across her knuckles, and his face darkened as if night had fallen.

For a second Pa seemed to rally. His fingers fumbled, then pulled Clint's hand against his side, against the six-gun still holstered there. Janet gasped.

"Shhhh." Clint frowned at her. His fingers closed around the handle of the gun. "Got it, Pa."

"Get Pa's hideout gun," he murmured. His gaze flickered to the two men talking quietly a few feet away, then to Pa's boot.

"I—" Janet closed her eyes a moment. Her stomach twisted into a tight knot. She'd never had to kill anyone, never even shot anyone, and these weren't men who would be stopped with anything less than death.

Clint's eyes met hers across their father. She firmed her lips and nodded. Resting her hand on Pa's shoulder, she surreptitiously curled her fingers around the pistol tucked into his boot.

"Good." Pa sighed. The wrinkles around his eyes eased into peace. His breathing changed, roughened like a green-broke bronco, halting, jerking, slowing. "Oh, hell—" His body spasmed, then went limp.

In anguished disbelief, she watched the clear blue of his eyes change, muddy into death.

"Oh, God, Pa." Clint's breath hitched; then he yelled, "Now!" He snatched up Pa's pistol and fired at the marshal.

Even as Janet jerked at Pa's other gun, she heard the sickening smack of a bullet hitting flesh, a grunt from the lawman. As if kicked by a mule, the marshal spun backward into the mud.

The other one roared, "Goddamn you!" and shot at Clint. Janet choked as her brother fell sideways, arm streaming blood.

"No!" She yanked and pulled, and the pistol finally came free of Pa's boot. She lurched to her feet. Her vision narrowed to the cursing man who aimed at Clint again. In her mind, she heard her father's voice. "Always shoot to wound; the Garret gang doesn't kill." Without even aiming, she lowered the barrel slightly and pulled the trigger.

The gun bucked in her hand. Garish blood and white bone exploded from the man's leg, and she stared in horror. His gun dropped from his hand and he fell to the ground.

"I—oh, God—what have I—"

Something tore into her chest; pain erupted like fire and she staggered a step back. Jaw clenched against a scream, she raised her pistol. The lawman—

The marshal, wavering on his knees, leveled his gun at her.

She shot him. A fresh burst of blood erupted from his shoulder and he went down.

She gagged, sick in heart and body. Forcing her eyes away from the unmoving, gory remnants of men, she turned to look for her brother. Her left arm wouldn't

11

move, and she spared a glance down, then looked away. Too much red.

"Clint?" Her ears ringing, she staggered, blinked at her brother. "You're alive?" He was on his feet, blood running down an arm, but the wound wasn't mortal. She glanced back at the bodies behind them and shivered. "Let's get out of here. The shots will attract anyone around."

She holstered Pa's revolver, then shoved Clint toward the horses and helped him mount. Wide-eyed, her horse shied away. Cursing behind gritted teeth, one arm agonizing and useless, she pulled herself up in her saddle.

Turning for one last look at Pa, she froze. *That marshal just wouldn't die!* Shirtfront bathed in red, he was standing. He staggered sideways, but the pistol pointed at her was dead steady. Desperately, she spurred her horse.

The blast of a pistol sounded.

Chapter One

Fall 1861

"Marshal! Marshal Blackthorne, look what we found!" Peter skidded to a halt in front of Dagger's desk.

"And what have you brought me?" Marshal Dagger Blackthorne set down his ink pen and grinned at the grubby boy and girl bouncing up and down in the jail office.

The nine-year-old boy dropped a muddy kitten onto the desk. "See?"

"Ah." Dagger glanced at the filthy footprints the animal left on the query he'd planned to send to San Francisco. Looks like he'd have to rewrite the letter.

"Isn't it darling?" Amelia's big blue eyes shone with delight.

Dagger picked up the cat. Pretty young; it fit right into his hand. "Where'd you find this one?"

"In the schoolyard. Meowing." Amelia reached out to run a hand down the dirty fur. "I don't think it's been eating. It's awful skinny."

"Appears that way." Dagger could feel each tiny rib under the thin coat. Given a chance to bathe, the beastie might be white, and it had blue eyes almost the color of little Amelia's. "Looks to be about a couple months old, I'd say. In the schoolyard, huh?"

He pulled out his pocket watch and checked the time. "Shouldn't y'all be in class right now?"

"Nah. Miss Tate done quit," Amelia said.

"She what?"

"Yeah, Marshal. When she found that rattler in her desk, she got all upset," Peter said earnestly. Amelia giggled, her eyes dancing with mischief.

"A rattlesnake?" Dagger assessed the gray autumn day through the window and frowned. "A mite late for a rattler to be around, isn't it?"

"Pike found one all snugged down in a hole when they were digging a new privy, so he put it in Teacher's desk." Peter chortled. "You should have heard her scream!"

Dagger winced, surprised she wasn't at the door demanding he do something about the miscreants. A born and bred easterner, the schoolmarm had been in his office—in spite of her fear of him—every other day, insisting he control her pupils. He'd heard that scream of hers a time or two. What child could resist trying to provoke one of those amazing shrill wails?

Still, he was a man of the law. He attempted to pull his mouth into the necessary firm line. "You know she could have been seriously hurt, don't you?"

"Oh, hell, Marshal," Peter protested. "Since she never comes early to start the fire, the room was cold as a witch's tit. That snake was dead asleep; hardly rattled, even when she dropped the drawer."

The image was too vivid and he choked back a

laugh. "Ah, right. Well, then, I guess I'll take this little one home and feed it. Either of you need a cat?" he asked hopefully. He set the cat down clear of his papers.

They shook their heads. "We asked Mama," Amelia confided, "and she said we'd already 'dopted two of your strays and not to let you sweet-talk us into any more."

"Well, shoot." He'd rather have a good gunfight than end up with any more abandoned animals, but as marshal in Shasta, California, both activities were part of his job. And he had no talent for talking to people. Hell, most of the townspeople acted like he was going to shoot them—or scalp them.

Damn his brother Bowie for not warning him of all the extra duties of a small town marshal.

" 'Bye, Marshal." The children jostled out of the office, laughing and shoving, obviously planning what mischief they'd create now that school was out.

School. Dagger raked his hand through his hair and scowled. Now the town would have to find a new teacher, an impossible task with the school year already begun. The head of the school board, Arnie, would probably be stopping by later, expecting him to attend some meeting to discuss this most recent fiasco.

With a sigh, he scooped the kitten off his desk and snuggled it in one arm. "You surely made a mess of my letter." His gaze was caught by the last sentence he'd finished: *Any word on the location of the Garret gang?*

So far, all his inquiries as to the gang's whereabouts had gone unanswered. After the shoot-out last spring they'd disappeared like ghosts. A bit poorer, as they'd left the gold behind, and each had been packing a bullet. Dagger's only regret was that the blond bastard who'd shot Blade hadn't caught the lead in his black heart.

But he'd fix that error yet. The two remaining members of the Garret gang would come to rue the day they'd crossed his path. The kitten's claws dug into his chest like the bitter memories dug into his soul. On that day Dagger had shown mercy, and they'd repaid him by crippling his brother. He'd never make that mistake again.

No mercy, no regrets.

Now what would she do?

Janet glared at the Whiskeytown express office where she'd picked up Clint's letter, then turned and stomped back down Main Street.

Main Street, hah! The so-called street was just a wide spot where men walked between the mishmash of tents and lean-tos. Buildings were abandoned and falling down since the miners flocked to the new silver fields in Colorado. She skirted one of the holes left by a gold hunter and ignored a miner's "Howdy."

Her skirt dragged in the dust of the road, dirtying the dull green material. With a grimace, she pulled the waist right again, wishing futilely to be back in her comfortable trousers. But no one would ever expect a Garret to wear a skirt, let alone have a bosom. Shoot, her chest kept startling her, the way it stuck out.

She deliberately bumped into another ogling, woman-starved miner and relieved him of his money pouch. Unaware, the stout man continued down the dirt path, his head plainly spinning at the unaccustomed contact with a soft female form. Janet dropped the pouch into her capacious skirt pocket.

With a hastily suppressed swagger, she continued down the street. Maybe a woman's garb wasn't such a bad notion after all. The miner hadn't even noticed his pocket being picked. Pa had been right; outlaws were a special breed, not like these slow-witted, civilized folk.

She winced at the memory of Pa, that hasty promise she'd made to go straight. But he'd been confused . . . surely.

Her next victim, wearing a red velvet gown with appallingly ample cleavage displayed, crossed the street toward her, reticule dangling from her waist. Janet thumbed her tiny knife open and glanced around, feigning being lost. She pretended to see her destination and started off quickly, so quickly she ran into the red-haired woman. The scent of cheap lilac perfume made her choke, but she still managed to cut the purse string and tuck the woman's reticule into her pocket.

Continuing on her way, Janet shook her head at the ease of it all. Much easier than the dramatic robberies her brother had favored. Tossing her long braid over her shoulder, she scanned the street for her next prospect.

"Ma, Ma!" Two little tykes dashed after the prostitute she'd just robbed. "Can we come with you to get food?"

The woman sighed, running a hand over her forehead. Janet frowned, taking a closer look. The woman looked exhausted. She was also rail thin, as were the two children.

The soiled dove gave her children a wavering smile. "We can go together, but remember, Sammy, we don't have much money. We'll only be getting some beans."

Not even enough money for bacon? Well, hell, the woman was even lower on her luck than Janet. Shaking her head, Janet veered into the street, near where the woman had crossed.

With a subtle movement, she let the reticule drop from her pocket. "Oh!"

The woman and children looked up at the outcry. "Ma'am, did you drop your reticule?"

The woman fumbled at her waist and found nothing. With a startled sound, she ran across the road. "It *is* mine," she said, her face still blank with shock. She took the pouch and held it to her powdered bosom. "I can't thank you enough!"

Janet nodded, ignoring the low growl from her stomach. Citizens were one thing, little 'uns another. She hadn't sunk low enough to deprive children of food. Not yet, anyway.

But Clint's letter had been mailed from a San Francisco jail. Might be her fortunes would be dropping much lower. Acquiring more money than a couple of bits here and there took a gang.

She tried not to let her mind dwell on how idiotic her brother must have been to try to rob anyone in the city. Yerba Buena used to be a peaceful little town, but when gold was found the place was renamed San Francisco and reborn as a civilized port city. They actually had a jail there now. Pa had always moved on when a town built a jail; he'd said the officials would be looking to fill it.

And they'd done just that with her youngest brother. He shouldn't have left her; how could she watch over him? They hadn't been so low on cash that he needed to try a city, no matter what he thought. He could have waited a little longer till, she'd recovered and could ride.

She detoured around another miner's hole and crossed the road. Her horse was tied in front of the large tent that served as a grocery in the mining town. Her right shoulder ached and she rubbed it. The bullet she took last spring had left her with a nasty scar and some achy muscles. The doc told her the muscles had been blown to bits. Shoot, she could have told him that and saved herself a couple of dollars.

Brownie whinnied quietly when she walked up. "Well, old girl," Janet murmured, "where should we go now?" She'd been staying with an old woman whose house Pa had used a time or two. "We've pretty much used up the money Clint gave us before he left. And now he'll be in jail a while." Jail! That stupid boy.

She rubbed the mare's forelock. "You have anyplace in particular you'd like to visit?"

As she stared glumly at the road, a man and woman crossed in front of her. She glanced at the man, then looked again. He was so big, he made the burly miners around him look like children. He wasn't wearing the usual slouch hat of the miners, but a rancher's wide-brimmed hat. The lady with him had on a blue-green calico dress and a bonnet that matched her eyes, and a pang of envy stabbed Janet. The woman's clothes fit as well as Janet's didn't.

"I'll get us some vittles for the trip back at the grocery," the man said to his . . . wife, Janet decided, seeing the wedding band on the woman's hand.

"You're a brave man. Between unwashed miners and old meat, the stench in there is worse than your sheep pen after a week's rain." The woman grinned at him

19

and batted her eyes. "Can you get me something sweet, my darling?"

The big man laughed. "Hannah should never have given you those flirting lessons. You were hard enough to deal with before." Then he gave her a puzzled look. "I thought you didn't like candy."

"I just . . . feel like having some today." The woman smiled as the man snorted. He strode into the tent serving as a grocery. The woman took a seat on a massive log laying beside the road.

A loud yell drew Janet's attention. Dust billowed up from a noisy fracas in the road. After a minute of trying to sort out the various arms and legs, she realized two husky boys were pounding on a small lad.

"Yer a bastard! Your mama didn't have no husband!"

Janet frowned. Being a bastard seemed to be a poor reason to have bodily harm inflicted upon one. But the bigger boys were certainly winning. She smiled slowly, pleased she had a way to work off some of her irritation at Clint.

Two steps put her behind the big boys. She grabbed one by his collar and with a twist of her wrist tossed him in the dust behind her. He landed with a high-pitched yell and a puff of dust. The other burly boy turned, enabling her to grab his ear. She pulled, and he followed his ear right up onto his tippy-toes.

"I do believe you should apologize and then leave this little lad alone," Janet admonished him. Damned if she didn't sound like her mother had. The thought made her smile.

Blocking his punch with her free arm, she gave his ear a twist.

"Ow! All right, ma'am, all right!"

20

"Apology, please?"

His mouth in a sullen pout, he mumbled, "I apologize, Matt."

Still on the ground, little Matt nodded. "S'okay."

"Very nice," Janet said. "Now take yourself off." She gave him a hard push to start him on his way.

She turned to check on the other bully. He lay facedown in the dirt, much closer than where she'd thrown him. The lady who'd been with the rancher was standing right next to him, one foot on his back. Looked like the lady had kept the boy from attacking from the rear. Janet was shocked. Kids or not, she should never have forgotten to watch her back.

The woman fastidiously brushed dust off her skirts before giving the rascal a nudge in the rear with her boot. "I think you should follow your friend's example."

He raised his face from the dirt and turned to glare at the woman. She smiled sweetly at him.

He glared at Janet. She smiled sweetly at him, too.

With a low growl of rage, he pushed himself to his feet and ran off after his friend.

Reaching down, Janet pulled the small boy to his feet. "Are you hurt, child?"

"No, ma'am." He wiped the tears from his eyes hastily. "Thank you."

"You're welcome. Do you—"

But the child had turned and darted off in the opposite direction from the two bullies.

Janet shook her head. "It's hard being little."

"Or alone," the other woman murmured.

The two women exchanged a look of perfect understanding.

"I'm Susanna Blackthorne."

"I'm Janet . . . Danner. Uh, thanks for your help."

Susanna had a low, infectious laugh that made Janet smile. "You know, I've found the nicest people interfere in fights and then forget to watch their backs. It was a pleasure to be able to help. Really." Janet saw from her face that she meant it.

This was a woman unlike any lady Janet had ever met. Most women would be far too dignified to interfere, would never have risked themselves by tripping a bully.

"I didn't realize there were any women up here. Are you mining?" Susanna asked.

Janet shook her head. "This is the closest mail drop to where I've been staying."

Susanna resumed her seat on the log, smoothing her skirts with enviable skill. "A mining camp isn't a good place for a woman alone." A dimple appeared in her cheek as she added wryly, "Trust me, I know."

At her inviting gesture, Janet sat down beside her. "Well, since I have my mail, I'll be . . ." Doing what? She'd brought her few belongings out of Millie's house, thinking Clint would have written where he'd be headed. Instead, there'd be no meeting. "I'll be moving on, maybe to the city, I guess. There's work there." Better pickings.

The pickings in Whiskeytown were a bit thin and the population too low for safety. Janet looked quizzically at her new friend's clean skin. "How about you? Are you mining?"

"No. My husband brought me up from Shasta to see the mine he and his brothers invested in last year. The men talked so much about the place that I wanted to see what it looked like." She smirked a little and motioned to a wagon tied up nearby. "I also got a good profit on some vegetables."

Janet imitated the woman's earlier gesture and smoothed her own skirts. There was so much to being a woman that she hadn't learned. Her times in dresses had been few and far between ever since Pa had figured out she was safer being a man. "You sell vegetables?"

"Yes. I like to garden," Susanna said.

"Oh. I've never tried that." Although most people had at least a little plot.

Susanna pursed her lips. "I'm sure you have other talents. You know, you were very good with those children." Suddenly a sparkle lit her eyes and she leaned forward. "What kind of an education do you have? Can you read and write? Read and write really well?"

"Of course," Janet said with assurance. Her mother, although she'd fallen for a dashing outlaw, had been a lady. She'd taught her children their letters and even made Pa bust into bookstores for the classics. Evenings, they took turns reading around the campfire. With a pang of loss, Janet remembered how Ma'd been partial to Edgar Allan Poe's *Nevermore*. "Why do you ask?"

"Well, our schoolteacher up and quit; she ran back East last week. The whole town's upset, especially since school's already started. You're looking for work, correct?"

"A schoolteacher?" Janet was stunned. Although she'd made that promise to Pa to go straight, she'd never really thought much about it. But this . . .

A schoolteacher was a more-than-respectable job. Could she, who'd never attended a day of school, take on a position like that? She sat for a moment, dazed with the possibilities, seeing herself actually a member of a town, greeted politely by people, needed by the community. Her mouth went dry as a whole new world opened in front of her—a world she had never thought to enter.

Sure, she knew she could never truly be a town citizen. Pa had made it perfectly clear that outlaws were a breed apart, would fit into a civilized society like wolves in a sheep flock. But teaching would be . . . oh, somehow it just sounded so tantalizing.

Janet pulled her braid forward and played with the end. Life had taught her never to accept something that came too easily. Best find out the hitch. "Why did the teacher leave?"

"Hmmm. Some of the older boys are a trifle feisty, and Miss Gable was an Easterner." Susanna laughed ruefully. "The boys had her stampeded before the first day was out."

She gave Janet a level look. "Somehow I don't think that would be a problem for you."

Janet's mind worked furiously. A place to hole up until Clint was out, and a way to keep her promise to Pa, at least for a time.

She wanted this job.

What would she have to do, to say, to get it? "I was a teacher for a short time down south," she said smoothly.

Her ability to lie had been finely honed by a master of the craft. Pa took pride in the fact that he'd never had to kill anyone. He said duping a person took much more skill than shooting him, and Janet did love being skillful.

"I quit my job when Pa took sick." Uh-oh, she

thought; refined people said "Papa" or "my father." "My father died just recently." She didn't have to contrive the tears, which sprang to her eyes under Susanna's sympathetic look. "I—I found I enjoy the mountains," she said truthfully. "A job teaching out here might be perfect."

Susanna's eyes were steady on Janet, a glimmer of doubt in them; then she shrugged and said, "This is the West, land of new opportunities and new beginnings." She tilted her head. "Having an experienced teacher would certainly please the members of the school board. When do you think you could start?"

"Hmmm. I would think immediately. Of course, I'd need to find lodgings."

"Well, this might work out very nicely. The school board had already arranged for the teacher to be housed at Priscilla Malvern's boardinghouse. I don't think she's had a chance to let the room out yet, since it's on the women's side."

Susanna turned at the sound of footsteps behind them. "Bowie, guess what? I think we've got a teacher for the school! Oh, Miss Danner, may I present my husband, Bowie Blackthorne?"

"Pleased to meet you," Janet murmured, suppressing the urge to offer a handshake. Something about him looked familiar, although she was sure she'd have remembered meeting someone his size before.

"Ma'am," he said, touching his hat brim. He turned his gaze back to his wife and chided, "Susanna, you can't just give her the job. There are—"

Susanna raised her eyebrows. "Why not? Lord knows we need a schoolteacher. I haven't seen anyone else coming forward with a prospect."

"She still has to go before the school board and get

formally hired. That's the way it works."

"Spavined snails, dam—" Susanna muttered.

She wrinkled her nose at her husband's murmured, "None of that in public."

Janet watched the two in astonishment. She'd never met a couple like this before. Susanna seemed a lady in all respects, but she swore and she fought. She had a core of toughness and independence Janet hadn't seen in a woman before. And her husband, for all his size, clearly doted on her.

A trickle of longing eased through Janet. No man had ever looked at her like Blackthorne looked at his wife. Shoot, aside from her brothers, most of the men she'd met thought she was a man, too.

"So, how long will it take them to hire her?" Susanna demanded.

Blackthorne stroked his mustache. "Arnie sounded rather desperate; could be they'll hire her right away. But they have to have all the members present for a vote."

Susanna pouted and kicked at a dirt clod under her feet. "Well, spit. Dagger was going to take that prisoner of his south; who knows when he'll be back. As slow as people move, our son"—she patted her stomach—"will be too old for school by the time we get a teacher."

Blackthorne straightened as his darkly tanned face turned an odd color of purple.

"Our what?" His roar stopped everything on the street. "Susanna!" A horse broke loose from the hitching rail and fled down the road.

"Um . . ." Susanna frowned down at her hands. "Well, that just slipped out. I wasn't planning to tell you quite like this."

He raised her chin so he could look into her eyes. "Are you serious?" he whispered in a husky voice.

"It might not be a boy, you know."

"Hell, who cares!" He threw his hat into the air with a howl of glee. Another horse neighed in protest and headed south.

Janet shook her head. If someone didn't shut the man up, there wouldn't be any saddle stock left in Whiskeytown.

After a moment, he sobered. "Miss Danner, would you care to ride down with us to Shasta? I'll talk with the school board and get them moving. Dagger said he'd be back today in time to see Blade off."

He grinned at his wife. "The matter of hiring a schoolteacher has just increased in priority."

27

Chapter Two

In front of the stagecoach office of Shasta, California, Dagger waited for his brother to limp across the road. Cane in hand, Blade slowly made his way toward the stage, detouring around the deeper ruts.

Dagger's teeth clenched every time Blade put weight on his injured knee, each time he faltered.

Finally turning away, Dagger tossed his brother's satchel up to the driver to stow away. "Take it easy over those ruts, won't you, Hank?"

"Sure thing, Marshal."

Standing beside the coach, Blade growled a curse under his breath, and Dagger winced. He knew how much Blade hated being treated like an invalid, but damned if he could help it. His mouth dry, he cleared his throat of the bitterness of loss. "Looks like it's time to move out."

"Looks like." Blade held out a hand, softened now by lack of labor.

Dagger took it firmly in his, took a last look at his younger brother, the faded tan, the way his clothes hung loosely. Dammit, Blade shouldn't return to school yet. "Are you sure—"

"Yes, you worrywart of an Injun, I'm sure!" The laugh lines around Blade's eyes erased some of the lines of pain. "And I'll be returning to the medical school with a much better knowledge of the *other* side of the scalpel. My future patients should appreciate all the hard-earned experience, eh?"

The lump in Dagger's gut hardened. It was his fault that Blade had that kind of experience. Why hadn't he checked old Garret for weapons? "Bowie and Susanna aren't—"

"They said good-bye this morning before they headed up the mountain."

"All right, then." Dagger stepped back far enough to let Blade enter the coach, close enough to grab him if he fell. He was rewarded for his concern with a hard elbow to his already churning stomach. Holding the stage door from moving, he waited while his brother took a seat.

After propping up his leg on the seat, Blade flashed him a grin. "Never thought you'd turn into such a nursemaid."

"Just . . . take care of yourself."

"Don't be such a stump. You're the one who lives by the gun." Blade leaned out to yell, "Hank! Let's be about it!"

"Gee-up!" A crack of the lash and the stage lurched forward.

Dagger slammed the door and stepped back. The swirl of dust behind the moving stage felt like his own thoughts. Dry and dusty. Gray.

"Take care, brother," he muttered. Damned if Blade wouldn't be safer back at college anyway. Look what coming home had done for him. He'd been crippled by his big brother's total incompetence. All those years of being a lawman and he'd fallen for their lies like an easy mark. He should have known an outlaw wasn't to be trusted. But he'd been taken in, and his little brother had paid the price.

If Blade had blamed him, the guilt might have been easier to bear. As it was . . .

After the third person greeted him, Dagger realized he was still standing in the hot sun, watching the fading dust trail.

"Hell!" He turned on his heel and stalked toward the Miner's Saloon. Maybe a whiskey would cut the dust, the ache from his throat.

Maybe two.

A time later, Dagger gingerly set another empty glass beside the stack piled on the table before him. He frowned when the glass pile wavered a little and split in two. When had he made two pyramids? He blinked, pleased when the stack firmed right up into one again. Reaching for the half-empty bottle, he noticed his fingers felt numb.

A movement caught his attention. Boots. Two of them moving back and forth. This time the jiggling wasn't caused by his eyes, he decided in satisfaction, no—the owner of the boots was fidgeting. He pushed himself a long way up to see who was so antsy.

"Harv. Good to see you," he said cordially. Damned if the man didn't look surprised. Just because Dagger wasn't as friendly as his brothers didn't mean he couldn't be polite.

"Uh, Marshal . . ." Harv glanced at the stack of glasses, undoubtedly in awe of the skill involved, and cleared his throat. "Damn, man, I've never seen you take more than one—oh, never mind. We've got us an altercation across the street."

Dagger shook his head in admiration at the way *altercation* just rolled off the man's tongue. Downright pretty. "A fight?"

"Yessir. Couple of the Smith boys all likkered up. Got into a ruckus over who'd go upstairs with Happy Hannah." Harv glanced nervously out the door toward his Golden Nugget saloon. "Can you come now, 'fore they tear the place up good?"

Dagger smiled as the chance of a fight cleared his head. He pushed himself to his feet and was pleased when the floor didn't move . . . much. "All right, let's go talk with your would-be loth-lothar—hell, lovers."

As he followed Harv out the door and squinted in the overly bright sunlight, anticipation bit at him. Whiskey hadn't taken away all the frustration or the guilt. Or the loneliness. But a ruckus?

Oh, yes, he'd very much enjoy a good fight. He needed it right now.

"Have you seen the marshal?"

Janet's attention wandered while her new friend Susanna queried the storekeepers along the four-block-long Main Street in Shasta.

Her head was still spinning from the speed of events since she'd agreed to apply for the position of school-teacher. They'd hitched Brownie to the back of the Blackthornes' wagon and headed down the mountain to Shasta.

Pretty little town, at least the town itself. Farther out—well, that was where the miners lived. The long Main Street had side streets branching off filled with nice houses; townies' well-kept houses. The mountains rose on each side, with the miners' shanties straggling up the hillsides like ugly thistles.

The town wasn't quite as busy as it had been three years earlier, she noticed. The bank would probably still hold a fair amount of cash, though; lots of prosperous businesses here. Lord knows her older brother, Harry, had boasted about the haul.

But, no, she was done with that line of work for now. The jingling harness and clop of hooves down the busy street seemed to keep time with the fluttering in her stomach, and her skin tingled in the brisk autumn air. Anticipation of her new job heightened all her senses. She'd played many parts in her life, but this—being a respectable female—would surely be the strangest.

She pulled at her shirtwaist, feeling fidgety in female clothes. Still, dressed in her dark green skirt and discreet white shirtwaist, she figured she looked just as well as the other women on the boardwalk. No one needed to know that two skirts were the sum total of her ladylike wardrobe.

"I saw him . . . uh . . . walk over to the Golden Nugget a few minutes ago," the owner of the dry goods store reported. "But, Miz Susanna, I don't think you should—"

"Come, Janet," Susanna said. "We'll just go and get him. Bowie should have most of the other school board members rounded up by now, but they won't start the meeting without Dagger."

Janet dutifully trailed Susanna down the boardwalk, past several bars, a bookstore . . . the same one where she'd almost been caught. Pa hadn't been pleased with her detour from the bank, and her hide had surely suffered. But the Charles Dickens she'd lifted had been worth it.

She felt a little strange walking so calmly out here in broad daylight among people she'd robbed. Pa had always said it was a mistake for outlaws to mingle with the common run of man. But now she was part of them.

"Ma'am." A man in the pastry shop grinned at her.

She smiled back. Oh, yes, she'd always liked this friendly mountain mining town. Colorful wooden storefronts alternated with buildings of yellow and red brick. Signs hung from the awnings and creaked pleasantly in the mild breeze, while upbeat music floated out of a saloon they passed. She licked her lips. Pity she couldn't wander in there and order a whiskey to buck up her nerves.

"The school's just down that street." Susanna pointed at a quiet tree-lined street. "At the very end."

Janet nodded in feigned approval. "My, yes. The farther from all these bars, the better."

"Exactly. And speaking of bars, there's the Golden Nugget." They crossed the dusty street, stopping once to let a mule train pass slowly by. Janet evaluated it with an experienced eye; goods for the miners up in the mountains. Nothing valuable.

As they stepped up to the boardwalk in front of the bar, Janet heard the high-pitched sound of glass breaking. Something wooden crashed with a thud.

"Oh, dear," Susanna said. She moved to one side of the door, pulling Janet with her. "Last time I heard that kind of noise, a man came—"

A man came flying out the swinging doors. He landed facedown in the muck in front of the saloon. The horses tied on either side shied away.

Janet pushed down a forlorn desire to wade into the brawl and have some fun, too. She gave a ladylike sniff instead. "My, these miners do behave badly, don't they?" She couldn't suppress the smile that pulled at her lips.

Susanna grinned back. "I do love a lively town, don't you?"

Propelled by an unseen force, another man staggered out the door to trip over the first one. "You son-of-a—"

"Jackass!"

The two men sorted themselves out and struggled erect. One spat out dirt, glared at the saloon, then lurched away down the street. The other picked up his hat and set it firmly on his head. Unlike the first, he planted his feet and waited.

"Oh-oh," Janet said. The man looked mad as a caged weasel.

Susanna's hand squeezed Janet's arm. "You don't suppose Dagger is—"

A man swung open the bar doors and stood there, silhouetted like a dark angel in a frame. Against the black shirt, the star on his shoulder glittered viciously. Blood covered his face, leaving only eyes ablaze with anger. "All right, you sumbitch, head for the jail."

"Sure, Marshal," the man answered casually. His hand dove for his gun.

The lawman yanked out a knife and let fly. Steel flashed across the boardwalk and, bellowing loudly, the man fell backward with Dagger's knife buried in his shoulder.

"Hell," the marshal muttered. "Now I got to drag the bastard."

The lawman stepped off the boardwalk and leaned

34

over the downed man. He yanked out the knife, heedless of the gush of blood.

Janet's stomach twisted uneasily at the gory sight. Damned if her guts hadn't been queasy ever since the day Pa died. But the cussed lawman hadn't even winced when he pulled out the blade. Cold bastard.

The marshal grabbed the man's arm and pulled him carelessly to his feet, ignoring the moan of pain, the curse of hatred.

Janet remembered the feel of hands like that, closing on her arm like a hunter's iron trap. The nightmare mingled with the present and her skin chilled. She'd been caught just once . . . but . . . oh, this marshal was like that, like all lawmen. Brutal. Finding pleasure in hurting others. The blast of hatred she felt shocked her.

"Move out." The marshal shoved his prisoner again.

"Damn you!" Suddenly the man turned and slammed a fist into the marshal's jaw. The lawman's head snapped backward. He staggered, tripped over the boardwalk and landed in a sprawl at Janet's feet.

Dazed and bleeding, he looked up at her, and—God help her—she laughed.

His eyes narrowed, and even with his features half-covered with blood, she could sense the menace. Then he shrugged and rubbed his jaw where the skin had split. He wet his lips; the lower one was already puffing up. " 'Scuse me, ma'am. I didn't mean to 'most knock you over," his words slurred together.

He closed his eyes for a second, then pushed himself to his feet and glanced around for his prisoner.

"He's halfway to Sacramento by now," Susanna said.

"Susanna? What are you doing here?" The marshal

straightened further, brushing futilely at his clothes.

Anger gone, Janet couldn't help but delight in his befuddled expression. She'd never seen a lawman so taken by the drink.

Susanna put a hand on his arm. "Are you hurt, Dagger? Your face is covered with blood."

"Nah, I'm fine. Just a gash where he hit me with a bottle."

"Oh, of course," she said in a dry voice. "Only a bottle. Here, wet this down and wipe your face before you scare Miss Danner away."

He took the offered handkerchief and dampened it in the nearby horse trough. The first few swipes over his face yielded an impressive amount of blood, enough so he finally just dunked his entire head in the trough. Coming up drenched, he used the handkerchief to dry off before turning around. "Is that better?"

Janet smothered a smile. With thick black hair hanging down to his shoulders, he looked like a shaggy dog. Now the blood was gone, she could see he had a dark complexion, a strong nose and jaw, eyes the color of . . . a . . . She felt the blood drain from her face and a roaring in her ears. He was . . . oh, hellfire!

This was the bastard lawman who'd shot her. Her hand grabbed her throat; God, she couldn't breathe! She took a step back. Her horse was at the livery, she could—

"Miss, are you all right?"

She stopped, halted in place by the concern in his eyes. Her heart hammered so loudly he'd surely hear it. But he couldn't. Her brain started to work—he'd said *miss*. He didn't know her.

And if she didn't make a jackass of herself, he'd never guess.

She wet her lips and endeavored a smile. "I'm all right now, thank you. That was a bit more blood than I'm familiar with." She certainly couldn't tell him that she hadn't seen that much blood since she blew his buddy's leg to pieces, or that she still had nightmares about that day. New nightmares to add to the old ones. Her nights were a joy to treasure.

"You look much better, Dagger; almost presentable," Susanna pronounced. "Now, Miss Danner, I'd like you to meet the marshal of Shasta City, Dagger Blackthorne. Dagger, this is Miss Danner, who has applied for the position of schoolteacher."

"Ah. I'm pleased to meet you, ma'am," he said. "And you're interested in being our schoolmarm?"

"The school board is to be meeting right now, Dagger," Susanna announced. "That's why we've been looking for you."

"Now?" He sounded appalled.

"Now."

Chapter Three

A few minutes later, at the jailhouse, Dagger did up the last button of his black shirt. He was clean, at least, even if he didn't present a respectable appearance. Not with a fat lip, a gashed forehead and sporting purpling bruises here and there. He slugged down some luke-warm coffee to take the taste of whiskey and blood from his mouth. Why the hell had he gotten into that fight anyway? Fighting wouldn't give Blade back the use of his leg.

Opening the door, he stepped out onto the board-walk. The two women were waiting patiently, speaking in soft voices. Probably snickering at the mighty marshal.

"There you are." Susanna turned at the sound of the door, a wide smile on her lovely face. Her fiery hair was decorously tied back for a change, and Dagger grinned. His conservative brother had bitten off more than he knew when he married this woman. Dagger had to admit to a twinge of jealousy now and then. He didn't like prim and proper misses much, and

Susanna had a wild streak that appealed to him.

He glanced at the woman beside his sister-in-law. Speaking of prim and proper, this young woman had taken the idea and vamoosed with it. She looked like every man's notion of a spinster schoolmarm. Shorter than Susanna, her hair was pulled back into a rigid golden braid.

"Marshal Blackthorne." Miss Danner nodded regally. She seemed extremely pale, her sky-blue eyes wide and a tad nervous. But then, she'd just witnessed a fight and now had to be interviewed by the school board. At least she didn't appear to be a screamer like the other schoolmarm.

He motioned for them to lead the way down the narrow boardwalk and they all started for the school. Dagger hung back slightly, his jaw too sore for him to enjoy talking.

The aches in his bones faded as he focused on the view. He slowly realized that the potential schoolmarm might be short, but she had a nicely trim shape. Her hips moved in an intriguing figure eight under the ankle-length skirt. Pity she was wearing those rigid undergarments that good women considered so necessary.

Dagger dodged a dog and stepped over a pile of horse dung. Unfortunately, Miss Danner didn't seem much different from the teacher who'd just left. How long would this one last? Did she have any idea what she was getting herself into? He stepped up beside her as they approached the schoolhouse. "What experience have—"

She looked up at him, and at the sight of her water-clear blue eyes, eerie cold crawled up his spine. "Miss Danner." He tilted his head, studying her face. A pretty face, really, with what the old ladies called peaches-and-cream skin livened by a spatter of golden freckles across her nose and cheeks. Surely he'd re-member—"Have we met before?"

Her look of dismay at the thought dealt a hefty blow to his ego. "No, absolutely not."

Well, she sounded certain. In fact, her reply seemed a little too vehement. Slowing his step, he eyed her carefully, his lawman's instincts rousing like a panther scenting deer.

A small flush had colored her face a creamy pink. Her lips were folded tightly together, keeping in all sorts of information. Was she hiding something, or just shy? A tingle of enjoyment ran up his spine. Damn but he loved puzzles. "To return to what I was about to ask, what experience have you had teaching?"

"My teaching experience?" she asked faintly, then lifted her eyebrows and gave him a snooty look. "I worked in a small school in Stockton until my father took ill."

What kind of woman stopped with one sentence? He frowned at her. "Do you enjoy teaching?"

"Oh, very much. I can't think of anything more worthwhile."

"So what brings you to Shasta?"

"I came out to see my father before he died." An-other one sentence answer, dammit. Was this really a woman? He gave her a hard look and had to concede the well-rounded form couldn't be anything but fe-male. Of course, he could check better by running his hands over that plush little as—he cleared his throat and looked away.

"Dagger, I have to run a few errands before I go, so I'll leave you both here." Susanna gave him a stern look. "You take good care of Miss Danner, now."

"Yes, ma'am," he said, giving the flourishing salute he'd perfected as an army scout and earning himself a swat on the shoulder.

"Good luck, Janet." Susanna turned and went back down the street, her long stride making her skirts swing.

Janet watched, her gut tightening. Susanna had given her a sense of safety that was now gone. Instead, Janet stood here, unarmed, next to this clever lawman. No one else had picked up on Pa's side trails before. What was he liable to pick up next? How the hell had she gotten herself into this mess?

She glanced at him, her nose wrinkling at the scent of stale whiskey. A drunk marshal. What was the world coming to? Shoot, maybe picking up Pa's trail had been an accident.

With a firm nod to herself, she decided not to worry about a pickled marshal. "Who all is on the school board?"

"There are five members." The marshal nodded at a woman bustling down the street toward them. She had gray hair with several strands falling loose, round pink cheeks and a starched white apron with one conservative ruffle. "There's Jenny Perkins. She and her husband run Perkins's Diner. They have two children."

Janet eyed her and decided she wouldn't be too hard to fool. An obviously straightforward and hardworking woman, one of Pa's "honest citizens."

The schoolhouse was a small square building of newly cut lumber. Built at the end of a short street, the wide schoolyard boasted two massive live oaks for shade. She caught a glimpse of two outhouses behind

41

the school and had to suppress the urge to make use of one.

They met the older woman at the schoolhouse steps. "Jenny, may I present Miss Janet Danner?" the lawman said, turning to the gray-haired woman.

"Oh, I was so pleased when Arnie told us about you," Mrs. Perkins bubbled, taking Janet's hand in both of hers. "And look at you! So pretty and young."

She studied Janet for a moment with experienced eyes. "But she's not so young that our older boys will rout her, I think."

The marshal looked at Janet dubiously. "Mebbe, mebbe not."

Janet raised her chin. Stepping into the schoolhouse, she came to an abrupt halt. The rest of the school board had already gathered.

"Ah, everyone's already here," Blackthorne said, stepping up behind her. He gave her a small push farther into the room, and she resisted returning the favor with an elbow to his gut.

She glanced around the room, automatically checked for exits, assessed the people present for weapons and noted what materials might be used for defense before stopping herself. She was here to teach. She wasn't an outlaw any longer; well, at least for the moment.

Three people sat at the long tables that filled the room. A massive desk dominated the front, with a long bench facing it. A small potbellied stove sat across from the door. So this was a schoolhouse.

With an effort, she forced a smile to her lips and folded her hands in front of her. "I'm Miss Janet Danner," she said in the haughty voice she'd heard Pa's favorite brothel madam use.

The marshal moved to stand beside her, and she was unexpectedly comforted by his presence. "Miss Danner, over there is Arnie Fromm. He runs the bookstore."

She nodded to the bookseller seated at the far side of the room.

Mrs. Perkins took a seat beside him. The marshal motioned to the two people sitting closer to the door. "Mrs. Emily Wilson. She and her husband own the clothing store, and beside her is Mr. Gus Grotefend, who owns the St. Charles Hotel."

Mrs. Wilson smoothed a hand over her very starched waistfront and nodded regally. Janet's stomach sank. That one wouldn't be easy to please at all. The hotel owner was a portly man with thick muttonchops and keen eyes. He also looked too smart for her peace of mind. But she'd come too far to back out without raising all sorts of questions.

Moving with all the dignity she possessed, she took a seat on the front bench, facing the inquisition. The marshal abandoned her to take a seat away from all the others.

Janet took a deep breath. Surely this couldn't be worse than robbing the French Gulch Bank. Plastering a serene smile on her face, she asked, "What would you like to know?"

"Can you explain how to divide a number by three?" The hotel owner began with questions about math.

"Of course—" After a few more questions in that vein, Janet relaxed. Years of counting money, weighing gold dust, dividing coins and dust among the gang members, buying food, horses and clothing had given her an excellent background in the practical uses of money.

In fact, she would play upon just that! "I must say, Mr. Grotefend, I have found in the past that sometimes too much attention is given to the higher maths, when first we must attend to basic arithmetic. If our children can't tell when they're being cheated of their change, then we have done them a disservice."

She suppressed a smile at the pleased look on the hotel owner's face. One down.

Mrs. Wilson's concerns were directed at deportment, manners and rules. Janet managed to subdue her with her agreement that children must not be allowed to sass.

"And what about Latin and geography?" Mrs. Perkins, the diner owner, asked. "Will you be prepared to help the children into higher learning?"

Janet blinked. Latin? "Well—"

Marshal Blackthorne interceded. "I believe Miss Danner said she'd been the instructor in a small school out here in the West. I doubt she taught Latin."

She wet her dry lips, feeling a sinking feeling in her stomach. She could probably bluff the rest of the studies, but Latin would expose her immediately. "I'm afraid I'm not qualified to instruct students in Latin."

Mrs. Perkins looked disappointed. "Well, I did have a forlorn hope, but I appreciate your honesty. I'll just have to find Benjamin a tutor when the time comes." She smiled at Janet. "We hope to see him off East to school in a few years."

"How wonderful," Janet said faintly. Did this mean she was still in the running?

"You can instruct them in geography, can't you?" Mrs. Perkins asked. "I feel very strongly that each child should understand where we are in relation to the rest of the world. And have some history also."

"I am quite capable of that." Janet gave a firm nod. She was damned good at deciphering maps.

Mrs. Perkins nodded back and waved at Arnie. The bookstore owner had a myriad of more intricate questions about the classics, but there Janet was on strong ground. She loved to read and usually had anything from a penny dreadful to a classic stuffed in her saddlebag. When Mr. Fromm nodded his satisfaction, she figured she was in the clear.

"Well, if no one has any other questions—"

"Oh, but I do," came a lazy drawl from the one person she didn't want to hear from.

"Marshal Blackthorne," she gritted out, "what would you like to know?"

"What was the name of that school in Stockton?" He'd found a piece of brown wrapping paper and a quill pen.

She thought frantically for a second, cursing herself for not having thought of a name yet. Last year, they'd gone past a little school on the outskirts of town— Clint had waved at a group of boys. What was the name she'd seen on the sign? "The Maple Street School."

He wrote, then tucked the paper into his shirt pocket.

What was he planning to do with that information? She chewed on her lip, then stopped herself. Dignity; remember dignity.

The marshal leaned back in his chair. "Gus, if you want to hire her, I have no objections."

Mr. Grotefend turned to her. "Miss Danner, I would like to offer you the position of schoolteacher for our town. How soon can you start?"

Chapter Four

The meeting adjourned rather quickly after that, with Miss Danner committed to starting on Thursday, the day after tomorrow. Arnie volunteered to post flyers and notify the parents that school would be resuming. Dagger figured there'd be a few long-faced children around supper tables tonight.

Dagger locked up the schoolhouse after the last board member, then turned to find the new schoolmarm wandering around the yard. "May I walk you to your boardinghouse, Miss Danner?"

"No, thank you. If you'll just give me directions, I'm sure I can find it myself."

He suppressed a grin. The lady didn't want to be around him, did she? "I'm going that way. It's just across the street from my house, and I need to stop there before going back to work."

He jauntily tossed the schoolhouse key in the air and fumbled the catch. Hell, not all that whiskey had worn off yet. If that wasn't a snickering sound she'd just made, then he was a damned horsethief.

"I need—"

"You can send a boy for your bags," Dagger interrupted.

"Well, then . . . thank you," she said, her pretty pink lips tight with displeasure. A small curl escaped from her bonnet, golden-white like a vagrant sunbeam.

He watched her tuck it away. How long might her hair be? He envisioned only hair of sunlight clothing her naked body. Her breasts would be—hell, what was he thinking? This was a schoolmarm.

Leading the way down the walk, he turned onto Main Street. "Ah, that's Arnie's bookstore over there." He pointed to the small brick building farther down the street. "He does a fine business, especially in the fall, when the miner's stock up on reading material for a long winter."

"All those days when they're snowed in," Janet said reflectively. "I read *Moby Dick* during one snowstorm."

Dagger frowned. "I hadn't realized it became so snowbound around Stockton." He'd taken two months to read that novel.

"Oh, well—I became ill that winter also. I had lots of time for reading," she said hastily, her cheeks flushed.

Dagger chewed on the inside of his cheek for a minute, regarding her thoughtfully. Her response had been too fast. If she'd been a criminal, he'd have voted guilty.

But she wasn't a criminal; she was a schoolmarm, and a pretty one to boot. He shook his head. He'd better get some sleep tonight, before he started suspecting everyone he met of some crime. A mangy dog under a bench rolled his eyes up as they passed. *That dog there—obviously a thief.*

Dagger chuckled and took the schoolmarm's arm to help her off the boardwalk and into the street. She jumped, and damned if he didn't think it was a guilty start, not an innocent miss's jump. He had to get some sleep!

Janet almost decked the man—God, she hated having a lawman touching her—then hastily pulled her face into a frown. "Did you just take the lord's name in vain?" she asked primly as they crossed the street.

"Ah, yes, ma'am. Please forgive me," he said contritely, and she smothered a grin. This being a lady might have all sorts of delightful fun hidden in it.

As they crossed the street, she held up her skirts to keep the hem from the muck underfoot. After crossing bustling Main, they walked down a quiet tree-lined street.

"Here's your boardinghouse," the marshal said, motioning to a large two-story whitewashed house. "And I live over there." His house across the street was a well-built dark green two-story with white trim. A covered porch the width of the house was occupied by several sleeping cats. Picket fences surrounded each yard.

"That's a lovely house," Janet said sincerely. What would it be like to feel so settled, to actually know where her bed would be each night?

The marshal pulled open the boardinghouse door and bellowed, "Mrs. Malvern! Got your new boarder." Pulling off his hat, he held it at his side.

A short, buxom woman slightly older than Janet walked out of a room off the hallway. "Stop that noise insta—oh, Marshal Blackthorne, it's you." Her irate expression faded immediately. She smoothed her white apron down over her gray poplin gown. "What were you saying?"

"I've brought you the new schoolmarm, Miss Janet Danner. Miss Danner, this is Mrs. Priscilla Malvern, your landlady."

"I'm very pleased to meet you," Janet said, watching the impeccably dressed woman intently. This was a woman she could take lessons from. Such a dignified and correct appearance.

"Welcome to Shasta." Mrs. Malvern motioned to the stairs. "Let me show you to your room."

"Thank you for escorting me, Marshal."

"It was my pleasure," he said. He took her hand gallantly, bowed over it. A glance up, and he grinned at her expression, which no doubt looked rather . . . sour. In the hour or so that she'd known him, the damned lawman had touched her more than anyone besides her family ever had.

He settled his black hat gingerly on his head, avoiding the gash in his forehead. "I will be seeing you, Miss Danner."

"Um," she answered. *God forbid.*

With a polite nod, he took his leave.

"Come, Miss Danner." Mrs. Malvern led the way up the stairs. "I have six boarders normally, although right now there are only four. The men have rooms on this side." She motioned to the right of the long hallway. "You have the front room on the women's side."

As she entered the room, Janet fought down a surge of fear. What was she doing in this genteel place? She'd never be able to manage.

The large room was lovely and feminine, with a massive armoire that would swallow her two dresses.

A matching dresser in one corner awaited the clothes she didn't own, but a large four-poster by one wall with a small nightstand beside it looked very inviting to her weary eyes.

There was a small writing desk with a lamp and a comfortable chair for writing to Clint. By the door stood a washstand with a porcelain pitcher and basin. A rag rug covered the golden pine floor in front of the bed. Janet cast about for the proper words, then went with her heart. "It's lovely."

Mrs. Malvern's tight mouth pulled upward in a pleased expression. "Well, that's good, then. The last schoolmarm we had here was just full of complaints. Thought she should be able to eat in her room. Imagine!"

"Imagine," Janet echoed. So she'd be eating downstairs. "When are meals?"

"Breakfast is at seven, dinner at noon and supper at six." The short woman eyed Janet, then folded her arms over her bosom. "I run a proper house here. Gentlemen visitors are received only in the parlor, never upstairs. The men and women keep to their own sides of the house. My personal quarters are downstairs, off the parlor."

"Of course."

"EmmaLou and Harry Catkins run a respectable bathhouse down the street with separate doors for men and women, and of course there's the necessary out back," Mrs. Malvern continued. "The parlor here is for our boarders' use in entertaining or for evening use."

"Of course."

"Do you have any questions?"

"Oh, not right now, thank you," Janet said faintly.

She'd rarely stayed anywhere in public as a woman, and certainly never anywhere so respectable. The very rules were overwhelming.

"We'll look forward to seeing you for supper tonight. I'll introduce you to the other boarders then." Mrs. Malvern glanced around the room proudly, then closed the door behind her. Her solid footsteps thumped down the stairs.

Eyeing the door warily, Janet tiptoed across the room, then slid the bolt home.

Safe.

Feeling as if she'd strolled a trail and had it turn to quicksand under her feet, she sank down into the chair. What in tarnation had she gotten herself into? She was the new schoolmarm for the town of Shasta, a boarder at Mrs. Malvern's boardinghouse and a respectable member of society. So many new roles to learn all at once.

She sighed. Well, all of them required the same behavior, at least. She had to bear herself with dignity, primness, be above reproach. She pointed her toe at the ceiling, admiring the trim black boot, although the sight of her leg with no trousers shocked her for an instant. A woman.

But damned if she didn't have a woman's leg, shapely calf, little ankle and all. Amazing. Why had she never noticed before?

Tipping her head back, she studied the ceiling, the flower-lined borders. What with Pa keeping the gang moving, with always another job lined up, she'd never gotten a chance to behave like a woman and . . . she really wanted to. Surely she could pull this off. After all, they were just law-abiding citizens here. Dumb as dirt, Pa would say.

But then there was that marshal with those all-too-keen eyes. She'd caught him studying her, dissecting her like some naturalist with a new magnifying glass. Each time those silvery-gray eyes landed on her, her stomach twisted.

She smiled slowly. But he hadn't known her, now had he, so he wasn't all that smart.

Wouldn't he be shocked to discover who she was? She rubbed her shoulder, remembering the bullet he'd put there. He sure didn't die worth a damn. How many bullets had she put into him?

She grinned, imagining showing him her shoulder. They could compare scars, count coup. But he probably wouldn't see the fun of it, even if she could.

Shoot, she couldn't blame him for doing his job, had always known that robbing carried more risk than any other occupation. She'd never expected someone being robbed to up and cower like a beaten dog, although it would have been nice.

They'd gotten away from the lawman, after all. Pity they'd lost the gold.

Settling back onto the bed, she reviewed the day's events. Susanna, the school board, the fight in the street, the marshal's face as he'd thrown his knife, so cold and determined. Not a man who gave up easily. Not a man who would let his quarry escape without pursuit.

No, he'd not have her sense of humor, if he had one at all. What was she thinking? Imagining comparing scars with him? He was a *lawman*.

God, what if he did recognize her? A chill settled over her, taking up icy lodging in her spine.

She firmed her lips and cast the fear aside. Some silly supposition like a marshal figuring something out wouldn't prevent her from going after what she wanted, and she wanted to live here. Be respectable.

So, she'd cut down on the chance he'd remember her—she'd just stay away from him. Far away.

On Thursday, Janet rushed through her breakfast like a posse was after her. She tossed greetings at the other boarders on her way upstairs to snatch her cloak. Mrs. Malvern had mentioned last night that the town expected the school bell to be rung right at eight o'clock, and as the new schoolmarm, Janet intended to do just that.

The morning was bloody cold. A frigid wind from snow-topped mountains bit at her cheeks. White frost tipped the brittle grass stems and crunched underfoot as she hurried past the awakening Main Street.

She was the only person in the schoolyard and felt a measure of satisfaction at that. She must be on time. Stepping up to the door, she beamed at the white clapboard school.

Hers.

Putting out a hand, she turned the knob and scowled. The door was locked. Someone had locked her out of her own school.

In the east, the sun was rising steadily, it was almost eight o'clock, the school bell was inside and she was locked out.

"Well, hell," she muttered. Rummaging in the unfamiliar reticule she had bought yesterday, she pulled out her leather packet of skeleton keys and picks. With her small, sensitive fingers, she'd been the best lockpick in the Garret gang.

She tried one, then another, finally catching the edge of the lock with the last one. The sound of the bolt sliding back made her feel good, brought back memories of Pa's praise when she'd opened her first door.

It was just going on eight.

Shoving the door open, she darted inside, snatched up the bell from the desk—her desk—and stepped outside again. Holding the heavy bell up high, she swung it madly back and forth, setting up a hearty clamor. She turned each direction, north, south, east and west. Wouldn't want any student to miss school, she thought righteously.

Like a beacon of hope, the sun crested the eastern mountains, streaming gold over the white peak of Mt. Lassen. Janet lowered the bell. Her chest pinpricked with quivers, anticipation and a little fear.

Her first day as a schoolteacher was about to begin.

"I thought I locked the door," a voice said from behind her.

She jumped and turned in the same instant. Her hand dipped into her skirt pocket to her hidden derringer.

"Marshal! You scared me!" She didn't have to pretend to be overwrought. She'd almost put a bullet through the blasted man, and wouldn't there be hell to pay then!

He stood there, unaware of how close he'd come to death, his eyes narrowed as he stared at the open door. "I thought I'd locked the door on Tuesday," he repeated, holding up a large key.

Janet shrugged. "It appears you didn't." She gave him a tiny smirk and added, "You weren't in the best of shape, after all." Brushing past him, she reentered the schoolhouse.

Dagger glared at the door, then the schoolteacher's

trim figure disappearing inside. He hadn't missed the way her hand had flashed down into the pocket of her skirts when he scared her. He rubbed a finger over his mustache to suppress a grin. Wouldn't it be fun to delve into the folds of her skirt to locate whatever she was hiding in her pocket?

The thought of what he might find there—slim, velvety limbs, and the place where those limbs met— he took a deep breath. No, she wouldn't be letting him rummage through those skirts. Pity. Just the thought had warmed him.

Stepping into the doorway, he examined the lock of the door carefully. The jamb was intact. He knew damn well he'd locked the door after the meeting. So how'd she gotten in? Another mystery for him to ponder.

Clicking his tongue against his teeth, he looked up. She had found the chalk slates and readers and was just holding them, staring blankly around the room. "Ready for your first day?" Must have nerves, he figured. Trying to be helpful, he took some of her load and started laying a reader and slate at each place at the long tables.

She watched closely for a second; then her sudden smile struck him like a bullet in the chest.

Her clear blue eyes danced with excitement, her light complexion flushed pink and she fairly radiated excitement as she placed readers on the tables. He felt as if someone had thrown a lasso over his shoulders and jerked him several steps into the world. If this was what just teaching did to her, what would making love do? But schoolmarms, good women—damn, he had a one-track mind.

He repeated his question, "Are you ready?"

She made an obvious effort to settle her anticipation. "Oh . . . the first day at a new school's always hectic," she said, "but I think I'm ready."

The first child dashed through the door, and she dropped the books she was holding like she'd seen a cougar or something.

Dagger knelt to pick them up.

Books forgotten, Janet beamed at the boy. "Hello. Um, I'm your new teacher, Miss Danner."

Janet heard a snort from the marshal beside her and ignored him. Her heart was hammering so hard in her chest, the town must hear it. "What's your name?" Her first student, with big brown eyes like a hound dog. Oh, this was glorious!

"I'm Richard Wilson."

"Well, Master Wilson, do you have a place where you usually sit?"

"Yes'm. The boys sit on the right and the girls on the left."

"Fine. Then take your seat and you can start looking at the reader."

His lip poked out.

"What's wrong?"

"We usually play in the yard until it's time to come in."

Janet glanced at the marshal beside her. Her first mistake. Bloody hell, why didn't the stupid man leave? "Oh, silly me, I quite lost track of the time. We certainly don't start yet, so go ahead. I need to finish setting up anyway." Hadn't she been holding some books?

Richard dashed outside, greeting some of the other students with hollers. "The new teacher's name is Miss Danner and she's really pretty."

Handing her a slate, Blackthorne gave her a mischievous look. "Seems like you've made a conquest. The lad had good eyes, at least."

She almost fumbled the slate at the compliment. "Well—"

"You'll have more students each day for a week or so, as the news spreads to the outlying areas. We weren't able to contact everyone on such short notice." The marshal moved toward the door, surveyed the bunch of children running here and there. "Looks like you have around a dozen here today."

Janet tried to swallow; her throat was too dry. "A dozen," she repeated faintly. What would she do with a dozen children, and more to come? Holy hellions.

She caught the marshal's questioning look and straightened her back. "Seems like a small number for all that noise." The yard outside sounded like an entire bar of high-pitched drunken miners.

"You'd best call them in," Blackthorne said.

She glared at him. "I can handle my classroom, sir. Don't you have some outlaws to chase or something?"

The left corner of his mouth quirked upward and he nodded. "Yes, ma'am, I surely do." He gave a doubtful look toward the yard. "Ah, good luck."

"Thank you." She moved to the door and watched him head down the street. He did move nice, didn't he? Smooth as a panther.

She called the children in and they quit their games and came running. When she saw the number of children filing past her, she had to repress the urge to call after the marshal.

Lord, but some of the children were big. Bigger than she was. And a couple looked just plain mean. A particularly loutish specimen seated himself at the back table, and she looked away with a frown. Even her fellow outlaws looked more civilized than that.

"All right, children. Quiet now." She waited a second for the noise of voices and sliding benches to subside. "My name is Miss Danner and I am your teacher. Good morning to you."

The entire room stood and chorused, "Good morning, Miss Danner."

She blinked in surprise. Was this normal? "Uh, thank you. Please be seated now."

"Aren't we going to sing?" a youngster with a reckless cowlick questioned.

Sing? "Of course we will," she declared heartily. "You—what's your name?" She pointed to the young man.

"I'm Ben Perkins."

"What's your favorite song?"

He bounced onto his toes. "I love 'Oh, Susanna.' "

"Good enough." She knew this one. Clint liked it, too. "We'll sing that."

Several songs later, Janet motioned for them to be seated. "So which *Reader* are you in?"

They gazed down at the books in front of them.

"Anne?" Seven years old and full of giggles and wiggles.

"I'm in the *Second Reader*. When Mrs. Tate left, the big kids had gotten to *McGuffey's Fifth Reader*, and us little 'uns are partway through Chapter Three in ours. Sarah and James still have to learn their letters, so they're not anywhere."

Janet lifted her eyebrows. She guessed reviewing everything from the beginning made sense after the long summer.

She sat down on the long bench in the front of the

classroom, wondering idly why it was so long. Several of the students looked surprised. "All right, Sarah and James, you come up here and we'll see about your letters. The rest of you work on your books."

She should be able to handle this teaching business right handily.

Friday night, Janet dragged her body up the stairs to her room. The scent of the meal being prepared turned her stomach. She couldn't feel worse if she'd been dragged through the desert and left to die.

How could she ever have thought she could be a teacher? Her hopes, so high in the beginning, were flattened like storm-battered grass at her feet. Dropping onto the bed, she flung an arm over her face.

Damned if turning a chipmunk into a cougar wouldn't be easier than turning an outlaw into a schoolmarm. Her classroom was a bedlam; the students weren't learning.

How could she teach one child if the entire rest of the class went mad? How could she deal with Pike, the plague of the classroom? How in the world did real teachers keep fifteen to twenty children in line?

She could quit. She considered that for a while. Hell, they'd probably fire her at the rate she was going, especially when Pike picked on the little 'uns.

And what had she done? She'd remonstrated with the bastard, tried to keep her temper and her words ladylike as a teacher must. He laughed at her. Told her she was just like the last teacher they'd had—the one who'd headed back East.

Little did he know how close he'd come to having his nose busted.

Janet's jaw clenched. She'd never been a quitter in

her life, and Pa had always said that determination would win over talent any day.

So, all right. She wasn't a talented teacher. Sitting up on the bed, she looked at her hands, lean and callused—determined hands on a determined woman's body. She closed them into fists and gave them a firm nod. She would learn to teach and to teach well, damned if she wouldn't.

Susanna had said she came into town every Saturday, and had mentioned meeting for tea. Janet tapped a finger on her cheek. Susanna had undoubtedly attended a regular school and would know what a teacher should be doing. Surely there'd be a way to get that information out of her.

Janet smiled, the idea of seeing Susanna again lightening her spirits. Her first woman friend.

Laughter and the clinking of silverware from down the stairs reminded her of the evening meal, and she bounced off the bed. All of a sudden, she was hungry!

Chapter Five

The next afternoon Janet walked up and down the boardwalk in front of Arnie's bookstore. The enticing scent of fresh-baked apple pie from the bakery next door made her stomach rumble.

A man brushed by her with a muttered, "Ma'am," and a hand touching his hat brim. She nodded sweetly. Amazing. She'd never been treated like this when she'd been disguised as a man.

So, where the hell was—there she was, coming down the boardwalk with a dark-haired woman. Janet waved her hand. "Susanna!"

Susanna Blackthorne looked around, spotted her, and a grin broke over her face that made Janet's heart lift.

"Janet. Oh, how nice you look." Susanna pulled the other woman forward.

"Janet, this is Miss Hannah Emie Laviolette, a dear friend of mine. Hannah, this is Miss Janet Danner, our new schoolteacher."

Janet's friend was short and buxom, with rich mink-colored hair pulled up into a bonnet. She had lively brown eyes and an infectious smile. "I'm pleased to meet you, Miss Danner."

"Oh, please, it's Janet." Janet turned to Susanna. "I was hoping you'd have time enough for tea."

"Surely, and I've been looking forward to talking with you."

The easy agreement warmed Janet through and through, and relief rushed through her. Surely she'd get her answers.

Hannah's eyes narrowed, then she said, "I'll go in and see what I can find to read while you two talk. Take your time."

Janet studied Hannah for a moment. She'd learned to read people early and well. Although just a young woman, Hannah had wise eyes, a strong chin and a mouth that looked like it kept secrets with the best of them. And she undoubtedly had gone to school also. Perhaps another mine of information. "Why don't you join us?"

"How about we go have some tea and dessert, and you can tell us how your first days of teaching went." Susanna motioned to the bakery.

Janet automatically steered them to the back corner and took a chair facing the door. They waited until plump Mrs. Chappell served them fragrant lemon pie and steaming tea.

Janet fidgeted with her tea, trying to figure out how to start. She'd never had any women friends, never asked advice from anyone but family. And revealing anything of her past went against all she'd been taught. How in the world would she get them started speaking about their past? "I—"

"How did you get along with your students?" Susanna prompted.

"Oh, fairly well," Janet said awkwardly. "I'm not used to having older boys." That sounded correct. She'd told them she'd been teaching at a girls' school. Now, would either take the bait?

"Oh, Pike and Albert. I bet they're a handful." Hannah shook her head. "Would you believe their fathers bring them into the saloon? They've already been upstairs—" She clapped a hand over her mouth and turned red.

Janet suppressed a grin and pursed her lips, trying to emulate the shock a well-bred schoolmarm would show, but she couldn't—her laugh burst right out.

And Susanna was laughing so hard that Hannah had to join in.

Was this what it was like to have friends? Were friends like family? But her family never lied to each other; Pa had whupped them good if he caught them in a fib. Her pastry suddenly tasted like chalk. If these two women were to be her friends . . . could she be a real friend if she tried to sneak information?

The other two sobered. Susanna took a sip of tea, then cocked her head. "You look so serious, Janet."

Caught in her quandary, Janet realized Susanna's face held sympathy, concern. She cast her doubts aside. "All right. I'm putting my cards on the table here. I've never taught school before, but I needed the work and really, I *have* had a good education. It just wasn't in school."

Susanna took a sip of tea, studying Janet over the rim of the cup. "I'm not surprised; I figured you were bending the truth a tad."

Janet looked at Hannah, who shrugged. "Needs

must, as my mother always said. If you can do the job and teach the young 'uns, then no harm done. I can't see how you'd do worse than that fancy experienced teacher from the East."

Relief blew through Janet like a warm wind. She hadn't been willing to admit how worried she was about losing Susanna's newfound friendship. "Thanks. Both of you."

"So, what advice do you need?" Hannah asked, putting them back on a practical basis.

"I'm lost as to how to run a schoolroom," Janet confessed. "There are so many children. Each time I work with one, all the rest of them tear the place apart."

Susanna grinned. "And you probably kept trying to be a lady, correct?"

Hannah looked confused, but Janet had to laugh. "That's exactly it."

"She knocked a little hoodlum into the mud when I first met her," Susanna explained to Hannah. "That's why I thought she'd be good for the job, but I noticed she's been real prim since then."

"Hmm." Hannah nodded. "Well, I'll start the advice, then. What you do in the classroom is your business. Do what you need to do to maintain order. Considering the scoundrels you have in your class, being a lady is impossible. But . . . on the street and in town, you need to act like you starch your drawers, especially around Mrs. Wilson."

Janet snickered. She should have known Susanna wouldn't have any stuck-up friends.

Susanna took over. "You need to appoint one or two helpers from the older students. They'll maintain order and keep the children at their lessons while you're occupied with one group—one group, mind, not just one student."

Hannah added, "And it's best if you establish some penalties for bad behavior. If they don't get their work done, they eat lunch inside with no recess, or stay after school, or sit in the corner. You can come up with some pretty creative punishments if you think about it." She grinned wickedly and tucked a bite of pie into her mouth. "Oh, this is heavenly, isn't it?"

A group of students at a time? Janet suddenly realized what the long bench in front of her desk was for. "So, I take all the younger students and have them sit on the bench?"

"For recital, right. Have them read aloud, spell aloud." Susanna drank some tea. "I was quick at numbers, so when I was done with my math lesson, I'd listen to the older children saying their lessons. That way I had a head start when I got to their part of the book."

A shadow blocked the sunlight streaming in the open door, and Janet looked up. How typical. Just when things were going well, out crawls a lawman.

He grinned at her, white teeth in a darkly tanned face, and her heart gave a thud. He probably got his job on looks alone.

"Afternoon, Mrs. Chappell. Can I have some lemon pie?" he asked, leaning over the counter and pointing.

The shopkeeper beamed. "One lemon coming up."

He turned and smiled at the group in the corner. "Susanna, Bowie's looking for you in Arnie's."

"Oops." Susanna gulped the last of her tea. "I'd better get over there. Let Hannah answer some questions and I'll try to stop back before we leave."

"Thanks, Susanna."

"Can I join you?" Dagger sidestepped Susanna and took her chair without waiting for an answer. Ignoring the fork, he picked up his pie like a biscuit. "How's the teaching going, Miss Danner?"

Hannah answered for her. "She's doing fine, Dagger, except for Pike and a couple of his friends. I was starting to tell her to be quite firm with them."

Dagger frowned. "Define *firm*."

Hannah laced her fingers together and gave Janet a laughing look. "Personally, I'm in favor of rubbing their faces in some cow pucky."

"Ah." Dagger nodded. "That kind of firm."

He turned his dark gray eyes on Janet, and a funny quiver woke in her stomach, a type of feeling she'd never had before. She hadn't noticed he had laugh lines beside his eyes, eyebrows that arched—why did he seem so . . . different? She yanked her wayward thoughts back and focused her attention.

"I had a mule up in the mines once. Good hauler, but a contrary beast. I'd have to thump her now and again to keep her from going off the trail. I figure Albert and Pike are like the mule. If you need to thump them here and again, the board will raise no objection."

He studied her for a minute. "Little bit like you, I doubt you'll do much harm."

Janet raised her brows. "I can thump them," she repeated for clarification's sake.

"Yup. Try not to break any bones if you can."

He didn't take her seriously, but she had her permission. "No broken bones. I think I can manage that."

He swallowed his last bite of pie. "Well, I need to be off. It was nice talking with you ladies." The smile left his face. His hands flat on the table, he leaned over. "All joking aside, Miss Danner, if you need me to take Albert or Pike out back and instruct them in some western etti-cut, let me know."

He was serious. He'd help her tame the scoundrels. The thought shocked her through and through. The law had never been on her side before. "Thank you," she said softly, "but I think I can handle them."

He shrugged and stood straight. "The offer's good if you find a need." Touching Hannah's shoulder lightly, he nodded. "Good day, ladies."

Janet watched him walk out of the bakery. The air in the room seemed lighter when he left, as if a powerful animal had moved on down the trail.

"He's a bit of a loner, but quite a handsome one, don't you think?" Hannah commented, following her gaze.

Janet twisted her mouth to one side. Oh, yes, he was. "I was never much interested in lawmen."

"Mmmm, but he certainly fills his shirt out nicely." Hannah's eyes met Janet's across the table, and they burst out laughing.

Hannah put her hand over Janet's. "I like you, schoolteacher. I'd like to be your friend, but you should know, I'm considered disreputable."

If she only knew, Janet thought with a grin. Couldn't be more disreputable than an outlaw. "And why's that?"

"I deal cards down at the Miner's Saloon."

"Oh." A card-dealer and not yet twenty? Janet hesitated. A schoolteacher was supposed to have only ladylike friends, she guessed.

She shrugged. She'd never had friends before. A person shouldn't turn down a gift. "I'd like to be friends." Her lips turned up into a smile. "Maybe we can talk Susanna into joining us for a ladies' tea and poker party."

Hannah giggled and the friendship was sealed.

On Monday, Janet trudged through a cold drizzle to the schoolhouse, glumly figuring the weather portended a bad day. Last week sure hadn't ended well. Then again, she had plans now, thanks to Susanna and Hannah, and her pupils were in for a surprise.

She caught sight of Pike and Albert lumbering toward the school, and her smile tightened. Lord help her.

The children arrived one by one, wet and chilled, huddling around the fat potbellied stove to warm up.

Taking a deep breath, Janet started the day.

"Rosie, I'd like you to take Richard, Flossie, Sally and Billy and work with them on their reading." She hoped Richard wouldn't give his big sister too much trouble.

The slender brunette looked up from the front table, then nodded. "Yes, ma'am."

"Albert and Pike," Janet said to her seventeen-year-old troublemakers, "we'll begin with your recitation. Please sit on the bench." Feeling like she was grasping a nettle with both hands, she took her place behind the teacher's desk.

After a moment, the large boys awkwardly plopped down on the long recital bench facing her.

"Albert, you may begin with page one hundred twenty-five," she told the blond, stocky boy dressed in rough clothing. He tended to do anything the cannier Pike suggested. Anne had told her that the older children read from *McGuffey's Fifth Eclectic Reader*, going a little further each season.

" 'For a moment, the blood was seen mounting to the face of—' " He slaughtered the page.

"Albert?" He couldn't read any of the bigger words, Janet quickly realized. "Try page sixty-six," she suggested. Face flushing, he leafed back through the book.

" 'The boy who will peep into a drawer, will be tempted to take something out of it.' " He could read most of the words there, although he struggled, and she rather enjoyed the moral here.

"I think this is where we'll start this year." He glared at her, but she met his gaze blandly and he finally nodded.

"Pike, let's see where you should be placed. Start with chapter seventeen," she said.

The youth already looked like a man, she thought, and should be out doing a man's labor, not causing problems in her schoolroom. He scowled at her from under black, shaggy hair and opened his reader.

He, too, missed words, especially further into the chapter. Not as badly as Albert had, but obviously he'd almost memorized the first page of the chapter rather than reading it. Janet frowned. Seems there was a negative side to listening to everyone reciting before you. "Try chapter nine."

He glared at her. "I ain't gonna read back with the brats."

"You can't read chapter seventeen. If you can read chapter nine, then we'll move forward." Chapter nine appeared to be just about the right place for him. "Excellent." The two boys stood and began to move to their designated back corner. "Wait." Hell, she'd almost forgotten another point Susannah had mentioned.

She pointed to the far back corner, away from the stove. "Albert, you sit over there. Pike, you may move your plunder to right there." She indicated the closest table.

Pike would be under her nose where she could watch him, and he couldn't plot with Albert, two tables directly behind him, unless he turned full around. The sullen expression in his eyes told her he'd figured out her scheme, too. She smiled at him. "Please work on your new chapter, and we'll see how far you've gotten in the morning."

The rest of the children all seemed to be further behind than what Hannah and Susannah had suggested, except for the Perkins children, who were smart as whips. After everyone had recited, and Janet had written down their assignments, she surveyed her classroom arrangement with satisfaction.

Turning, she indicated the painted blackboard behind her, where she'd chalked a variety of math problems. "I'd like you all to take out your slates and do these problems. Get as far as you can, then bring me the slate when you're done." She'd put up simple addition all the way to some algebra, planning to learn exactly where each child needed to be working. As each child came forward, she marked more information in her notebook.

By the time noon rolled around, everyone had finished and been sent out for lunch and recess except Pike, who was washing down the blackboard as punishment for throwing a spitball.

Janet pushed the notes she'd taken to and fro on her desk with the metal ruler she'd found in the desk drawer. She had a righteous mess here, she did.

A couple of very bright students, two at the right level, most behind and a couple very far behind. Albert needed to be reading with Richard, the ten-year-old. Six-year-old Thomas couldn't do math, although his reading wasn't too bad and she could swear he was a smart boy. Mrs. Malvern's fancied-up daughter couldn't add anything, for all her big nine-year-old size. How in the world did these teachers manage?

Just then the shouts outside rose to a pitch that yanked her attention back with a start. Sally was screaming, someone was roaring and everyone was shouting. She dashed outside.

Oh, hell. Albert was pounding on smart little Ben Perkins. Anne hauled on Albert's shirt from behind, shrieking her head off, "Stop it! Stop!"

At that moment, Janet's temper snapped like the chalk she'd dropped earlier. Her eldest brother, Harry, had smacked on her just that way. She hated bullies!

Striding up behind Albert, she yanked Anne away, then kicked the boy in the back of the knee with her sharp-toed boot.

"Eooouh!" His knee buckled. She smacked his arm with her metal ruler and he snatched his hand back, releasing Ben.

Albert spun around, his fist pulled back.

"I don't think so," she muttered. Blocking his punch with one arm, with the other hand, she lifted her skirts enough to kick him solidly in his manly treasures. With a wheezing bellow, he collapsed in upon himself like an overripe peach and landed in the mud with a satisfying splat.

"Well, now." Tapping her ruler against her palm, she frowned. Now, what had Hannah said about the rules—what was that word she'd used? Oh, yes.

"You are expelled from school for fighting, Albert," she said sternly to the moaning boy. "If you can conduct yourself properly, you may return tomorrow."

Reaching down, she hauled Ben to his feet. His cheek was bruised and his lip was split and bleeding. Well, growing up with three outlaw brothers, she'd had plenty of practice tending wounds. "Let's go in and get you doctored up, young man."

She glanced around at the wide-eyed children. "Come along. Lunch is over and we have much work to do."

Chapter Six

That evening, she stepped outside the boardinghouse and took a seat on the porch. The air was chilly and damp, but welcoming after the stuffiness of the dining room. From Main Street, she heard the distant sounds of nonstop revelry, somehow a pleasant accompaniment to the closer hooting of a barn owl.

Drawing her shawl closer, she tipped her head back to study the dark sky. A cloud, all alone in the sky, made its way toward the cold light of the crescent moon, moving slowly but inevitably toward its goal. Much like her.

She gave a small sigh of satisfaction. The day had been a success. In spite of all the energy in the classroom, she'd managed to keep the children in hand and moving through their lessons. With Albert gone, Ben relaxed and did his work. Pike had sulked rather thoroughly, but quietly, at least.

She had a few more tricks to try on them tomorrow, some suggestions Hannah had made.

Movement from across the street had her sitting up

and peering through the darkness. Looked like a child was on the loose. The figure ran up the steps of the marshal's house, and knocked on the door.

The door opened to the glow of lamplight and the marshal stood in the entrance, a big dog at his side.

What was going on? Janet wondered. Trouble at the child's home? Appears a lawman didn't get much rest.

After a brief conversation the lawman disappeared back inside and returned a minute later with a small kitten in his hands. He handed the kitten to the child, ruffled the hair on both and then watched as the boy darted away.

The dog at his side, he leaned against the door frame, apparently enjoying the night, and Janet couldn't help but smile at the idea that they had something in common. Only crazy fools would enjoy a cold night like this. After a quiet moment he patted the dog on the head and pushed the door open to go in.

Suddenly he stiffened and turned, his gaze sweeping out through the darkness and meeting Janet's with a force like a gut blow. When he tipped his head and sent her a grin, her muscles went quivery as jelly.

After lifting his hand to her, he disappeared inside. Janet let out a breath and pressed a hand to her stomach. Wasn't that . . . something.

Unsettled, she rose. Time and past for bed.

At the door she glanced back over her shoulder. The lawman's lamp had been extinguished and the house was dark.

Overhead, the lonely little cloud had covered the moon, but instead of darkening the sky, moon and cloud glowed together with a soft shimmering light.

* * *

Two days later, Janet bounced out of the schoolhouse and stopped on the steps. Wonderful cool late afternoon air. The clouds had broken apart and shafts of sunlight patterned the damp grass.

She'd released the children an hour earlier, but hadn't been able to bring herself to leave. Her plan for each child was almost finished.

A movement from under the big oak caught her eye. She stopped. Her hand slid into her skirt pocket, wrapped around her revolver; then she realized who the man was.

Blackthorne. Her heart thudded hard, then slowed.

Dressed in his usual dark colors, he'd blended in with the tree's shadows. Hell. He was lucky she hadn't perforated him before she'd recognized him. Good-looking would only carry a man so far, after all.

Of course he was *very* good-looking, what with those broad shoulders and that gray-eyed aloof look. Amazing that some woman hadn't snagged him already. But then, most of the townspeople seemed to be uneasy around him. Pity; her little brother would give his eyeteeth to have people look at him with that faint anxiety.

She tilted her head to one side. What was the lawman doing watching her schoolhouse, anyway? "Marshal Blackthorne?"

He pushed himself away from the trunk, his gaze scrutinizing her closely. "Heard you whupped Albert Johnson."

Was he here to arrest her? She tensed, fingers still curled around the butt of the pistol.

He took her elbow and assisted her down the steps. His lean face broke into a grin. "I'm ready for your confession."

He was teasing her . . . wasn't he? "Uh . . . yes, I whupped him, in a way." Lordy, how could she explain how a proper teacher kicked a male's pride and joys? "But I didn't break any bones."

Any bones? Dagger winced, figuring if it had been him, he'd rather have the broken bones. Then he grinned, enjoying the flush of color that had pinked the pretty schoolmarm's cheeks. "Well, now, I guess you didn't. And I doubt Albert will give you much trouble after this. His father might, though."

"His father?"

Dagger pulled her to a halt on Main Street, trying to find a path across the muck that followed a rain. "Let's do it this way," he said, and hefted her into his arms. She gave a gasp and stiffened.

His arm touched the solidity of a corset, the crumple of petticoats and a very feminine shape under it all. Round, soft, sweet . . . he felt as if he'd grown an extra few inches.

Her hair, pulled up on top of her head, smelled like flowers.

"Marshal! Stop it!" she hissed. Her squirming caused him to slip in some horse dung and he almost dropped her.

She gasped and flung her arms around his neck. "Don't drop me, you fool!"

"No, ma'am," he agreed contritely, thoroughly enjoying himself. Her bosom pressed against him with each breath she took, and he considered how much nicer her breasts would feel freed of their constraints. She surely did have a nice figure. He stopped for a buckboard, then stepped back as the afternoon stage from Red Bluff splashed past.

"You looked . . . happy when you stepped out today," he commented, unable to find a word to describe the glow in her eyes. The glow that appeared again with his words. Her lips curled into a smile, for all the world like a barn cat with a mouse trapped in the grain.

"The children and I have had a couple of very good days."

"Really?" What kind of teacher could say that after being in a fight with someone who outweighed her by a good hundred pounds?

Dagger reached the boardwalk and reluctantly set her down.

She smoothed her skirts before looking up at him. "I've placed all the students where they belong and made lesson plans for each." Her face showed a wealth of satisfaction, more than he'd seen on any teacher's face before. Well, she was fairly new at teaching.

"Sounds like a good piece of work." He steered her down the boardwalk.

"Oh, my, yes." She glanced back as curses from a mule skinner seared the air.

She continued. "Do you realize many students are behind the level they should be at?" She pulled her pretty face into a frown and scolded, "You're on the school board. You all should be ashamed."

Dagger sighed. She might smell like flowers, but her voice was pure schoolmarm. "I am—"

She stopped suddenly. "Where are you going? My boardinghouse is down that street back there!"

"Yes, ma'am, but you have a letter waiting at the express office."

"A letter? For me?"

"That's what Ernie Short said. Addressed to Janet Danner."

Janet clasped her hands together tightly. Only one person would be writing, and that would be Clint. Just in case she'd gotten the job, she'd written him at the prison before she'd left Whiskeytown.

Her feet sped down the boardwalk, then slowed when she realized Blackthorne had kept step. "Uh, I can find the express office, Marshal."

He grinned at her, his rare smile putting a crease in his tanned cheek and making her mouth dry. He sure was one fine-looking man.

"I'm sure a smart lady like yourself could find just about anything, but I needed to talk with Leroy next door at the livery."

"Isn't that where Albert Johnson's father is employed?" Janet's stomach clenched. A cocky Albert had returned to school the next day, and she'd heard him tell Pike that his pa was going to "have it out with the schoolmarm."

Janet hadn't had a chance to speak with Albert's family—well, maybe she'd been avoiding it—but perhaps today would be a good time. She gulped. "I really need to speak with his parents about Monday."

Dagger gave her a keen-eyed look, then patted her shoulder with a callused, long-fingered hand. "Don't worry, schoolmarm. Big Al isn't an unreasonable man."

"Big Al?" Janet said faintly. She'd kicked Big Al's son in the . . . private parts, and he wouldn't be unreasonable? "I hadn't realized how . . . interesting this profession could be."

Dagger chuckled, a deep, gravely sound that tightened her stomach. Why did she keep having these funny reactions to him? "People out West are a bit

78

more lively than back East, it's true. Want me to tag along?"

His offer made her feel less alone, although the last thing she wanted was a lawman's company. She just knew, down in her gut, that one day he'd look at her and see the outlaw he'd shot, one of the gang who'd crippled his friend. Every moment she spent in his presence kept her fear alive, yet he was a likable man.

He seemed aloof with the townspeople, but she was beginning to realize that he was just a quiet man. For some reason he'd relaxed enough around her to tease her like he did Susanna. His informality made her feel warm inside, against her better judgment.

"No, Marshal, I'll handle this myself." She smiled to lessen the rejection. "But thank you for the offer. If you hear a scream from the stables, come and rescue me." She suppressed a grin. The day some lawman had to save her would be a cold day in hell.

He touched his hat brim and moved on down the boardwalk while she entered the express office. The bell rang over the door when she walked in, stumbling slightly over the roughly planked floor.

A head popped up from behind the counter, then back down. ". . . right there," came a muffled call.

Canvas bags with stenciled lettering, crates and bags packed for mule trains lined the back of the room.

She leaned on the wooden counter in a patch of sunlight falling from the dusty window behind her.

The head popped up again, followed by a lanky body. Young Ernie Short. "Yes, ma'am?"

"Have you received a letter for me?" Janet asked the clerk. "My name is Janet Danner."

"Oh! Yes, ma'am." The young man, barely into his twenties, flushed like a girl and dived back down behind the counter. "Here it is!" He reappeared, waving the letter like a flag of victory.

"Thank you." There was no return address, but the letter had been mailed from Sacramento. Relief and pleasure raced down her spine. Clint must be out of jail already.

She nodded at the boy, then walked out of the office, ripping open the envelope. Outside, on the boardwalk, she sank down onto a rough-hewn bench, heedless of her clean skirts. The letter read:

> *Sister,*
>   *I take pen in hand to inform you that I'm out and on my way to see you. I have a project or two in mind and could use your assistance.*
>   *As you had mentioned in your previous missal, I will be most discreet about contacting you in person.*
> *Sincerely,*
> *Your brother.*

She dropped the letter into her lap, slumped back against the bench and closed her eyes in futile anger. How could this be happening to her? How could the wretch be making plans that involved her?

It wasn't fair! The teaching was beginning to work, she was enjoying her job, the town. She wasn't ready to quit yet.

She couldn't wish for him to have stayed in jail longer, not her little brother, but couldn't he keep doing his robberies by himself and elsewhere? Surely she deserved some time off, some time to explore being a woman.

A ghastly vision appeared to her of aging, ending up an old woman, still in man's garb, shot in the back when her arthritic arms couldn't haul her into the saddle one more time. She had to laugh, but the sound seemed bitter. She flexed her fingers in reassurance. No arthritis, she was still young, and there was time to make decisions yet.

Maybe. Then another appalling thought took her breath.

Dear sweet heavens, what would happen if Clint came face to face with Marshal Blackthorne? Blackthorne was sure to recognize him and, worse, Clint would never forget the man who had put a bullet in him.

"Miss Danner, how nice to see you," a woman's voice said.

Janet opened her eyes to see Mrs. Perkins standing in front of her with her sweet eleven-year-old daughter.

"My Sally is just delighted with your class, and she's working hard at learning her multiplication tables."

"She's a delightful child," Janet said with a smile. "And bright as a store-bought button."

Sally beamed at the compliment.

"Thank you." Mrs. Perkins walked away, then stopped to say, "We're so very pleased you're here."

There! *See, Clint*, Janet said mentally. She belonged here now, not with him, not with a posse on her trail or people shooting at her. She didn't want to camp out, hide out or shoot out anymore. Smoothing her skirt, enjoying the sound of crisp petticoats, she muttered, "I'm respectable and I'm going to stay that way."

She sighed. Pa had often called Clint "the little mule" as a boy. As a man, his stubbornness was un-

rivaled. She'd have a fight on her hands when he arrived.

With a grimace, she tucked the letter into her reticule, then frowned at the nearby livery. The day was
rapidly going to hell in a handbasket and she hadn't
even met the ominously named Big Al.

The darkness of the stables left her blind after the
glaring sunlight outside. The familiar dusty scent of
hay and horses comforted her as she moved past a
stall. "Mr. Johnson, are you in here?"

"In the back," a bellow came from the murk.

Running her fingers over the stall planks, Janet
picked her way to the end of the stables, stopping for
a quick pat of her mare. An imposing figure stepped
out of a stall and she caught her breath. Lordy but the
man was big!

"I'm Miss Danner," she said primly. "Your son's
schoolteacher."

He scowled at her in disbelief, thick black brows
pulling together over a beaklike nose. "You're the one
who hurt him, had him walking bowlegged for two
days? He was just funning, and you almost crippled
him, woman!"

She straightened to her full height, managing to
reach at least to his shoulder. "Crippled him? Hardly,"
she said scornfully. "And if you call punching a puny
young 'un like Ben Perkins in the face *funnin'*, then
you have a wretched sense of humor."

No wonder Albert was such a bully if this lout was
his father. She scowled at the man, rocking up on her
toes, ready to dodge a punch.

Damned if she wouldn't do her best to cripple the
father, too.

But Big Al deflated like a grape in the sun. "Ben? Albert was punching on little Ben?"

She nodded.

"Oh, he—" He stopped. "Excuse me, ma'am."

A horse poked his head out of its stall, and Big Al stroked its neck, his massive hand surprisingly gentle and slow. "I know you're hungry, Thunder, just let me settle the missy here."

Janet waited, unsure what was happening. Something had changed.

After a moment Big Al turned back to her, his jaw working from side to side. "Pike told me you whupped Albert cuz he couldn't read his book right and tried to make a joke."

Eyes steady on the man, Janet shook her head.

He growled something under his breath.

She grinned and then put the nail in Pike's coffin. "I'd kept Pike in to clean the blackboard. He wasn't even outside."

Big Al snorted. "Pike, huh? Two-faced little whelp."

Totally in agreement, Janet nodded. "But that's beside the point. The point is, I can't have Albert picking on the smaller students. And quite honestly, I wasn't about to let him punch me, either."

His jaw dropped. "He tried to *hit* you? My—" He stopped. "But he didn't succeed, did he?"

His rumbling laugh jiggled the big belly under a pair of bright yellow suspenders. "Well, now, we've needed someone at the school who could take the boy down a peg or two."

He leaned against the stall and rubbed his cheek with a dirty paw. "He's gotten caught up with that Pike. A scoundrel Pike is, and too smart for his own good. Leads my Albert astray."

"I've noticed Albert tends to follow Pike's lead."

"Oh, yes." He looked into Janet's eyes earnestly. "My Albert's a good-hearted lad. Not too bright, mind you, and neither am I. After Grover Walsh took over the horse market and Pike started school, Albert ran amok. His ma and I can keep him behaving at home, what with chores and working here, but he and Pike have pretty well had a free hand at school."

He frowned at his shoes. "It's been an embarrassment to the missus and me, knowing our son was part of the reason we've had so much trouble keeping schoolmarms."

Janet smiled. "Your son is old enough that you can't dictate his every action. I think he'll soon find out that Pike might not be the best person to use as a role model." She tilted her head. "But he may catch a few lumps in the process of learning, Mr. Johnson."

Big Al chuckled. "Miss Danner, you have the missus's and my permission to give our son as many lumps as needed in order to teach him to walk the straight and narrow." He looked at the ceiling for a moment, and she was startled to see the gleam of tears in his eyes.

"He studied last night," Big Al said quietly. "He hasn't cracked open his reader since last year."

"Well." Janet wasn't sure what to say. "I—I'll do my best to see he has a good year."

"Thank you, miss." Big Al ducked his head and turned into the nearest stall, hastily grabbing his pitchfork.

Equally embarrassed, Janet retreated back outside with a sense of relief. The one thing she'd never expected from this day's meeting would be gratitude from Big Al.

She stopped outside the door, savoring the warm feeling inside. He'd thanked her for helping his son. Said his son needed her. The sense of satisfaction made her want to march right down to the school and get started.

Chapter Seven

"Join me for a cup of coffee?" Dagger asked the schoolmarm as the boarders rose from the supper table. He filled two mugs from the pot on the table.

"Well—"

He smothered his grin at her glance up the stairs. She plainly wished she could escape but was too startled to be able to come up with a quick excuse. As he handed her a cup, he savored the sight of a schoolmarm at a loss for words. Her face when he'd shown up for supper had been priceless. No one had told her that one of the marshal's benefits was thrice-weekly meals at Mrs. Malvern's fine table.

"All right," she said.

The parlor was as stuffy as the landlady, with immaculate doilies covering every surface and a sofa harder than a bench. No wonder the boarders shunned the room.

The schoolmarm stiffly settled into a chair to one side of the fireplace and tilted her head.

"How did it go this afternoon with Big Al?" Dagger

poked at the fire and tossed another log on, sending sparks flying up the chimney.

"Very well."

Damn, there she went again with those short answers. "I take it he didn't take you to task for the way you . . . punished his son."

With her laugh, she relaxed and was a different person. How did she do that? One second all starchy and the next she glowed with humor and energy. Her smile, her face was so vivid, like a spring morning when the sun first clears the mountains. Two persons, light and shadow. He tore his eyes away from her face and poked at the fire again.

"So he wasn't angry?"

"Nope, not after I explained." She grimaced. "Apparently Pike told him I'd done . . . well, *that*, because Albert sassed me, not because he had beat up Ben and then tried to punch me."

"He tried to what! You?!" Dagger found himself on his feet, his fists clenched. He'd do more than jostle Albert's pride and joys, he'd—

"Relax, Marshal. He didn't get anywhere, remember?"

He let out a huff of breath and settled into the chair next to hers. "I still want to beat on him a little," he grumbled.

Her amused smile softened. "I'm used to taking care of myself, but it's . . . thank you for wanting to protect me."

For a moment she looked so alone, he wanted to hug her.

"Didn't your father take care of you?"

She blinked. "Oh, he did—he watched over me like a hawk. But he was ill there—at the end."

"Ah." His eyes narrowed. Sounded like the truth about her father, but he'd never seen a pampered woman act quite like her. She had a self-assurance that spoke of competence, of independence. She was much like Susanna, who hadn't been protected at all. Something didn't add up here.

"Well, aside from Albert, how are the children doing? Are you enjoying teaching in Shasta?"

"Oh, yes." Her eyes lit up. "You should have seen Flossie today. She tattled on Richard—he'd put a toad in Sally's lunch pail."

"And you did—?"

"Well, nothing. I just let the toad out the door."

Dagger gaped. The last schoolmarm had almost fainted at the sight of spiders, bugs, snakes—when would he learn that this little miss was very different.

"Anyway," she continued, "Richard found the same toad again at recess, and this time he put it into Flossie's coat pocket." Her nose wrinkled up as she snickered. "She put her hand in her pocket and let out a screech—well, I'm surprised the whole town didn't show up to find out what was going on. It took me a half hour to quiet down the classroom."

"That would—"

Mrs. Malvern interrupted in a frozen tone from the doorway. "I hardly think that type of incident is a laughing matter, Miss Danner."

Instantly the schoolmarm turned into her reserved shadow. "You are perfectly correct, Mrs. Malvern, I shouldn't have laughed. Flossie had quite a scare."

"You know, she could get horrible warts from touching those creatures," Mrs. Malvern said. "I made her wash her hands in lye soap several times."

Dagger could see the schoolmarm biting her lip,

and damned if he wasn't having trouble himself as he choked out his agreement. "That was probably wise. No sense in taking chances." He turned to Miss Danner. "I trust the miscreant was punished?"

"Oh, my, yes."

Mrs. Malvern gave a stiff nod. "Well, I'm glad to hear that." She started to leave, then turned.

Dagger snatched his hand away. Darned hard to pat someone's hand under Malvern's eagle eye.

Mrs. Malvern pursed her lips. "It's getting late, Marshal . . ."

She was booting him out.

"I understand." He rose, holding out his hand to help Miss Danner to her feet. Her hand was tiny within his, sending another flash of fire through his veins.

She walked with him to the door, then paused. Her eyes were wide with uncertainly as she said, "Good night, Marshal."

Taking both her hands, he lifted them, pressed a kiss to the back of her fingers and savored the quiver under his lips. "Good night, Miss Janet Danner."

Janet stepped out onto the landing in the alley behind the general store and turned back to call out, " 'Bye, Billy. Do your schoolwork like I showed you and get well soon. I miss hearing your voice during recital time."

Maude Tucker, attired in an eye-catching gown of purple and yellow, stepped outside and shivered at the brisk wind. "Thank you so much for bringing Billy's schoolwork."

Janet smiled. "He works so hard in school; it seemed a shame to let him fall behind."

"He's looking forward to coming back, especially since you set that Albert in his place." Maude gave a pleased nod.

"When did the doc say Billy could return?"

"He'll be over the grippe in a couple of days, so he should be back by Monday." Maude swiped a hand across her hair and sighed. "I'll be pleased to hand him back to you. Young boys make terrible patients."

Janet grinned, remembering the last time she'd taken care of Clint when he was ill. "Old boys, too. Sick men are whinier than a cat in season."

Maude let out a high snort of laughter.

A thin wail sounded from inside, "Mama, I need some water."

Maude nodded good-bye and disappeared back inside.

Janet shook her head. The child was running poor Maude ragged.

As she trotted down the splintery wooden stairs, the sounds of the general store below drifted upward: miners dickering over prices, something heavy slamming to the floor—probably a barrel—old-timers gossiping by the wood stove. How much rest could Billy get above the busy store?

At the bottom, she turned down the alley, then stopped and snapped her fingers. Hellfire, and how could she have forgotten to pick up the pastries for the children?

The night's snow had dusted the ground white and now it glimmered with the sunlight. Taking a happy breath of crisp air, Janet twirled her way down the alley, her skirts billowing around her legs. As she emerged onto Main Street, the townspeople nodded to her, calling greetings from across the street. Men tipped their hats. Her pleasure at the welcoming faces dimmed as she remembered who she was. Would these people still be so nice if they knew about her past? A painful sensation gripped her stomach at the thought of losing their respect. How long could she keep on as a schoolmarm before her past caught up to her?

She shoved open the door to the bakery and stopped in the doorway. One sniff and her dismal mood lifted. The heavenly scent of fresh bread, cinnamon and apples filled the air.

"It's a hard decision, but I'll take the gingersnaps."

"You're spoiling those children," the bakery owner said sternly, and then her pudgy cheeks wrinkled into a smile as she filled a sack and handed it over. "And I'll bet they just love it, don't they?"

Janet patted the brown paper bag that held the treats. "They work very hard to get one of your sweets." She winked at the big woman and whispered, "And if it's been a hard day, sometimes I treat myself, too."

Mrs. Chappell's hearty laughter followed Janet out of the bakery.

Janet glanced into Arnie's bookstore longingly. He had the newest Mark Twain displayed in the window, but her salary didn't extend to new books. Not this month. She'd be needing a new dress soon, and clothes for work came before fun.

She skirted a bony mongrel dog asleep in a patch of sunlight, then stepped down into the street. The cold had frozen most of the muck, making the crossing much more pleasant than usual.

She resolutely turned her eyes from the Shasta jail. Last time she'd walked by, she'd seen the marshal hard at work at his desk in front of the cells. As if alerted, he'd looked up, his eyes meeting hers, and she'd felt odd, like snow melting under a hot sun. The disconcerting feeling seemed to be coming over her more and more often around him.

He wasn't there today. She stepped up onto the boardwalk on the other side of the street with a feeling of relief and disappointment that she hadn't seen him.

"Hello, Miss Danner," a soft voice said from beside her.

She glanced around. Little Thomas sat on the boardwalk beside the land office. He had rags wrapped around his feet, one small exposed toe red with cold.

"Good afternoon, Thomas. What are you doing in town?" He usually hitched a ride to school with Sarah, his mother having died of the fever the year before.

"Pa is filing a new claim. Ours didn't show any color."

Janet frowned. Most of the gold had been panned out in the decade after the rush. The only mines producing now were deep, requiring equipment and financing. "Isn't he still working at the Jackass Mine?"

"Oh, yes'm, but we work on our own mine in the evenings and on weekends."

No wonder he never got his arithmetic done, smart as he was, Janet thought. The boy was just skin and bones, with a multitude of bruises. Mining must be rough work.

"Well, I hope you find some gold in your new mine," Janet said sincerely.

"Are those treats?" Thomas eyed the brown bag under Janet's arm.

"Yes. Better study those spelling words tonight."

He tossed his head to get the shock of black hair

out of his eyes and grinned. He was the best speller in the younger group.

Janet moved away, then stopped at the sound of a high yip. "What's that?"

"Uh, nothing," Thomas said. His loose homespun shirt moved, and a small head popped out of the top. Big brown eyes, floppy ears and a shaggy brown coat. Janet's heart melted.

"A puppy! Isn't he darling! Is this your dog?"

Thomas glanced at the land office door, then lowered his voice. "No. He was hiding under the boardwalk. He's so skinny, I don't think he's had anything to eat."

On the boardwalk lay an empty tin pail, the ragged bottom edge bent into an artistic attempt at scallops. "And I suppose you fed him your lunch?"

"Well—"

"What!"

Janet jumped at the bellow. In the doorway, Thomas's father scowled at his son. "You fed dat mongrel good food?"

Scrambling backward, Thomas set the puppy down.

The man snatched up the dog and tossed it behind him. A high yelp sounded. Turning, he hit Thomas between the shoulder blades with a huge hand, knocking the boy sprawling. The sound of the boy's head thumping hard on the boardwalk released Janet from shock.

She slapped Mr. Boudreaux's hand away before he could grab his son again. "You leave him alone, you mutton-faced coyote."

"Whut you say?" The stocky miner staggered a step sideways, and she realized he must have spent some time in the saloon.

"I said," she enunciated clearly, "leave the child alone. He hasn't done anything to warrant a beating."

Red creeped from Boudreaux's collar up into his beefy face. "This my son. You don't poke your pretty nose in where you got no business, missy." He shoved her back.

Thomas stood slowly, leaning against the building with a green look on his face. His father fastened his hand into the boy's shirt and slammed him against the wall with a thud.

"Enough, you jackal!" Swinging from the hip, she punched Boudreaux dead in the chin. Arms windmilling, he fell backward into the street. He landed hard, the icy muck cracking under his weight.

Janet shook her hand. Every finger felt busted. By golly, the man had an iron jaw.

He sat up, rubbing that jaw, his brows lowered over close-set eyes like an outraged bull. Considering the angry stream of French spilling out of his mouth, Janet was relieved she'd never learned the language.

She brushed the mud off her skirt and frowned. She'd enjoyed punching him, but losing her temper would never do. Engaging in fisticuffs wasn't considered schoolmarmlike behavior. She'd lost her temper, he'd lost his temper. This was getting out of hand.

Unfortunately, Boudreaux wasn't taking time to think. He rose, his eyes mad with rage, and yanked a double-edged knife from the sheath at his belt. "You want to have fun d'en, little missy?" he asked softly.

Oh, hell. She gave Thomas a push. "Get out of here."

The boy cringed, then took a few steps away. She turned back, knowing she was in trouble. Fear was a cold piece of ice in her stomach, a familiar companion she'd hoped never to feel again.

Eyes narrowed, she waited for Boudreaux to make his move. She'd have to duck and—

He lowered his head and charged straight at her. She steeled herself for the pain, she—

A body crashed into Boudreaux, knocking him back into the muck again. Ice and water burst under the impact and he let out a roar like a wounded grizzly. He was on his feet in seconds, lunging at—

With a gasp, Janet recognized the marshal.

Light on his feet, posture almost casual, the lawman lithely evaded Boudreaux's knife. As the miner stumbled past, Dagger hammered his fist into Boudreaux's neck. Another crash for the miner.

Covered with stinking mud, Boudreaux came up roaring and swinging his blade. Dagger kicked the knife out of his hand and it flew up into the air. With one punch, Dagger knocked the miner flat, then caught the knife on the way down.

Janet sagged against the wall, mouth open in awe. She'd never seen anyone with such deadly grace.

The marshal flipped the knife end over end into the air and caught it again. "Poor balance," he commented, then dropped the weapon beside the groaning miner.

He looked at Janet, his gaze running over her so intimately that she felt her cheeks burn, then squatted down beside Boudreaux. She couldn't hear the conversation, so she turned to pull Thomas into her arms. He shivered and clung to her. "It's all right, honey," she whispered. "The marshal will take care of everything."

Both men were looking at her now. The miner's

face was a study in fury before he grudgingly nodded.

Dagger stood. He motioned for Thomas to come closer.

Thomas pulled himself loose and went to stand beside his father. With a low groan, Boudreaux pushed himself to his feet, and the two headed down the street.

"He'll use a lighter hand on the boy," Dagger said to Janet. "I've warned him before, but there's no law that says a man can't beat his son. He won't get near you again, at least."

Janet gazed at the marshal's lean face, the dark brows drawn into a concerned frown, and her resolution to avoid him slipped another notch. "Thank you for the help."

White teeth flashed in a grin. "My pleasure, ma'am. It gave me an excuse to abandon my paperwork."

He wasn't even mussed, Janet realized. "Your way of fighting—" She paused. "Where did you learn to fight like that?"

"I lived with the Commanches for a while."

"Oh, my," Janet said faintly.

"Knife-fighting's a real sport. Being the only whiteskin, I got to practice a fair amount."

Uncomfortable with his past, Dagger took a step away. How could he tell her that although he'd returned to the white world, he didn't seem to belong there any more than he had with the Indians? He had no home, no place to be comfortable.

But he didn't feel that way with this woman, he realized. How could this be?

A soft sound registered a minute later. "What's that?" He turned his head, trying to locate the source.

"Oh! I almost forgot you, little one," Janet exclaimed. She crouched down next to the edge of the boardwalk, unconcerned at the way her skirts trailed in the mud. "Come here, baby."

Dagger squatted next to her. A pair of sad brown eyes peeked out from under the porch. His heart sank. Another stray. "Oh, hell."

"Excuse me?" Features arranged in a prim mask, the schoolmarm frowned at him. A dimple appeared briefly before she tightened her lips.

Dagger's lips curled in response. He was starting to realize this young miss had all sorts of hidden traits, one of them a well-developed sense of humor. "Sorry, ma'am."

She tried to coax the dog out from under the boardwalk, but the puppy cowered back from her hand. "You can't stay there, baby. You'll starve," she said softly.

Dagger gave a grunt. "C'mon, mutt," he growled, holding out his hand.

"You can't get him out by growl—" Janet's reprimand stopped short as the puppy sniffed Dagger's fingers, and his tail thumped on the ground.

Dagger inched backward and the little mutt followed eagerly. With an annoyed sniff, he picked up the dog. A cold nose buried itself in his neck and he sighed.

"What will you do with him?" Janet asked anxiously. He smiled at the concerned look in the pretty blue eyes. She caressed the puppy's ears with a gentle hand, and Dagger wanted to push his head against her hand for a pat, too.

He cleared his throat. "As marshal, I'm responsible for stray animals. We had a shack and fencing on the other side of town, but—"

"Got another critter for your house, eh, Marshal?" Jenny Perkins called from the doorway of her diner. "By the way, I think old Billy was looking for a dog to keep him company. Not a puppy, though."

"Jenny, you're a wonder," Dagger said. "I have an older dog that needs someone just like Billy." He held the puppy up and eyed the big, ungainly feet. "This one's going to be a fair size; he'll need some space to run." The puppy nestled back against him.

"Let's get him home," he said, rubbing the soft ears. "Want to see where I keep the strays?"

Janet nodded and bent to pick up a brown paper package before joining him.

In companionable silence, they strolled down Main Street and turned onto the quieter McKay Road toward his house.

Enjoying the sight of her graceful walk, Dagger commented, "He'd make a good dog for one of your children."

Her eyes were soft and the dimple winked again in her cheek. "I'll keep my ears open," she promised. "How many animals do you have?"

Dagger glanced at his house, then held open the gate for her. "The number varies. I find them homes as soon as possible. Right now there are three cats, two older kittens and three dogs, not counting this one."

At the sound of the gate, all three dogs rounded the house, running like a pack of wolves in pursuit. The hunting dog tried to leap on Janet, but she sidestepped him with impressive ease. He saw no fear in her eyes as she bent to pat the eager dogs.

They, in turn, almost knocked her flat with their enthusiasm. It appeared she had almost as much appeal for animals as she did for children—and for him, he admitted reluctantly. She was a woman of contradictions. He'd seen pretty women before, but this one had more than just a pretty face. She had a big heart and a sense of humor. He was beginning to think her primness was more of a disguise than an inbred trait.

He could still see that punch she'd thrown. Absolutely beautiful. And the way she'd faced Boudreaux's charge without cringing. There were few qualities the Blackthorne men admired more than courage.

"They're all very sweet," Janet said, giggling at the squirming huddle.

Dagger laughed, too. Tanner, the big and bony hunting dog, sat at her feet, tongue lolling halfway to the ground, shoving his ugly head under her hand every few seconds. The terrier, Casey, had two paws planted on the schoolmarm's dress and trembled all over with excitement.

Old Blackie, some homely mixture of hound and shepherd, lay on the ground, waiting patiently for his turn.

"I think Blackie there would make old Billy a fine companion," Dagger said, motioning to the older dog.

Janet paused in ruffling Casey's ears to hold out her hand to Blackie. Without raising more than an inch off the ground, he crept forward until his head was under her hand, then gave a massive sigh of pleasure. Janet chuckled, a low infectious sound. "You look so mean, but you're just a big pussycat, aren't you?" she murmured to the dog.

His tail thumped the ground so hard, Dagger was surprised it didn't break off.

"Will Billy be good to him?" she asked anxiously.

"Billy lost his wife last year after fifty years of marriage. He's kinda like Blackie here; looks like a grizzly and has a pudding-soft heart. They'll do well together."

"Oh, good."

Out of the corner of his eye, Dagger saw a woman moving down the road, her dark dress making her look like a crow. Mrs. Wilson. Of all the poor timing. Just when the schoolmarm had begun to soften toward him.

"Marshal Blackthorne." The paragon of virtue waved a furled umbrella, then came to a startled halt in front of his fence.

"And Miss Danner." Disapproval oozed through the words like mud in a cow pen. "Fancy meeting you here."

Janet stood unconcernedly and brushed dog hair from her skirts. "Hello, Mrs. Wilson. Did you see the puppy we just rescued?"

Grinning inwardly, Dagger held up the puppy. Startled from a heavy sleep, it yipped, and Mrs. Wilson drew back quickly.

Janet slipped through the gate, smiling at the dogs' disappointed chorus. "Now that I've met your beasties, I'll be seeing if any of the children would be a good match for them," she said to Dagger.

He tilted his head, less in agreement than in respect for her quick thinking.

"Are you going to the boardinghouse, then, Mrs. Wilson? Is this Mrs. Malvern's day for the ladies' tea?"

Mrs. Wilson tugged at her shirtwaist and gave a brief nod, her lips pursed in disappointment over losing a juicy piece of gossip.

"I'll walk across with you," Janet said. "Good day, Marshal. And good luck with Blackie and Billy." She inclined her head in as decorous a fashion as he'd ever seen.

His lips pulled straight to hide the grin, he gave a stiff bow. "I appreciate your assistance, Miss Danner. Good day, ladies."

Turning quickly before he started to snigger, he hurried into the house with the puppy. Putting the wiggling bundle down by the food dish, he poured in some scraps from the butcher. "So, pup, are you hungry?

He leaned against the table, his eyes on the window, still feeling . . . happy. Still feeling anger toward Boudreaux. So many emotions.

Usually he could keep his temper, maintain a distance from the world. Truth to tell, he felt like an observer most of the time, like when he was a scout for the army, viewing an encampment through the distance lenses. Not involved.

But whenever he was with Janet . . . seemed like she yanked him right into what was going on.

The loneliness that was so much a part of his life dissipated like fog in the sun when she was around.

The pup put a foot into the bowl of food to anchor it for a thorough cleaning and Dagger smiled. "You know, maybe I should take dinner at the boarding-house tonight. Miss Danner's quite a woman." He frowned, remembering the small discrepancies about her. "And she appears to be much more than what I first assumed."

Chapter Eight

Across the street, Janet handed Mrs. Wilson off to her landlady with a relieved sigh, adding, "It was good to see you again, Mrs. Wilson. Your children are a delight to instruct, and Rosie is a wonderful helper. She'd make a fine teacher herself."

The pinched look faded from Mrs. Wilson's face and she beamed.

"Would you care to join us for tea?" Mrs. Malvern asked reluctantly.

"You are too kind." Janet motioned to her muddy skirt. "However, I assisted the marshal in rescuing a puppy and I fear I am sadly mussed."

"The marshal?" Mrs. Malvern's lips thinned. "I do not believe that serving as the marshal's deputy is part of your duties."

Still glowing, Mrs. Wilson demurred. "Charity toward unfortunate animals is a fine trait in a lady. In fact—"

A knock sounded on the front door. When Mrs.

Wilson and Mrs. Malvern turned to greet the caller, Janet made her escape.

"Phew." After closing her bedroom door, Janet tossed her skirts onto the floor. She'd have to rinse them out quickly or the muck would stain the material. It was good that the laundry woman would be stopping by to pick up the wash tomorrow.

A giggle escaped her as she thought about how Boudreaux had looked. If the mud stank so badly on her gown, what must Boudreaux smell like? He'd been virtually covered in the stuff.

She wrung out a rag and performed a swift wash using the water in the basin. Her day to visit the bathhouse was Friday, so far away. Maybe she could sneak out of town tonight and visit the creek. The water would be more than freezing, but, oh, how she enjoyed being wet all over. She'd bathed in streams and lakes in every type of weather all her life.

After finishing her ablutions to her satisfaction, she donned her chemise and drawers and dropped down into the small chair, then stood again. She walked over to the window, then back to the bed.

The day was almost over, and she was pretty happy about that. Good thing she wasn't the type of woman to get overwrought. But she couldn't seem to calm down now that everything was over.

At least school had gone well. Both she and the students had settled into a routine, and she saw visible progress in their lessons. She'd never known such a feeling of satisfaction, not even from a successful robbery.

So that wasn't what was making her feel so unsettled.

More likely her fight with Boudreaux and then . . . being with the marshal.

She tipped her head back, enjoying the feel of her hair hanging loose, tickling her back. No itchy hairpins, no weight on the back of her head.

Marshal Dagger Blackthorne. Dagger. Rather funny name, actually, and his brother was called Bowie. Huh.

Hannah had told her he'd been raised by Indians. No wonder he'd picked up the gang's tracks that day.

Shaking her head, she pulled her thoughts back in order. The problem wasn't his odd name, but the fact that she liked his name . . . and him. She didn't *want* to like him.

But she did.

For one thing, he'd kept her from being hurt. Hell, he'd jumped in front of a knife for her! She could feel her pulse speed up at the memory of his courageous actions. She admired bravery. Her brother Harry would still be alive today if that extra man Pa had picked up for the break-in hadn't run like the yellow-belly dog he was.

She couldn't see Dagger running from anything.

And the way he'd cuddled the puppy to his chest had melted her heart. She'd known men who were gentle and weak, and men who were hard and brave, but she'd never met a courageous, deadly man with a gentle heart. Being with him was . . . different, her senses all aroused. She felt like a woman, and darned if she didn't like the feeling.

But . . . she sighed. He was also a man who could never have any tender feelings toward her or her family. She was being downright stupid about him.

In exasperation, she blew a wayward lock of hair out of her face. How in the world did she keep running into the man anyway? The way she felt around him, so wool-headed, meant she was more likely to be foolish, let something slip. She needed to keep her distance from him.

Humming "Sweet Betsy from Pike," Janet sifted the flour into the large wooden bowl the next evening. After checking the receipt Mrs. Chappell had written out for her, she added a small spoonful of soda, then started stirring. The large kitchen was quiet, with only the subdued crackle of the fire in the cookstove. From the parlor, she could hear the other boarders' murmurs, punctuated by an occasional shout when someone drew a good domino.

Turning the bowl, she scraped the sides and stirred quickly, then slower as her arm tired.

"Need help?"

She spun around, the spoon clattering onto the table and her hand whipping to the derringer in her skirt pocket.

"Exactly what *do* you keep in that pocket?" Marshal Blackthorne raised an eyebrow and sauntered into the kitchen.

Damn the man, one of these days she *would* shoot him, just for the fun of it! "That's a most impertinent question," she said, pursing her mouth into a stiff line to keep from laughing.

"Well, ma'am, I do apologize," he said with a straight face. But the way his eyes creased at the corners, she doubted he would fall for her prudish act any longer. She wondered briefly why the thought didn't bother her as much as it once had.

Stopping in front of her, he glanced at the bowl of spice cake dough. "Ah-ha! Mrs. Chappell said you were making treats for the children. But didn't you just buy them gingersnaps?"

"That's different. This is for David Verne's birthday tomorrow."

"Of course, entirely different." With a flourish, he presented her with the bouquet of roses he'd kept hidden behind his back. "May I bribe you into taking on an assistant and bowl-licker?"

"Ohhhh, how pretty!" She buried her face in the blossoms, inhaling the rich scent.

He flashed a wicked grin. "I stole them from Susanna's garden before I left. Valley roses are still blooming. So, is this an adequate incentive?"

"You want to help me cook?" Surely she was missing something. "Why?"

"Aside from the delight of your company"—Dagger made a little bow—"I'd wrestle cougars for sweets." He gave her an endearing little-boy grin. "I used to help my mother when she was cooking—there's nothing better than cake dough. Purty please?"

Dear heavens, how could she resist the appeal in those silvery gray eyes? "Well . . ."

A smile creased his tanned face.

She sighed and pushed the bowl toward him. What had happened to her resolve to stay away from this man?

He scooped up a finger of batter and popped it into his mouth with a murmur of delight before starting to vigorously stir the bowl. "Lucky children," he murmured, licking the sugar from his lips.

She couldn't take her gaze off his firm lips that looked soft at the same time. A shadow of beard blurred his strong jawline, gave him a rougher air.

"They think you're a fine teacher," he said, his head

bent over the bowl as he stirred. "The children are full of stories about the classroom, and their parents are quite pleased with the children's progress."

"Why . . . thank you, Mr. Blackthorne." The rush of pleasure at the compliment was as heady as a quick shot of whiskey.

"Dagger."

"Excuse me?"

"My name is Dagger. This 'mister' and 'marshal' is getting tiresome."

She wet her lips, uncomfortable under his steady gaze. "I don't believe that would be proper."

"Ah." He considered for a moment. "How about just in private, like now?"

"Well . . . I suppose that would be acceptable."

"And what is your handle?" He laughed at her confused look and added, "What do you like to be called?"

Why did this feel like she was revealing an intimacy? "Janet."

"Janet. That suits you fine."

Hearing Dagger say her name sent a warmth through her, like riding up the last path to a mountain hideaway. A feeling of coming home. Only her family and Susanna called her by her first name, Janet realized. And her last name was one she'd made up, so it still didn't seem quite real.

"Did you hear about the fight in the Gold Nugget? Apparently . . ." Still stirring, Dagger started in on the news from around town. Seating herself, Janet tilted her head and listened, strangely content in the warm kitchen with her unaccustomed companion.

A few minutes later, while Dagger finished telling her about Arnie's first bookstore in a mining town tent, she checked the coals and the heat in the cookstove, then popped the cake in, managing to avoid Dagger's last-minute attempt at more thieving. The man was a bottomless pit.

She dipped hot water from the reservoir in back of the stove, poured it into the dish basin and began the cleanup. Leaning back in his chair, Dagger related another tale of the livelier members of the town.

She slowly washed the dishes, enjoying listening to his faint southern drawl.

"Ah-ha, there's more." Beaming, Dagger scooped up a fingerful of spilled batter from the table.

Laughing, Janet slapped his hand with the wooden spoon she'd been drying. "Shame on you," she scolded. "You're as bad as Clint."

"You have brothers?" With an unrepentant grin, Dagger tucked the finger into his mouth.

The question brought all Janet's worries back. "Just one left," she murmured. "One out of four."

Dagger whistled. "Did they die in an epidemic?"

"One died soon after being born." Her mother had cried over little Joshua's tiny body. Harry had fallen in the streets of Sacramento after an aborted bank robbery. Dan had broken his back in a frantic getaway and had never woken up. And Clint . . . well, Clint was alive and just out of jail.

"The rest . . . died of a type of sickness." A sickness called crime.

He pressed his hand on her shoulder. "I'm sorry. It's hard to lose the people you love." His eyes darkened to the color of fog.

"Did you lose someone . . . ?"

He hesitated, and she knew this quiet man rarely spoke of old wounds. His hand still rested on her shoulder. She reached up and laced her fingers through his.

As if her touch had opened something within him, he said, "My wife."

She straightened. "You were married?"

"Shocking thought, eh?"

"N-no, I—"

He smiled, a dimpled line appearing in his cheek. "It was quite a few years ago. I was just nineteen at the time. Uh . . . she was an Indian."

Janet blinked. She was curious to know more about Dagger's past, but she refused to pry. If he wanted to continue she would listen. She waited quietly, allowing him time to collect his thoughts. The silence seemed to pull further words from him, opening a door she suspected he kept barred most of the time.

"She was beautiful, slim and quiet as a moonlit lake. That was her name—Moon on Still Waters. She didn't like to be around a lot of people."

A wry smile tugged at his lips. "Not at all like you. The thought of those children you tend would have sent her to the hills."

"What happened to her?"

"The Indians don't do well with our childhood illnesses. There was chicken pox someone brought from a trip to the nearby fort—the tribe lost half its people, Moon included. I . . . mourned her for a while."

He stared out the window, obviously recalling a very painful time. Janet felt an ache in her chest. God, how he must have missed her. Her eyes filled with tears; she wanted to comfort him, to take away his pain. She reached out and squeezed his hand.

He looked up at her and attempted a half smile. "Well, hey, darlin'. It was a long time ago."

She tried to smile at him, and her lips quivered. "What did you do after she died?"

"My brothers showed up shortly afterward. They'd been hunting me off and on for years—ever since I'd been captured."

"Captured? If they'd been looking for years, well, you must have been just a boy."

His jaw tightened. "Old enough, and probably what I deserved."

Janet longed to ask him more questions, but she only murmured, "Your family must have been frantic."

"Like I said, they searched for years."

In the silence that followed, Janet checked the cake, then removed it from the oven. Thinking about what he had said, the look on his strong face, she picked up the basin and carried it to the kitchen door. The night wind struck her face, cold against the heat of the kitchen.

She glanced out into the alley to be sure it was empty. She didn't want to toss the dirty water on some poor man's head.

A movement beside the house caught her eye and she hesitated, then gasped as a figure stepped forward into the spill of light from the door.

"Clint," she whispered.

He looked thin, his trousers patched, his hair jaggedly cut. What in the—

"Is something wrong, Janet?" Dagger called from behind her. He stepped to the door beside her and peered over her shoulder.

"N-no," she stammered, hastily stepping in front of him. "I-it's so cold. Let's get the door shut before Mrs. Malvern has a fit."

He gave way as she pushed him back into the

kitchen. Even in her shock, she noticed how hard his chest was under her fingers.

"You look pale." He touched her cheek with gentle fingers. "Did you see something that frightened you?"

"No." She shook her head vigorously. "I was just surprised by how fast the temperature dropped. I got cold, see?" She put ice-cold fingers over his warm ones.

"You're freezing." He enfolded her hands between his own, rubbing her fingers gently. His gray eyes studied her face and she forced her expression to remain still, her gaze even.

Dammit, she had to get rid of him. What if Clint actually knocked on the door?

She'd stopped seeing the silver star on his shoulder, but now it flashed at her with an unholy light. This was the marshal, and Clint was a Garret. If they met, blood would flow like a river.

What was she thinking about so intently? Dagger wondered. There was a pucker between her eyebrows, and her lovely pink lips had lost their smile. Was it him?

Watching her closely, he brought her hands to his lips and pressed a soft kiss into each of her palms.

A lovely flush warmed her cheeks before she gasped and snatched her hands away. "Oh, no—you mustn't." But he noticed that her gaze kept flickering to the kitchen door, to the window.

Dagger suppressed a frown—whatever was bothering her now, it wasn't him. What had she seen out there?

"Well." She rubbed her hands absently. "The dishes

are all done. The kitchen is clean." She took a step toward the door.

"Here's your hat, what's your hurry?" Dagger said wryly.

"I—" She flushed, then gave him such a sweet smile, he felt like a low-down coyote. "I am rather fatigued."

He politely excused himself and retrieved his hat and coat from the hook on the wall. Showing the same courtesy, she escorted him to the door. All the closeness of the evening had disappeared and he felt the lack.

Why had she changed?

He headed toward his house just until the door closed behind her; then he sprinted toward the back of the boardinghouse.

The sour odor of a perpetually damp street surrounded him as he moved into the alley. Lanterns in the windows cast a dim and flickering light across the muddy lane. Farther down, a door closed, and a second later the window next to it darkened.

He counted houses and doors. The door that had closed had been Mrs. Malvern's. Well, now, if Miz Janet wanted to retire for the night, why had she opened the back door again?

A shape moved nearby, and Dagger tensed, only to grin as a raccoon lumbered away between two houses. The alley was now silent, except for the drip of water from the roof, the rustling of mice behind an empty can. He knelt near the back door of the boardinghouse and peered at the ground, silently cursing the dim light. Nothing by the door. He moved back.

There!

In the middle of the alley, footprints were slowly filling with the water that trickled down the back street. The prints weren't full; someone had been out here not long before.

Dagger glanced at the door and rubbed his mustache thoughtfully. Obviously Janet'd seen something out here—someone. And if that someone had been a mere drifter, she wouldn't have hesitated to mention it to him.

He recalled the way she'd shoved him backward, away from the door, her tiny arm surprisingly strong. Whoever had been here, she'd not wanted him to see.

His lawman's suspicious nature roused like a bloodhound on the trail. He put his hand down into the muddy water of the footprint, feeling edges, the heel. Rider's boots. Not a shoe, not a miner's rubber boots. The left heel had a small notch. Dagger smiled in satisfaction. He'd know this boot if he came across it again.

He let himself into his own house, built up the banked fire and settled into his favorite chair. Hawthorne's *The Scarlet Letter* sat on the table, waiting for him to continue reading it, but he couldn't get interested. When the lean cat called Mouser jumped into his lap, he stroked a hand down its gray back. "We have a lot in common, cat. Curiosity will be the death of us."

Not deigning to reply, Mouser kneaded Dagger's legs thoroughly before deciding his lap would be adequate for a nap.

"On first sight, she seems like a perfectly normal schoolmarm, don't you think?" Dagger asked.

Mouser narrowed his eyes.

"Yeah, that's what I thought. Almost too perfect." He leaned his head back. "Have you ever seen such a sweet punch? Knocked Boudreaux right on his can."

Mouser took the time to clean a speck of dirt from between his claws.

With a touch of envy, Dagger admired the glint of light off the wicked weapons. "Why can't my knives be built-in? And what exactly does the little school-marm carry in her pocket? You think she might be packing?"

Mouser flexed his claws to show that only a fool leaves home without weapons.

"Uh-uh, and she's no fool, that's true. Took down Albert, too." Dagger ran his tongue over his teeth, tasting the lingering sweetness, and regretted that he hadn't been able to taste the sweetness of the teacher herself. She was much like a well-made apple pie. Full-bodied, sweet, with a touch of tartness.

He shifted uncomfortably and earned himself a glare from the napping cat. "Sorry."

Who had she been meeting out there in the alley? And what was she hiding, because he was damned sure she was hiding something.

The lights of the boardinghouse were visible through his front window. "Well, Miss Danner," he muttered, "seems we'll be doing a tad more talking." Pleasure slid through him at the thought.

Nothing he liked more than digging into a good mystery.

Chapter Nine

Janet woke with a start, her heart thudding. She tipped her head at a grating noise. Dammit, that was her window!

She raised herself up on an elbow and slid her pistol out from under the pillow and cocked the trigger.

At the sharp click, the figure in the window froze.

"Janet? It's me." Clint's soft whisper had her uncocking the pistol.

"You fool. Get in here before someone sees you."

"No one sees me unless I want them too," he boasted like the boy he still was. "Got out of the alley fast enough, didn't I?"

"I guess. I checked after the mar—the man left and you'd already gone." She jammed the weapon back under her pillow. Rising, she pulled the curtains before lighting a candle. Damn, it was fine, really fine to see him again. She leaned on the wall and beamed at him.

"Whoee, sissie, look at you." Clint gave a low whistle.

"What?"

"I've never seen you in female fripperies—you look
. . . different. Pretty."

After glancing down at her nightgown, Janet
blushed. "Well . . . thanks."

He dropped down on the chair. "Are you ready to
shake the dust from this two-bit town?" He grinned
at her and tossed his hat in the corner. "I've got a job
lined up."

Hell, she'd known this was coming, and she still
didn't have a good reply. "How did you end up in jail
anyway? And in San Francisco of all places. Pa told us
not to go there."

"I thought it'd be the quickest way to pick up some
cash. Some damned vigilantes grabbed me; I almost
got strung up on the spot."

Her stomach tightened at the pinched look that
crossed his face. He'd been scared, and the thought of
losing him scared her. She didn't have any family left
but him, her little brother.

"I did manage to stop a couple of wagons on the
way here, though, and . . . do you need some money?"

Pride in him mixed with fear for his safety and a
touch of . . . shame? A concern that she might have
known the people he'd robbed? "No. I'm making do."

"Anyway, here's what I got in mind for us to do
next."

"Listen, Clint—"

"The plan's simple, smooth as a baby's bottom. I
figure we can—"

"No, Clint."

He stopped, struck silent at the harshness of her
voice.

"I'm not leaving here." She sat down on the bed

116

and pulled a blanket around her shoulders against the chill in the room. The surprise on his face twisted her stomach. She reached out a hand, then drew it back. "Clint—"

"But . . . we're partners. All that's left of the Garret gang."

His bewilderment hit her like a lead slug in the belly. "I have a job here, friends . . . respect."

He was so uncomprehending that her heart wrenched inside. A few weeks ago, she wouldn't have understood either. But somehow she had to make him see. "I don't want to leave here." That sounded too final, so she added weakly, "Not yet, anyway. I'm having fun."

He snorted and stood. "Fun, huh. And for a little *fun*, you'd let your brother ride into danger with his back unguarded." He bent over and retrieved his hat.

Guilt surged through her like wildfire. "Clint—"

"Nah." He yanked the curtains back and put one foot through the window before looking back at her. "Just think on it, Sissie. I got some things to do first, then I'll be back. I know you won't let me down."

He grabbed the tree limb and swung out. A creak of branches, then a thud, as he jumped to the ground.

She rushed to the window, her mouth open to call out . . . something . . . but he was already striding away, tall, broad-shouldered and so dear to her.

Her lip quivered. "Dammit!" she snarled away the betraying weakness. Furiously, she kicked the wall, stomped back to the bed, ripped the covers back and slid in.

The room felt empty without Clint's energy, and like a knife in the dark, loneliness slid between her ribs and settled in her heart. She had only one person in the whole world who loved her, who knew who she was, and she'd just sent him away.

She shivered and drew the covers closer. What if he was careless, tried something foolish? He was only a boy still, even if he'd managed to grow to a man's height. Rash, too. Like the time he'd been mad at Harry and had filled his boots with lake slime. She'd had to say she'd done it, since Harry wouldn't whip a girl as hard. Clint had been so sorry, she'd conned him out of dessert for a week.

Her lips curled into a rueful smile. The two of them had been closer in age and to each other. It had been the two younger Garrets against the older, harder brothers. Would that hardness happen to Clint?

She remembered Harry carrying her on his shoulders when he'd been oh, fifteen or so, letting her pull his curly yellow hair. And Dan, the way he'd take in sick animals, orphaned birds, and nurse them back to health. Then, all of a sudden it seemed, they'd changed.

Once they'd started riding the outlaw trail.

"Good afternoon, Mrs. Wilson." Stepping into Wilson's Dry Goods and Ready-mades, Janet took an appreciative sniff at the scent of new fabric and pungent shoe leather. If anyone had told her before how much fun shopping could be, she'd have laughed herself silly.

"And what can I help you with today?" Behind the counter, Mrs. Wilson tugged her shirtwaist down over an ample stomach. "Material for a gown?"

The small sniff at the end of her sentence made Janet wince. She deserved it, too. What kind of schoolmarm only owned one skirt and one dress?

118

"Yes, but first I wanted to know if you could recommend a good seamstress."

"Well . . ." Pleasure at being asked for advice warmed the woman's sallow complexion. She lowered her voice and nodded at a woman across the room. "As it happens, Mrs. Harris, over there, is one of the best."

Janet glanced at the young lady. Mrs. Harris appeared to be a bit down on her luck in an impeccably sewn gown of faded color and fraying hemline. A hard twinge of sympathy moved Janet at the sight.

"A few months ago her husband fell down a mine shaft and broke his back. Lingered almost a month, poor man." Mrs. Wilson lifted up the hinged countertop and sailed through. "Let me introduce you."

"Uh—" She'd been saving up, but could she afford a new gown? Material and labor? Janet bit her lip, then obediently followed. She could always say no if the cost was too dear.

"Olivia, my dear, I'd like to introduce you to our schoolteacher, Miss Danner. She may have some work for you."

Mrs. Harris had eyes as timid as a cornered rabbit and a sweet smile. "Pleased to meet you, Miss Danner."

"And you, Mrs. Harris. Um . . . I'd like to discuss a possible gown, suitable for my classroom, of course." Tossing Mrs. Wilson a quick nod of thanks, Janet launched into her ideas.

Turned out the cost was more than reasonable. While wandering among the fabrics, they managed to set up a time for fittings. Janet couldn't resist touching, smoothing each soft bolt of material. She'd never known how different women's fabrics were from the rough clothing she'd worn as a man.

"Isn't this one lovely?" she murmured. Soft and white, perfect for a chemise.

"I also do whitework," Olivia Harris said, lifting her eyebrows.

"Heavens, I couldn't afford it right now." Janet drew her hand away reluctantly. "I can afford the material or you, but not both."

A flush climbed Olivia's cheeks, and she glanced over at Mrs. Wilson, who was busily doing her account books. "I . . . I'd be happy to exchange my labor for—"

"For what?"

Her voice dropped even lower. "Reading, Miss Danner. I'd really like to be able to read."

Who'd have figured? Janet thought. "Well, he—" she cut off the swear word and smoothly substituted, "Here's a fine chance for both of us." And then it was her turn to blush. "Would there be any chance of making some, um . . . frills?"

A slow smile grew on Olivia's face. "Ruffles? Lace? Pretty?"

The longing was too much for embarrassment. "Oh, yes! And I'll have you reading before Christmas." They grinned at each other in complete accord, and Janet swept up the bolt of material.

Olivia gave Mrs. Wilson the yardage needed of each fabric, then nodded good-bye.

"I'll see you in a couple days," Janet called.

Mrs. Wilson totaled up the sums of the material, muttering numbers and carryovers. "Looks like you owe—I almost forgot. Do you realize Thanksgiving is almost upon us?"

Janet tipped her head and frowned. Did that mean she'd need another dress or something? Lord help her. "Yes, I know that."

"And has anyone mentioned the harvest recital and dance?"

"Recital?" The floor seemed a bit soft beneath her feet, like she was standing in quicksand. "What kind of recital?"

Mrs. Wilson tsked impatiently. "A school recital, Miss Danner. For all your pupils. I'm sure you've been preparing. Everyone loves when there's singing as well, of course. There *will* be singing, won't there?"

The reply had to be forced through a very dry throat. "Of course." She wet her lips. "What date is this to occur?"

"We've always had it on the third Friday in November. You and the children handle the program; the women from the churches will help with decorations and provide food and drinks."

Janet glanced down at her feet; the quicksand seemed to have turned into freezing water and she was sinking fast. "Decorations, children's recital, singing. Anything else?"

"No, that should be it." Mrs. Wilson paused a moment and smiled slowly. "You may want to consider another gown . . . of course—for the dance afterward."

Janet leaned against a railing outside the store, her head spinning. Just when she was starting to feel like she had a handle on things, they went and changed the rules.

Mrs. Wilson seemed to think she knew what all a recital included, and here she didn't have a clue.

"How are you today, ma'am?"

She glanced up. "Um, fine, Father. Just . . . thinking."

Father Sean had halted in front of her, his graying eyebrows pulled in concern. His cross dangled and glinted at her, reminding her of the glitter of the marshal's badge. She'd best get off the street or the nosy lawman would be over here, too, butting into her business.

"You look ill, Miss Danner."

Seems there was a negative side to being a member of the town; people took too much of an interest at times. She shook her head and mustered a smile for the elderly priest.

"Mrs. Wilson just reminded me how close we are to the time for the children's recital. I hadn't realized how quickly time had passed."

"Ah." He patted her shoulder comfortingly. "You've been busy. May I say how pleased everyone in town is with the way you've handled the school?"

A warmth crept into her stomach at his words and then froze solid as he unwittingly finished her off.

"We're all looking forward to the recital. Bless you for your work." After nodding warmly at her, he moved down the boardwalk toward the pastry shop, on his way to indulge the sin of his life.

Janet let her head thud against the post holding up the boardwalk's roof and wished it would just crash down on her and put her out of her misery. How could she pull off a recital when she'd never seen one? It sounded like the entire town would be there to witness her incompetence.

She turned to head back to her room. Maybe if she talked to some of the people in the boardinghouse—

she bounced off something hard and was pulled upright before she fell. "Ooooph!"

"Well, if it isn't Miss Danner." The amused voice stroked her nerves like rum-laced coffee, soothing and arousing all at once, and she realized he'd caught her against his rock-hard body.

"Marshal." She looked up into gray eyes shaded by his black hat and had to enjoy the way the lines beside them crinkled at her. Seemed unlawful for a lawman to be so damned good-looking.

"You'd best watch your step," he said, allowing her to move back and steadying her with a firm hand on her arm. "Some of these men here might take advantage of having a pretty miss jump into their arms."

"I never!" She shot him a glare, still feeling the muscles of his chest against her tingling bosom. His fingers were warm, hard. "Let me go."

"Excuse me. Where were you headed in such a hurry?"

"I wasn't in a hurry. I was heading back to the boardinghouse."

"Well, maybe I'll see you for supper, then." His polite nod was erased by the wicked grin that followed it, a flash of white that sent shivers down her spine. What would it be like to—

"Oh, I almost forgot," he said. "Susanna's been asking about you. She's not getting out as much these days, due to her . . . ah, delicate condition, but if you'd like to ride out there, I'd be happy to escort you."

Susanna! The perfect solution. "Thank you, Marshal, but I'm sure you have work to do."

She couldn't suppress the blinding smile she tossed him before turning and dashing toward the livery.

* * *

In the late afternoon, Janet pulled her horse up before a large ranch house flanked by massive barns. Tying her mare to the rail, she strode up the wide porch steps just as the front door was flung open.

"Janet! How wonderful!" Susanna wiped her hands on her apron and grinned widely. "I've been so lonely for other women. Bowie won't let me go to town as often now, what with my being *enciente*. He's *much* too protective."

"I've missed you, too." Janet stopped, stunned. Damned if her friend wasn't wearing britches. "Uh—"

Susanna glanced down. "Oh. My trousers. I made a deal with Bowie that I'd only wear them on the ranch."

"Uh, what was his part of the deal?"

A dimple appeared in Susanna's cheek. She nodded to the side of the house.

Janet turned. If he was in a dress, by damn, she'd be leaving real quick. But she only saw the big man hard at work digging up a garden.

"He promised he'd help me with my produce business, and he's an honorable man."

He tipped his hat to them, and Susanna beamed at him before muttering to Janet, "And doesn't he have the nicest shoulders you've ever laid eyes on?"

Janet snickered. "You sound like Hannah."

"Oh, and who do you think pointed those shoulders out to me?" Susanna asked airily. "Come on in and tell me what's been happening in town."

A few minutes later, Janet settled down on a soft couch with a glass of hot peppermint tea. A fire snapped busily in a wide fireplace, sending out wonderful warmth to the entire room. She glanced around the cozy room. "What did the house look like before you arrived?"

Susanna laughed and rolled her eyes. "Bare wood and clutter."

"I figured." Lord knew she'd lived around men and seen their idea of decorating. This room was both homey and tidy. Well-crafted chairs were softly padded with bright fabrics and colorful weavings decorated the walls.

"So tell me what's going on."

Janet sighed. "Actually, I came out for a reason. I need help again. Mrs. Wilson tells me I'm in charge of a recital and dance." She bit her lip. "Sus, I've never even *been* to a dance."

"Oh, my. Planning this out is going to take a while. You'd best stay for supper."

A couple of hours later, Janet had a long list: recital ideas, decorating tips, traditions, who to ask for help. As they ate the tender roast beef supper, Bowie related stories of past fall dances. Apparently the event could become rather rowdy. She was beginning to like it already.

Bowie snatched another biscuit. "And then Arnie— he can't hold his likker worth a darn—started quoting Shakespeare. Would you believe he was doing Romeo and making sheep's eyes at Hannah?"

"Hannah?" Janet pursed her lips and glanced at Susanna. "Didn't she tell me that she can't stand when men moon around her?"

"Uh-huh. Been dealing cards too long with all those lecherous men. She likes to look, but she doesn't want them close. At least not most of them." Susanna passed Bowie the butter. "Poor Arnie. What did Hannah do?"

"She decked him and—" Bowie held up a hand to silence the laughter. "Horse coming up the lane."

While Susanna went with him to check out the visitor, Janet added another idea to the list sitting beside her plate.

"Damn, it's good to see you," Bowie said as he followed Dagger and Susanna into the room.

Oh, hell, the bloody marshal. Janet frowned at him. The lawman seemed to be turning up everywhere.

"You're here just in time for supper," Susanna said, fetching another plate and setting it beside Bowie.

"Well, now, that was the plan. I never miss your cooking if I can help it." Dagger seated Susanna, then picked up the plate, moved down the table and took a chair beside Janet. "And how are you this evening, Miz Danner?"

She could feel the warmth of his body, so close, and she shifted her chair farther away. "Just fine, thank you. What brings you out here?"

He pulled an envelope from his shirt pocket and handed it to Bowie. "Blade wrote." Glancing at Janet, he added, "Our brother. He's in medical school over in San Francisco."

After tearing open the envelope, Bowie gave the letter a swift perusal. "Looks like he'll be home for Thanksgiving."

Susanna gave a crow of delight; then her brows drew together. "It's such a long, bumpy stage ride. Should he really be coming back so soon?"

"Is he ill?" Janet asked. Surely a man around the marshal's age wouldn't take the stage; he should be able to ride his horse.

"Got a bum leg," Bowie explained. "He was—"

Dagger interrupted, his deep voice harsh. "Stinking, lying outlaws shot him."

Janet's fingers trembled at his angry response and she hastily put her hands in her lap. "Outlaws? What—"

"We went after a gang that robbed a mule train. The leader was dying and I . . . I stupidly gave them a chance to sit with him." Jaw rigid, Dagger's words were filled with self-loathing.

Her lips were numb as she asked the question anyone else would ask. His brother—that must have been his brother she'd shot—"Why was that stupid?"

"The two who were left—one took the old man's gun, the other had a concealed weapon, and they opened fire on us. Blew Blade's leg to pieces."

Janet's eyes shut. *She could feel her hand lower as she pulled the trigger. The blood and bone bursting out of his leg. His fall, so slow, so inevitable.* Bowie's brother . . . Dagger's brother. Her stomach churned and she held a napkin to her lips. "I—I'm sorry."

"Shoot, Dagger, what are you thinking of?" Susanna scolded. "You're getting her overwrought."

Dagger tore himself from his memories and frowned at the schoolmarm. Susanna was right; the little lady's face was the color of snow and her hand shook. "He—ah, I'm sorry, darlin'. I guess I got carried away."

He touched her hand, icy cold, and she jerked away, making him feel like a filthy cad.

She clasped her hands in her lap and took a breath. "Did you catch the . . . outlaws?"

"No . . . not yet." He felt a muscle twitch in his cheek and rage swelled up in him again. "But I will," he vowed. "And, by God, when I do, they'll hang by the neck."

She sank back into her chair—well, hell, he'd scared her again. She looked about ready to swoon.

Susanna glared at him from across the table. "Dagger, you are such an idiot; if I wasn't a lady, I'd smack you one."

She turned to the teacher. "Janet, are you all right?"

The schoolmarm smiled with a visible effort. "I'm fine, Susanna." She pushed back her chair. "But if you'll excuse me, I think perhaps I need a bit of air."

"Of course." A frown creased Susanna's brow. "I—"

Janet held up a hand. "No, stay there and finish your meal. I'll be back in a few minutes. I just need a moment."

She let herself out the front door quietly.

Dagger ran a hand through his hair and let out a sigh.

"Dammit, Dagger—" Bowie started.

"I know, I know. Not appropriate dinnertime conversation, and I'm too driven to get revenge, and—"

Bowie gave a grim smile. "Exactly. Couldn't have said it better myself. Whatever possessed you?"

"Well, hell—sorry, Susanna—but she asked, didn't she?"

"And you just had to tell her. Did you see how white she was? She's a schoolteacher, not used to our rough ways."

Dagger slumped in his chair. He hadn't thought about how a civilized woman might react to his need for violent revenge.

As the minutes ticked by, Susanna kept glancing at the door, obviously concerned about her guest.

Finally, Dagger sat up. "I'll go check on her, all right? And apologize."

Sus nodded and picked up her spoon. "Thank you, Dagger. I'd feel better."

Chapter Ten

Janet took a deep breath of the cold night air and heaved a sigh of relief at being out of the house. The anger and ferocious determination in Dagger's face had flat-out scared her. That was her neck he was talking about stretching on a gallows. Her life he wanted to end.

Her hands felt icy as she pressed them against her cheeks. This must be why Pa had never wanted to shoot anyone during a robbery, why he'd planned so carefully.

But his planning hadn't worked that last day, had it? She'd shot Dagger's brother, left him lame for life. There was no reparation she could make for that.

How would she feel if it had been Clint?

She could still remember the man she'd shot and could now see how his features were akin to Dagger's, but younger, leaner. The thought of Dagger limping, his powerful grace diminished, made her feel sick to her stomach. And she'd caused that harm to his brother.

With a glance back toward the house—no, she wasn't ready to face them yet—she stepped down off the porch. A giant barn stood off to one side, and she heard the stamp and snorting of horses. Without a thought, she headed that way.

Her mare had been tucked into a stall, watered, grained, with fresh loose hay. Brownie whickered as Janet approached and butted her head against Janet's shoulder.

Janet leaned her head against Brownie's neck and wrapped an arm loosely over her shoulder. "I feel so guilty, so evil," she whispered. "... And so scared. What if he finds out who I am? Or Susanna, or Bowie?" She'd lose her friends, the job she had come to love. Her heart squeezed at the thought of how they'd look at her—worse, how the marshal would look. His eyes wouldn't be that light gray but would turn the dark of a horrible storm. "Why do I worry about that lawman and what—" The crunch of footsteps halted her confidences.

"Ah, so here's where you went." Dagger stepped into the barn, the moonlight behind him illuminating his tall frame. She couldn't see his face.

"I—I thought I'd check on my horse." Janet unwrapped her arms from the mare, uneasily aware of how much the position revealed of her frame of mind.

"Mmmm." Dagger leaned against the stall and stroked Brownie's muzzle. "Pretty lady. You're a lucky horse to have so much attention, aren't you?"

The silly mare ate it up, and the muscles in Janet's shoulders relaxed at the soothing croon of Dagger's voice. His anger was gone as if it had never been.

He turned to her, the corner of his mouth pulling

into a half smile. "Want to stretch your legs before we go back in? There's plenty of light."

"That sounds fine." Her fingers shaking only slightly, she placed them on the offered arm and let him lead her out of the stable and into the crisp night air.

Over the eastern mountain range, a huge golden moon was rising, and she gestured to the hillsides, where manzanita bushes reflected the light in eerie miniature. "Fairy ballrooms."

"Rabbit holes."

She shook her head in mock sorrow. "No imagination; just like a man of the law."

Dagger led her past the house and down a quiet tree-lined path to a small pond fed by a gurgling stream. A rustling in the bushes, then silence, indicated the field mice were alive and well.

At a smooth-hewn bench, Dagger stopped. "We built this for Blade, so he could enjoy the pond while he was recovering."

"And to encourage him to walk this far?" Janet tried the bench and relished the view across the pond to a willow with gracefully drooping branches.

"Nah. He's not the type to need to be pushed; actually, the reverse was true. He'd drag himself out here, but then he had trouble standing up."

She heard the pride in his voice, the protectiveness for his brother, much like she felt for Clint. More even. Her feeling of guilt increased.

Above the pond, an owl swooped, feathers shimmering in the moonlight. A small animal darted and ducked the bird's talons, disappearing into the grass.

Her hands tightened in her lap. Instead of feeling like the hunter, today she felt more like the prey.

"You're unusually quiet," Dagger said. He lifted up her chin to meet his dark gaze. "Are you chilled?"

"N-no, yes . . . a little." He seemed awfully close, the heat from his fingers burning into her skin. That smile of his, a lopsided flicker—something so fleeting, yet it fogged her mind, made her breath come hard.

"Well, good," he murmured, and pulled her into his arms. "I'll try to warm you up a little then. Susanna'd have my hide if you caught cold."

"Oh." Heavenly warmth poured from his body and the arms around her were comforting . . . hard . . . exciting. She'd never been held like this, by a man not in her family. It was . . . different.

"How long have you been a marshal?" She tried to focus on who he was, what he did, but her thoughts kept fleeing from her like the bats dipping over the water.

"Mmmm." His warm breath ruffled her hair, his cheek touched hers. "Been a marshal for a while. When I left the army, seemed like the next best job."

"Carrying a gun?"

"I like things orderly." He hesitated. "I don't like seeing people picked on or taken advantage of," he said, as if he was confessing something shameful.

She recalled the determined look on his face when he stepped into her battle with Boudreaux—he'd looked like a man on a mission. And she suddenly understood something about what drove this man.

"Have I told you how beautiful you are in the moonlight?"

Her mouth pulled into a smile at the grudging tone, but at the same time his words took her breath away. No one had told her she was beautiful before.

She tipped her head up to look at him, and when

her eyes met his, she felt caught up in white water, tumbling over and over. "Dagger."

His breath fanned her cold cheek as his mouth descended. Lips firm, yet startlingly velvety. She moaned at the rush of desire, molten heat pooling low.

He nibbled her lips, teasingly, and she started to say . . . something, but the words were swept aside as he took possession of her mouth, firmly, completely.

A moment spun into forever as he kissed her senseless.

Then he lifted his head, pulling away from her. "I shouldn't have—"

"Ha." Trusting in the strength of his arms, she freed his shoulders. Lacing her fingers behind his head, she yanked him back to her waiting mouth.

A moment's resistance. His arms tightened. "Well, then—"

Damn, he was good at this kissing business.

She was melting from the heat, about to run out of his arms and puddle into the pond. Plastered against him, she could feel his heart thud against her breasts. His hands warmed her back, his fingers playing with her hair, stroking her shoulders, the sensitive nape of her neck. She shivered and the aching in her grew more acute.

She needed . . . something . . . something more. Her breasts felt swollen and she rubbed them against his chest, heard his breath catch. A shadow crossed overhead, the owl trying for another—

"Wait . . ." Her voice sounded husky, breathless in her ears. A lawman—she'd been kissing a damned lawman. "I—"

"Oh, he—shoot, darlin'." His voice was no better, velvety gravel. "I am sorry. Had no intention of this happening. I came out to apologize for scaring you earlier, not to attack you in the moonlight."

"I'm sorry, too." She leaned away from him and smoothed her skirts, as if the action would put her feelings back into a ladylike box. "We'd best get back, don't you think?" Damn it all, what had she been thinking?

He helped her to her feet, tucked her hand into the curve of his elbow. Just like she was a real lady.

As they moved down the path, she glanced back at the pond. Over the willow, the owl flapped higher into the night sky. The risen moon shone starkly on the small mouse struggling in its grip.

A short time later, Janet leaned back in the comfortable chair in front of the fireplace. After finishing the interrupted meal and enjoying dessert, the men had gone out front to smoke, leaving her alone with Susanna.

"That was one magnificent meal, Mrs. Blackthorne," Janet said with a happy sigh.

"And one scrumptious apple cake, Miss Danner. I'm glad you were here to make us dessert."

"Thank Mrs. Chappell instead; it's her recipe."

Susanna rummaged in the basket next to her chair and pulled out some knitting.

"What are you making?" Janet asked and saw Susanna hold up an incredibly tiny—"A sock? It's so small!"

"A bootie, you silly goose. And, last I heard, newborns are small."

"Yes, but—" Janet eyed the sock, trying to imagine the size of the foot that would fit into it. Babies had

135

been in short supply on the outlaw trail. Did they really come so little?

Then again, a person did have to carry them around inside—what would it be like to have a baby? She barely remembered when Ma was carrying Clint, but seemed like she was bigger. Resting her hands over her stomach, she frowned at Susanna's gown. "You don't really look like you're with child," she blurted out.

Susanna laughed and smoothed the skirt down over her front to silhouette a rounding abdomen. "It's started, but I'm not too far along the family way yet."

"Oh." Well, hell, she knew that. A woman didn't just suddenly turn into a waddling mass of flesh. She'd always felt so superior when she'd seen the rare pregnant woman out and about, but now . . . now she had a twinge of envy. A baby out of one's own body—a ready-made family. A feeling of homesickness washed over her. Not much family left to her anymore.

She snuggled back into her chair and watched as Susanna quietly knitted a length, the silence comfortable between them. The fire nibbled busily along the edges of hefty oak logs while a mantel clock ticked its own beat.

The ache of missing her family eased slightly at the thought that she had friends now, the first she'd ever had. The empty spot within her heart seemed to fill slightly. Life couldn't remain the same, not and be life, so all a body could do was move on.

After a while, Susanna looked up. "Did you and Dagger have a nice walk?"

Heat rose in Janet's cheeks. Hell, her face must be turning the color of a ripe tomato. "Yeah . . . I mean, yes. He showed me the pond. Very pretty." At a sudden thought, she straightened. Having seen animals going at each other, she assumed humans would perform the same. Surely kissing couldn't make a baby . . . could it?

With a soft cough, Susanna nodded. "Yes, it's a pretty pond. Very . . . romantic."

Janet studied her suspiciously. "Oh? I hadn't noticed."

Susanna looked up, her eyes dancing with laughter.

Janet gave in. "All right, you win. How did you know?"

"Perhaps the rash on your face? The Blackthorne men have heavy whiskers, don't they?"

Janet touched her cheek, remembering the roughness of Dagger's face, the exciting feel of that scrape against her face, her neck. He might as well have branded her. She shook her head.

"Dagger's a fine man," Susanna said softly.

"I'm sure he is, but I'm not interested in finding a man, fine or otherwise."

Susanna ignored her. "And those dark gray eyes— aren't they something?"

"Susanna," Janet raised her voice. "I'm telling you plain, I'm not marriage-minded." She suppressed the flutter at the memory of those eyes, fog-colored and fogging her mind. "Don't make a mountain out of a molehill here. It was just a kiss and there certainly won't be any more."

On the porch, Dagger paused, the match halfway to his cigar. The raised voice had cut through the still air like a knife. Not gonna kiss him again? He frowned at the half-open door.

"Appears you've lost your touch with women," Bowie commented mildly. He leaned against the porch railing and tilted his head to catch the high voices from inside.

Dagger finished lighting his cigar and took a puff. "The hunt's not over; that was only the first shot." He pushed the front door closed with his foot, cutting off the women's voices. "My quiver's still full."

His brother grinned. "This little deer might escape you. She seems pretty fleet of foot."

Dagger didn't know about her feet, but the woman had the softest lips he'd ever tasted. Just what the hell did she mean that she wouldn't kiss him again? He was darned well going to see her again and . . .

Putting his feet up on the railing, he leaned back and studied the moon. "Then it's just as well that I'm a fine hunter."

Chapter Eleven

Janet joined the congregation streaming out of the church and stopped for a moment to gaze at the glistening white snow on the mountain peaks and the cloudless blue sky. The air was amazingly warm and she took a happy breath, shaking off the unsettled feeling the sermon had left with her.

At the foot of the steps, Reverend Albertson waited, reminding her of a benevolent spider in wait. He beamed at the children, chided Randall Perkins, whose bloodshot eyes displayed his overindulgence the night before, advised and chatted with his parishioners. Janet, still humming some catchy hymn about a cross, stopped to give the preacher the expected words of appreciation although his sermon on honesty had been one she'd prefer not to think about.

Soon surrounded by the townspeople, exchanging nods and bits of conversation with the women, she felt very much a part of everything. A most unfamiliar and heady feeling.

"Miss Danner," Mrs. Tucker called, bustling up. In

her sedate church gown, she looked almost undressed without her usual starchy white apron. "Some of us are going to picnic at the creek and enjoy the warm weather. Would you care to join us?"

"Um," Janet hesitated, then grinned. "Surely. I would enjoy that very much. What can I bring?"

"Just yourself, dear. Let us old women show off our baking skills." She linked an arm with Janet's and pulled her over to the Tuckers' buckboard.

"Get in, Miss Danner!" Billy urged from the back, then leaned over the side to taunt another boy. "See, told you she'd come with us."

Mr. Tucker helped her onto the seat beside his wife and then took his place. A slap of the reins and the wagon rattled after several others down Main Street, toward the town's favorite picnicking area.

The wagons and buggies pulled up on the stream bank under a huge oak tree and people jumped down. As Janet helped unload the food, she smiled at the vibrant green grass that the fall rains had woken.

In just a few minutes, colorful blankets formed patterns like crazy quiltwork and baskets of food added lumpy texture. The smell of fried chicken, sweet cakes and the tang of coleslaw filled the air.

Shouting in high voices, the children played on the banks of the rushing creek, finding colorful stones, racing sticks, making mud pies. Under the noise of the children and the bubbling stream sounded the muted chatter of the adults. Women chatted with women, men conversed with men.

Settled on a corner of the blanket, Janet listened to the range of topics: crops, stomach complaints, livestock, gowns, politics, food, battle and back to clothing again. She'd never realized women were much more realistic about life than men.

"And how's the day finding you, Miss Danner?"

Janet jerked around at the sound of the marshal's deep voice above her. "Uh, fine. I'm fine, and how are you?" As usual, he was dressed all in black. Didn't the man wear any other color? she thought grumpily.

Thumbs casually hooked into his belt, he looked at her intently. "Not too bad. Enjoyed the sermon today."

Fascinated with the way the sun lightened his smoky eyes to silver, she had to think for a moment. Her throat closed as she recalled the sermon: honesty. Reverend Albertson had spoken about the sin of lying, the need for honesty, the—

"Maybe I've been a lawman too long," Dagger said, "since I hear a lot of lyin', but what the preacher said made sense to me."

"Uh." Her mouth was dry. "Perhaps a bit of a simplistic approach. There may be times—"

He raised his eyebrows and she stopped, stumped.

Maude Tucker waved from her blanket. "Miss Janet, can you get the boys? We're ready to feed the hordes."

Relieved at the interruption, Janet gave Maude a grateful look. "I'd be happy to fetch them."

As she headed down to the creek, the lawman kept pace with her. She glanced up at him and got caught again by the silvery gaze. Caught long enough to trip like an idiot over a rock.

Moving faster than a bee-stung dog, his big hand wrapped around her upper arm and he pulled her upright. Even through her sleeve, she felt the hardness of his fingers, and heat spread outward from where he held her. "Thank you," she murmured.

A glint of a white smile flashed in the dark face. "Well, it was my pleasure." One eyebrow arced upward. "Not like you to trip, though."

Better not be. Outlaws didn't live long if they were clumsy. One false step in getting away and the lawmen would catch you faster than a rabbit in a snare.

"Children." Janet clapped her hands in the way she'd seen Sally do when the girls were playing teacher-and-student pretend games in the schoolyard. Didn't work. They ignored her in their splashing.

Dagger grinned at her. "Let me try." He took a deep breath and let out a bellow, "Come 'n' get it. Chow's on."

Heads came up and a mass exodus took place, leaving behind shoes, stockings, half-built stick boats, dolls and bonnets.

"How was that?" Dagger asked.

Janet giggled, then brought herself back to reality. Schoolmarm; she was a schoolmarm. "My," she said primly, "that was certainly effective, Marshal."

He tilted his head and frowned at her. "Dam-darned if you don't seem to be two different women sometimes."

Her heart thudded. "Whatever do you mean?"

"One minute you're a bouncy, fun-loving lady; the next you're all starch and vinegar." His gaze swept over her, piercing in intensity.

He wasn't two people—he was all lawman, and a chill prickled up her spine. The last thing she needed was to get him curious. A bland answer might be the ticket. "I don't understand your confusion, sir. I am a woman and I am a schoolmarm. I do have a certain appearance to maintain, of course."

He turned and held out his hand to help her up the creek bank. "Of course. But your appearance sometimes seems more of a—"

She raised her chin and gave him a haughty look.

"Never mind. I don't know what I was talking about. That chicken smells good, doesn't it?"

In silence, Janet walked beside him back to the blankets. The man was too clear-sighted. He was beginning to see that the schoolmarm manners weren't who she really was. Chewing on her lip, she glanced at him out of the corner of her eye. He was watching her, his eyes steady on her face. Thought he had her figured out, didn't he?

"Join us, you two." Maude motioned toward an empty side of the blankets. Beside her, stiff in his black suitcoat, sat Peter Tucker, her husband. Laura, slim and lovely, graced one corner, and Billy and Richard jostled each other for space in the other.

Janet moved to sit down, then hesitated as Priscilla Malvern bustled up. Like a rotund shadow, her daughter followed.

"Marshal Blackthorne, how nice to see you," her landlady gushed, then nodded at Janet. "Miss Danner."

Priscilla plopped her stout body down on the blanket, arranged her flouncy skirts with precision, then patted a spot beside her. "Sit here, Florence. Mind you don't get your shoes muddy."

Janet watched the procedure, trying to grasp the method of lowering oneself to the ground while encased in a stiff corset and an overwhelming amount of useless material. Good lord.

"Let me help you down," Dagger said, holding out a rock-steady hand.

At his action, Mrs. Malvern's small lips pinched as if she'd been sucking lemons.

Janet couldn't resist. If she touched Dagger, would those lips get thinner, disappear altogether?

Placing her hand in the marshal's, she let him steady her as she settled herself on a corner. His hand closed over hers tighter as she started to let go. When he pressed her fingers gently, a flame ignited in her center.

"Thank you." She pulled her hand away, feeling her landlady's glare like a branding iron against her skin. Yup, Prissy Priscilla's lips were gone indeed.

Then again, rousing her landlady's anger might be a foolish thing to do. Being tossed out of the one respectable boardinghouse in town would be a disaster.

If the marshal would just leave, that would solve most of her problems. Perhaps he had somewhere else he had to be now, damn his curious nature and his bloody good looks. She was having trouble remembering he was the enemy, and if that wasn't foolhardy, she didn't know what was.

But Dagger settled right down beside her. Close enough to feel his hard thigh against her own. His wide shoulders brushed against hers every time he moved, and damn, but the man seemed made of iron.

She glanced up at him as he bumped her again, and he was staring straight at her. The ground dropped away beneath her as his dark gray eyes crinkled at the corners. She felt his breath on her face.

His lips looked firm, soft, firm—as they moved, saying something or other. She swayed closer—

"Miss Danner, do you—" Laura's high voice.

She blinked and jerked back. "What did you say?"

"Want a piece of chicken?" Dagger said, holding up a drumstick just as Laura repeated, "Do you want some coleslaw?"

What *had* she been thinking about? Feeling like a headless chicken, all flap and no brain, she snatched the drumstick from the marshal and held her plate out to Maude's daughter. "Thank you . . . both," she muttered.

He'd flustered her a bit, Dagger decided with satisfaction. Her cheeks were flushed with color, her breathing fast. His breath wasn't exactly steady either. She'd sent heat through him just by sitting next to him.

He watched her eat, mesmerized by the small, even teeth nibbling on the chicken. Imaginations were a cruel possession sometimes, he thought, as his presented him with images of those pretty teeth nibbling on various parts of his body. When they reached . . . lower, he had to shift uncomfortably.

What the hell was wrong with him anyway? He'd been around pretty women before, even beautiful ones. But something about Miss Danner yanked him around the neck like a leash on a hound dog. Maybe all that energy, a rushing torrent of vitality inside stiff corset and lacings. Even now, with her sitting and eating, she still seemed to be in motion.

"How's the hunt going for the Garrets?" Peter Tucker broke into his thoughts and Dagger glanced up. Pulled his thoughts back where they belonged.

"Gone to ground," he answered briefly. "Haven't heard a peep from them since last spring, when the old man bought it."

"Huh." Tuck pulled at his muttonchop whiskers. "You figure the gang broke up, then?"

God forbid—not before he had a chance to hang them. Dagger unclenched his jaw. "Doubt it. There are at least two sons left."

"Perhaps they quit?" Miss Danner's soft voice broke into the conversation.

Her eyes were lowered and he couldn't help but notice the long feathery lashes, the curve of a—his hand raised without command and he stroked his fingers down her velvety cheek. Out of the corner of his eye, he saw Priscilla Malvern's eyes widen, then narrow.

Startled, Miss Danner looked up, her eyes so clear it was like looking into blue glass. Worried eyes.

"You have a soft heart, darlin', but desperadoes like them don't just quit. They'll keep going until someone shoots them down or hangs them."

"And you'd be just the man to succeed," Mrs. Malvern proclaimed. "Bring them back and we'll break in that new hanging platform Abel Haws just finished."

When Janet shuddered, Dagger could have shot himself for letting this conversation continue. "Shoot, I'm sorry. I forgot how you don't like hearing about this."

"Oh, that's all right, Marshal. I live in the West, where such events are commonplace," she murmured. But the pinkness had fled her cheeks. "Mrs. Tucker, how about I go check on those little soldiers?"

Richard and Billy were fighting in the open area. Sunlight flickered off their hair, highlighted their swords—long half-eaten turkey legs. Every now and then the fighting would pause long enough for the warriors to snatch a meaty bite off their weapons.

slapped Randall's hand away from his revolver and appropriated it for herself. She was firing before he had time to blink, and pieces of rattler splattered across the rocks.

Skidding to a stop at the rock pile, Dagger paused, then holstered his Colt.

He heard Randall upchucking nearby. The rest of the adults converged like a hoard of locusts on a cornfield.

In the center was the heroine of the day, looking as sweet and young as the little girl she'd saved. With one arm, Miss Danner hugged Anne, who clung like a baby possum.

The other arm enfolded Ben, who was stammering, "We didn't know there were snakes in there. It's winter, isn't it?"

Dagger drew in a deep breath. That had been too close; visions of the ugliness of a snakebite still flashed in his head. "It's winter, Ben boy, but, it feels like summer right now. To us and to the snakes." His eyes ran over the large chunks of dead snake. "That old guy came out to warm his bones and y'all scared him."

Ben gave a high-pitched laugh. "He scared me back."

"Me, too," Dagger muttered under his breath. He rested a hand on the schoolmarm's shoulder. "Nice shootin', Miss Danner."

Fright still danced in her eyes and she hugged Anne tighter.

"Annie, my baby!" Emily Wilson shoved through the crowd and snatched the girl up into her arms.

From the other side, Randall grabbed Ben. The drunk couldn't seem to stop mumbling, ". . . couldn't get the gun out . . . fingers didn't work . . . drunk, damn me, Ben—" He buried his face in his son's hair and sobbed.

Dagger held out a hand to Janet. "Now that you've been abandoned, may I congratulate you on your ability with a gun?"

Miss Danner extended a rock-steady, warm hand, but her gaze was shadowed. "I can't believe I managed to hit that . . . thing. It's a miracle."

The rest of the crowd pressed around her, thanking her, patting her on the back while Dagger watched.

He glanced at the place where she'd snatched the revolver from Randall, then at the rattler. Twenty, maybe thirty feet distant. She'd emptied that six-shooter and each bullet had hit the snake. He'd watched the pieces fly.

His eyes narrowed. That wasn't the Lord's hand; that was the hand of a sharpshooter.

Her shooting skill was the topic of conversation all through supper that night, much to Janet's dismay. And to make everything worse, the marshal had shown up for the meal.

At the sight of him for a rare Sunday supper, the landlady had gone into a frenzy, and now the long boardinghouse table gleamed with her fancy silverware and Sunday china. Studying the fragile glasses, Janet mentally thanked her father for the expensive dinners, the reward for a successful robbery. She might not have worn a dress, but she did know how to handle the silverware. *Have to remember not to accept a cheroot after*.

The marshal sat at the landlady's right, plump Florence at the left. Janet wasn't sure if she was happy or not with his distant location. Worse, she found herself annoyed at the way Priscilla leashed him to her side.

"I heard the snake was chopped to pieces," Flossie said. "Weren't you just terrified, Miss Danner?"

"I didn't have time to be frighten—" She stopped and considered her words. A schoolmarm would be scared; she wouldn't have spent summers working on her skills by shooting rattlers for the pot. Her lips twitched as she considered the effect on Priscilla if presented with a snake to cook up for supper. "But afterward, I was so scared that I just shook," she finished demurely.

"Ooh, I can just imagine." Phoebe Patterson shuddered. "Don't you think she's just the bravest lady you know, Marshal?"

His eyes were narrow, piercing, as he considered the question, considered Janet. His gaze rested on her hands for a moment, then he smiled slowly in a way that made her heart quicken. "I do. Very brave indeed."

Then he had to go and spoil it. "Where did you learn to handle a pistol like that?" His chin tilted upward, his brows raised.

"Oh . . . when I was a child, my father let me shoot his gun a few times." Over and over, aided by a switch when she missed. "But I hit a rabbit one day and"— she gave a lovely shiver—"oh, my, the blood! I never shot a gun again—until this very day. And just think of how many times I pulled the trigger to hit that snake."

His mouth twisted, and she got the awful feeling that he knew each bullet had landed in the snake. "Well, Miss—"

Priscilla leaned forward, brushing the marshal's hand with her pink fingers. "But really, she should have left everything to you, Marshal." She frowned at Janet. "What would have happened if you'd missed, Miss Danner, and hit one of the children? That was a terrible risk you took with their lives."

Janet opened her mouth to retort, then stopped and fumed. She could hardly tell everyone that she could knock the tail feathers off a jay. The lawman was struggling not to grin and Priscilla looked too smug for words. Too smug to tolerate.

"Of course you're right, Mrs. Malvern," Janet cooed sweetly. "Next time I'll just stay right by your side and watch the men."

A silence settled over the table. Priscilla's mouth pinched down, like she'd bitten into a lemon.

Unfortunately, her words hadn't affected the marshal one bit. Although his mouth was straight, his eyes were all crinkled up in laughter. "Well, I'm sure we men would have managed to muddle through, but the children are safe, which is all that matters." He quirked an eyebrow at Janet before turning to Priscilla. "So, what's for dessert?"

Later, stomach pleasantly full of Mrs. Malvern's dried apple pie, Dagger bid the landlady good night. Past the stout woman's form, he saw Janet ascending the stairs, skirt lifted slightly. He caught a glimpse of a dainty ankle, a tiny, fragile, sweet ankle just like its owner.

A sweet sharpshooter. He closed the door behind him and stepped out into the chilly night. Thoughts of the intriguing schoolmarm filled his head as he crossed the street to his own house.

The dogs were waiting for him and he had to be buffeted, licked and pawed before they settled down to their accustomed places.

After adjusting the lamp, Dagger picked up his new book, *Frankenstein*, but his heart wasn't in it. He had a mystery right here in front of him to solve.

The little schoolmarm was lying to him.

Oh, she was an accomplished liar, he'd give her that. But that was a puzzle also. Where'd she learn to adjust the truth so quickly and skillfully? The others had fallen like gullible fools for her story.

Not him. Oddly enough, he was beginning to be able to hear her falsehoods. Her voice . . . changed.

He leaned back in his chair, one hand playing with Tanner's ear. That soft, husky voice . . . when she was lying, the husky note would disappear and her voice would . . . thin, like coffee brewed with too much water, with no body.

And her eyes—lovely blue eyes that never looked away, that didn't blink at the untruths falling from her soft lips. But he'd seen her eyes lose some of their glow.

He tilted his head, pulled off the mystery by the memory of her eyes. Bubbling, dancing, sparkling— like a high mountain waterfall—icy cold, shocking, exciting . . . fun.

Hell, he was in trouble.

Chapter Twelve

The note had read: *Meet me west of town at sundown. C.*

Janet urged Brownie into a trot as the sun rested for a moment just over the white-capped mountaintops. She pulled her coat closer and shivered. Damn Clint anyway; didn't he remember how cold the mountains got at nightfall? The warmth of the past few days had disappeared, probably for the rest of the winter.

The imposing pines threw long shadows across the road, hindering her search for the Garret sign. There! She pulled Brownie to a halt. Across the road stood a tree with a fresh wound in the trunk from a branch being cut. The cut branch leaned casually against the tree, pointing toward where Clint would be waiting.

Janet pulled Brownie off the trail and onto a narrow animal track. The darkness deepened as she moved into the thick woods. A startled deer paused, head up, then leaped gracefully away. "Hello to you, too," Janet muttered. Where the hell was her brother? The path would be dangerous until the moon rose and, even then, not very safe.

But just as she'd decided to head back, she saw a glimmer of light ahead. A fire. Urging Brownie ahead, they broke into a small clearing. Backed up against a boulder, Clint was seated on a log next to a crackling fire, and, all was forgiven, he had coffee boiling. She could smell the heavenly aroma already.

Swinging down from her horse, she strode over to the fire. "Give me a cup and then we'll talk."

He grinned. "I'm fine, and how are you?"

With a scowl, she accepted the cup and sipped the hot black liquid gratefully. The coffee burned a path all the way down to her toes, warming its way outward. "Move over."

She plopped down next to him on the log, shoving him aside until her toes were perilously close to the fire. Heat. She'd forgotten how cold the mountains were. She was getting soft, turning into a town person. A lady.

As if he'd been reading her mind, Clint leaned back and looked her over. "You look . . . different. Sound the same, but . . . your face is softer or something."

She bumped her shoulder against him in rough answer, careful not to spill her coffee. "Softer, my ass. What the hell did you haul me up here for in the dark—to complain about my looks?"

He laughed and gave her a mocking leer, stroking his long mustache. "Oh, no, *cherie*, you are beeeutiful." His French accent was deplorable.

"Fool," she said mildly, feeling a pain inside. He was only teasing, the way they'd done all their lives, but she found a regret there. Only one man had ever said that to her. "What are you up to these days?"

"Ha! I thought you'd never ask." He poured himself a cup of his horrible brew and she grimaced.

Now that she'd warmed up, the flavor of the coffee had become apparent. She nodded at the pot. "What did you put in there, your smelly old socks?"

"Shut up," he said. "This is business now."

She grunted. "All right. Shoot."

"Shasta—you live there now."

"Well, there's news."

Giving her a disgusted look, he continued. "As you know, your little city is the busiest place in the northern mountains. The stages and wagons have to stop there, and everything transfers to mule trains for the mountain roads."

"I know that. So?"

"So, all those goods are paid for when they arrive in Shasta. Lots and lots of money, mostly in gold dust."

A nasty ball formed in her throat; she had to force the coffee past it to swallow. "You're thinking of robbing one of the freight offices."

"You betcha." He grabbed a stick and diagrammed Main Street in the dirt. "Just think, Sissie, you're already on the scene and a lady. No one would even think of you helping out. All you'd need to do is—"

"No."

With an annoyed look, he went on. "Really, there's no worry on your part. After you—"

"I said, no."

"Shoot, Sissie, and I heard you. What do you mean? You haven't even listened to my plan."

She didn't need to. In her mind's eye, she could see the plan all laid out, even guess which freight office would be his choice: Abraham Verne's place. He'd stopped her on the street, told her how pleased he was with how David was learning. Boasted about his son knowing his alphabet already because of her. "I don't want to . . . soil my own nest, Clint."

That confused him. His eyes held such a bewildered look that guilt rushed through her.

"But you're not going to stay there . . . are you?"

"No. Yes. I don't know," she said.

"Then if you don't, it doesn't matter. And it's a really good plan. First we'll wait until a big freight train comes in and they start to load up the mule trains. Then—"

She lost track of his words as the image planted itself in her head. Load up the mule trains. That might be sweet Ernie Short. Just a baby, really, even younger than Clint. He'd been trying to grow a beard, but the blond hair came in too thin. Looked like mange-eaten, overworn fur, but he was proud of his whiskers. Always tipped his hat to her, and half the time tripped over his own feet afterward.

She set her coffee mug down next to the fire. How could she put him at risk? What if he got hurt?

Clint dug his stick into the ground to sketch out the escape plan and she thought how good it was to see him. He looked healthy, happy, his eyes dancing with his cleverness. Just the way she wanted him. Only his happiness would mean pain to people she'd come to like.

Dropping her head into her hands, she moaned.

"Janny, what's wrong?"

Clint touched her lightly on the shoulder, the flow of his planning halted for a moment. How could she combat the tide pushing her back into her previous life? "I don't want to rob my own town."

157

"It's not your town. Just a place you're staying."

"Nonetheless, I won't do it."

He threw the stick down on the ground. "Damn you're stubborn, just like Pa always said."

"Pa." She blinked back the tears.

But he saw anyway. "I'm sorry, Sis."

"S'all right. I don't quite understand myself," she murmured. How'd she come to . . . care about a bunch of townsfolk? To not want to see them hurt. "Pick someplace else."

He leaned back into the solid boulder behind him. "Hell, a perfectly good plan wasted. Are you getting all *girly* on me?"

Sounded like a filthy epithet. "No. Maybe." He was going to think she had no mind left at this rate.

Huffing out an exasperated breath, she added, "It's just I'm not through there, and I don't want to have to leave with a posse behind me, all right?" She glared at him.

Holding up his hands, he grimaced. "All right, big sister, I surrender."

Relieved, she punched him in the arm. "Good choice."

"How long are you going to be there? You *are* coming back, aren't you?"

The fire snapped, blowing glowing embers out to the side of the wood, leaving a hole. Like her plans for her life, blown apart in one moment in time, one death, one new life.

"I'm . . . I'm not ready to think that far ahead yet." She stood, and Brownie's head came up. "I'd best be heading back. Don't want my landlady wondering what I was doing out so late."

"Cheesh. A landlady. A reputation." His eyes glimmered with hurt. "I'm not sure I still know who you are."

"Me neither, little brother. Me neither."

The livery was dark and quiet, only the stomping of horses disturbing the peace. She shivered as she closed the barn door behind her and felt her muscles relax in the relative warmth. In spite of her riding gloves, her hands were numb and tingly. Darn Clint and his idiotic rendezvous locations. He didn't care; *he'd* gotten to stay by the campfire.

Albert, napping on a pile of hay in one corner, roused as she walked Brownie down to her stall.

"Miss Danner?" He stood and reached for the reins. "You're out awful late."

A flush heated her cheeks and she raised her chin. "I find that cold air helps me think, and I was working on the spring curriculum." Thank God for Susanna and her big, educational-sounding words.

Albert looked mighty impressed, too.

"And did you get your mathematics completed, Albert?"

He flashed her a smile, turning from a sullen boy into a fine-looking young man. "I did, ma'am. And I finished all my reading, too."

Her eyes widened. "All of it? I'm impressed."

"Well, that *Peter Parley* story was so interesting, I couldn't stop." He pushed aside some horse dung with his boot. "Pa yelled at me to get to work; then, when he saw what I was doing, he laughed and let me finish reading. Said he was proud of me."

Janet blinked back the sting of tears and squeezed the boy's arm. "I'm proud of you, too," she whispered, and escaped quickly before she embarrassed them both. What was it with these Johnson men that made her puddle up like a leaky pump?

She stopped outside the barn to wipe her eyes and gasped when a dark figure approached.

"You all right?" Dagger's deep voice with the hint of southern accent washed over her like a warm breeze in the cold night.

"Albert's reading . . . for fun."

"Ah, well, that'd make anyone cry." He gave her a half-perplexed, half-understanding look.

"That's not funny." But her lips curved up into a wry smile.

He took her hand and pulled her out into the street. "Sure it is. Did you know that you're cold?"

His hand was hot, wonderful, and when his arm came around her, she almost whimpered with the heat he generated, even through his coat.

"How'd you get so cold, anyway? And what were you doing at the livery at this time of night? It's almost ten o'clock." He guided her down Main Street toward their street. The businesses were shut down, their windows dark, and doors locked.

She didn't think he'd like hearing about her meeting with her outlaw brother. She had to lie . . . again; she was beginning to feel like a creekside tree whose roots were being undermined by a river of lies. One of these days her last hold would crumble and she'd topple right in. But until then . . .

"Oh, you know us women. I just felt like taking a night ride, blowing the cobwebs from my dusty brain."

His narrow-eyed look questioned her sanity, but at least he didn't suspect she was lying. "Next time you feel dusty, come over to my place and I'll see what I can do."

Did he mean that the way it sounded, so . . . she licked her lips, then noticed the way he was staring at her, at her mouth in a way that made warmth tingle along her nerves. "I . . . I'm sure that—"

He was going to kiss her again. Her breasts felt heavy, her skin sensitive. She could feel every small stroke his hand made on her shoulder and had to wonder how it would feel without the coat between them, without *anything*.

The wind rustled dry leaves down the boardwalk, bringing with it the sound of the nearby Miner's Saloon piano, the scent of cigar smoke. Without a word, Dagger pulled her off the boardwalk, and they made a detour around the pool of light spilling out of the tavern.

She gave him a questioning look.

"You don't want to be spotted roaming the streets alone with a man, Miss Schoolmarm," he said seriously. "Your reputation—"

"Of course," she murmured. How in the world could she have forgotten? She'd figured on sneaking back in so Mrs. Malvern wouldn't see her, but had totally forgotten about being out alone at night. Not strange, considering she was as used to riding at night as during the day. It shook her to have made such a basic error.

"Not that I mind escorting you wherever you want to go."

"Just to my boardinghouse, thank you, Marshal."

"More's the pity," he muttered and turned with her down the quiet, tree-lined street. Glimmers of lantern light echoed the light from the waning moon overhead and the sounds of Main Street faded. At Dagger's house, Tanner loosed a welcoming bark.

"Want to stop in?" Dagger nodded toward his house.

And wouldn't that just put the finishing touch on her reputation? "No, thank you." She ignored the way her heart had sped up at the invitation, at the way her skin tingled. "That wouldn't be proper."

He leaned against the arch over the boardinghouse walk. "And you're always proper, aren't you, Miss Danner?" His long arm blocked her path, forcing her to stop and turn.

"Always."

He leaned in, his breath warm against her face. "Always, always?" His lips grazed hers, sending a jolt of heat to her toes.

"Well . . ." She tilted her head, just enough to increase the teasing contact, to feel the velvet smoothness of his mouth, to brush against the roughness of his—

She jerked back. Damn, what was she thinking of? Last time she'd kissed him, he'd left whisker marks all over her face. Did she want the entire boardinghouse to know what she'd been up to?

"What happened?" He touched her cheek, turned her face toward his.

"I need to go in." Was that breathless voice hers?

A corner of his mouth raised and the appealing crease in his cheek appeared. "Cold feet, Miss Danner?"

"Cold heart, Marshal." She ducked under his arm and moved up the walk to the front door at an undignified speed.

Behind her, she heard him snort and mutter, "Like hell."

Chapter Thirteen

"That's perfect, Richard," Janet said the next day. "Now walk back to the end of the line and Florence will recite her poem." She nodded at her landlady's daughter.

Florence minced several steps away from the line and tossed her corkscrew curls back over a shoulder. "My poem is from Walt Whitman's 'Leaves of Grass'."

Listening with half an ear, Janet leaned against her desk and suppressed a weary sigh. Who'd have thought that preparing for a program was such hard work? But she decided the effort had been worth it; the room looked magnificent, all ready for the big occasion.

The walls were papered with the children's best efforts: handwriting and essays on one wall, elegantly prepared maps from geography lessons on another. The girls had brought in scraps of fabric and ribbons and added festive touches to the front of the room. They'd all worked hard.

Florence finished her piece. "Very nicely done," Janet said, smiling as the girl beamed. "Now let's work on that last song of the night, 'My Old Kentucky Home.'"

An hour later, she let the children escape into the schoolyard to eat their lunches and work off their energy. What wouldn't she give to be able to do the same? She glanced at the pile of uncorrected papers on her desk. "The heck with it." Grabbing her lunch pail, she followed the children out into the yard.

She stopped at the foot of the steps as the chill of an oncoming storm almost froze her bones. Dark clouds whipped across the sky overhead, the advance scouts for heavily laden clouds. She calculated the storm's speed and decided to call the children in early. They didn't have long before the rain would start, and with the chill in the air, it could easily be sleet.

She hoped the roof wouldn't leak. Old Mr. Haws hadn't shown up today to work on the shingles. He must have found some color in his mine and taken the day off.

"Miss Danner, Ben's hurt!" Panting, Sally Perkins skidded to a stop in front of Janet's feet. "He's bleeding."

"Show me." Picking up her skirts, Janet followed the girl around the side of the schoolhouse to where a group of children were tangled together like a briar patch.

Ben was bleeding indeed, from a swollen lip and a bloody nose that poured blood down his shirtfront in spite of the hand pressed against it. Janet fished out her handkerchief—now she knew why women carried the things—and stanched the flow. The nose wasn't broken. Well, she knew how to deal with noses, busted or bleeding. "All right, what happened?"

Over the gabble of responses, Janet could tell one thing: No one had been there except Ben Perkins and Billy Tucker. "So. Ben and Billy, stay here. The rest of you go back to the front and finish eating your lunches, please. You may go inside if you get cold."

Kneeling in the grass, Janet motioned for the two boys to join her. "Sit down and tell me what happened."

"Nothin'," muttered Billy, his pale face even whiter than normal.

Janet cocked her head to one side. "Not like you to be fighting, Billy. Richard—now I wouldn't be surprised if *he'd* managed to get into a fight—but not you."

He glanced upward, his gaze going past her to somewhere over her shoulder. "Uh, I . . . just got mad, that's all."

"Ben, is that what happened? What did Billy get mad about?"

Ben's eyes wavered to one side. Neither boy had skinned knuckles—not even red—so she knew the boys hadn't been fighting.

A burn ignited in Janet's stomach. They were lying to her. Two of her favorites and here they were, lying right to her face.

She slammed her fist on the ground, well pleased with the way they jumped. Pushing to her feet, she set her hands on her hips. "You're not telling me the truth here, boys. That makes me feel ill." And it was true. She was mad, yes, but knowing they'd not been honest with her—that hurt.

Ben and Billy exchanged glances. Ben's freckles

were smeared with blood, his face skinned up like he'd taken a . . . fall.

She circled them like a cat around cornered mice. "You didn't have a fight, did you? No, I don't think so. Want to tell me the truth now, before you *really* get into trouble?"

Ben slid over beside Billy, and two pairs of worried blue eyes watched her as she stalked closer. "I really don't like being lied to. Don't you remember the sermon the preacher gave on Sunday?"

Two heads nodded.

"How can I trust you if you lie to me? How can I even want you near me?"

Billy's gaze dropped, and guilt twanged through her like a loose guitar string. She knew he really liked her.

"But—" Ben whispered.

"But what?" Janet snapped

"But we promised we wouldn't—" Billy's elbow caught Ben in the side and shut off the confession like a stopped-up pump.

Janet turned away, her hands behind her back, while she thought. All right, there was more involved in . . . whatever, than the two boys here. And one of them had already gotten hurt over their reckless game. She couldn't afford to ignore this.

Their parents might not look kindly on her ignoring a lie, either. As the wind whipped her hair around, the first raindrop fell like a chill to her heart.

How was she supposed to handle this?

She knew what she'd been taught by Pa, but the parents of Billy and Ben probably wouldn't take kindly to their sons being horsewhipped. She doubted she'd have the stomach to do that anyway.

So. Intimidation without any back-up force. She

166

turned around and glared at them. Let them see her anger. "Billy, go stand with your face to the wall there." She pointed to the schoolhouse. He walked over, his feet dragging, glancing back every few steps.

"Ben, finish what you were saying." He looked almost as shaken as she had the first time she'd been caught lying by Pa.

"Teacher, I—"

"I'm waiting, Ben." She dropped her voice to a raspy threat. "My patience is not unlimited. How did you get hurt?"

"I . . . Anne, she climbed—" He glanced upward at the schoolhouse roof, and a cold chill slid into Janet's stomach.

"What did Anne climb?" Her eyes were on the steep roof. A feather of pink material caught on the rough shingle slabs jerked in the gusts of wind. "The roof? She climbed up onto the roof?"

His worried eyes followed hers. "Yeah. She really likes to climb, you know."

"Oh, dear heavens," Janet whispered. She frowned, her gaze searching. Where was the ladder the handyman Abel Haws had been using? This morning it had been lying on the ground next to the schoolhouse— she'd checked—but it wasn't there now.

To use the heavy ladder would have taken all three of them to lift into place. She walked closer to the building and froze. The ancient ladder lay shattered in several pieces.

A splatter of rain struck the side of the schoolhouse, chilled her cheeks. "Did the ladder break when you were climbing it?" she asked. Maybe Anne hadn't made it up there.

"When I was coming down. That's how I hurt my

nose." He touched his face gingerly, obviously startled to feel how his nose had widened.

Janet tried frantically to remember if giggly little Anne had been in the crowd. "Ben . . . where's Anne?"

Ben nodded at the roof. "Still on the roof. She made us promise not to tell you. Her pa said he'd whup her if she climbed anything again."

The light dimmed as the dark clouds eradicated the last of the sun. The trees dipped and cracked with the hard wind, and more icy cold rain whipped at Janet's clothing. If she squinted, she could see the girl's figure. Looked like she was hugging the chimney. The wind would be strong up there, the mossy-covered shingles slick as they dampened.

Janet bit her lip. She was a lot heavier than the children. The ancient shingles might well bust or tear loose under her weight.

But if Anne let go of the chimney now, she'd be liable to be blown right off the roof—and it was high enough to break her neck. The thought made her shiver. Lord, but she hated heights.

All right, then. "Ben, run and get the rope stored in the stable.

"Billy." She had to raise her voice to be heard over the gusting rain. A hard pellet hit her face. Another.

Sleet. This disaster was just getting worse and worse.

"Yes'm?" His blond hair was in draggles, his blue eyes anxious.

"I want you to run and get the marshal. Have someone bring a ladder, too."

"Yes'm. I'll be quick as I can."

She sighed. Not quick enough to keep her from having to climb that behemoth. There would be no way to get a ladder to the school in enough time. Why couldn't they have built a *short* schoolhouse? "I know. Git."

As he fled down the street toward the jail, Janet moved away from the schoolhouse. From just . . . here, she had a clear view of the chimney. In the murky light, she saw Anne shiver. How long could her fingers hold on in the icy rain? "We're coming, Anne," Janet shouted. "Just hang on there."

The child nodded, her face pressed against the bricks.

"Here, Miss Danner." Ben shoved the rope into her hands.

"Thank you, Ben." She quickly shook out a good loop and cast it high. It dropped down, and . . . the rope hooked on a corner of the chimney and caught. But not secure enough.

Janet flipped it up and off; a good stiff rope was worth its weight in gold. There! With a lovely whirl, it settled down around the chimney. Thank goodness she'd learned to rope. When her big brother Dan was eighteen, he'd talked Pa into rustling cattle for a summer. *Bless you, Daniel.*

Janet jerked the lasso to tighten the knot, then jerked again to test the strength of the chimney. No bricks fell off. She leaned with her whole weight on the rope. The chimney didn't topple.

"Ben, you stay right here," Janet cautioned. "I might need someone on the ground for help." Hell, she could use someone for help right now. Her hands were stiff, from fear, from the cold.

With a muttered curse, she strode directly under the roof. Pulling the back of her skirts through her legs, she tucked the fabric into her belt. Grabbing the rope, she swung loose and then climbed it, hand-over-hand, to the roof.

The rope was plastered tight against the shingles by her weight and she couldn't get a grip on anything except a couple of loose shingles to help her over the edge. Scrambling up and onto the roof dried all the spit in her mouth and left her breathless. She looked over the side, at Ben's small body, the ground so far away, and moaned. Her hands tightened on the rope and didn't want to loosen.

"Just a little more," she muttered, then raised her voice. "Anne, I'm coming."

The sleet blinded her, as did the wind whipping her hair loose and around her head. Her boots scrabbled at the slick moss-covered shingles, and she was kept from falling only by her grip on the rope. Her fingers were going numb and her breath came in frantic pants.

But finally she pulled herself up to the chimney with a massive lunge. Two shingles cracked and broke loose to fall . . . a long way to the ground. She inched over to where Anne cowered. "Come on, child. Let's get you down. Give me your hand."

Anne's face was pure white, eyes terror-stricken. She didn't move. Janet couldn't blame her. It took all her infinitesimal courage to release one hand from the rope and grasp the girl's wrist. "I've got you now. Let go."

Anne whimpered, and clung more tightly to the chimney bricks.

Making her voice as soothing as possible, Janet managed to coax Anne in to letting go of the chimney. They paused at the edge of the roof as Janet pondered how she could possibly slide over the edge hanging on to both the rope and the child. Anne shivered against her, a cold thin mass, too weak to hang on to the rope by herself.

And that was where Dagger saw them as he pulled up his horse. A small child held carefully in a small woman's arms perched on the very edge of the high schoolhouse roof in sleet and wind.

His heart almost stopped.

He took in the problem at a glance. Janet couldn't climb down and hold on to Anne as well. He spurred his horse to the side of the schoolhouse.

Grabbing hold of the rope, he shimmied up it. "Janet, let Anne down." He stretched out one arm. "Anne, grab my hand, honey."

After a moment, cold fingers latched on to his, and he saw a pair of tiny boots. Gripping the rope with one hand, he grabbed the child with his other, yanked her against his chest and slid down the rope.

"What's goin' on?" Arnie yelled. He, Gus and Randall Tucker had caught up.

"Take her!" Dagger ordered, dropping Anne into a pair of arms. He hauled himself back up the rope.

When Janet saw Anne enfolded into Arnie's embrace, she sagged in relief. She'd done it. The girl was safe, was on the ground.

Her turn now.

Involuntarily, her hands tried to tighten on the rope, but her fingers were bleeding, stiff, going numb. How the hell was she going to get down?

"Slide down to me."

She blinked the rain out of her eyes and realized Dagger had reached the roof again.

He beckoned to her. "I'll help you down."

She shook her head, frozen in place. Too high, too

scared, too vulnerable—and he was a lawman. A shiver wracked her body, and she slipped a little.

"Come on, honey, hang on to the rope and slide down." His voice was the soothing tone used to gentle wild horses. His eyes held steady on hers, not letting her turn away.

"You drop me and I'll—" she clamped her jaw shut before the damning, threatening words could escape. And gutting him like a coyote wouldn't do her any good. She'd still be splattered all over the schoolyard.

"Come on, Miss Schoolmarm."

She peered at him suspiciously, he'd best not be laughing at her. Clamping her jaw shut against the whimpers of fear, she changed position, inch by inch, until she lay, feet dangling over the edge.

Nerve-wrackingly slowly, she slid, belly-down, over the edge of the roof, and then, her useless, weak grip loosened. "Dammit!"

She could almost feel her body hit the rocks below and she tensed for the pain and the death.

When the hard arm clasped her around the waist nothing had ever felt better. Dagger pulled her against him and slid a ways down the rope; then they stopped, swinging in the cold wind, high above the ground.

After a moment she realized he was talking to her. "Let go, honey; let go of the rope."

She looked up.

"You need to loosen your grip on the rope. I won't let you fall, Janet."

The words slowly penetrated her fear. "I—" She risked a quick glance at her hands. They were gripping the rope so tightly her knuckles were white.

"That's right, let go," he murmured, and tightened his grip on her waist.

Gritting her teeth, she mentally told her fingers to release. Still, it took a while before they obeyed enough so that she and Dagger could continue their descent.

She let out a breath of relief as her feet touched the ground, but she sagged into Dagger's firm grip. Solid, wonderful ground—why did it feel so unsteady? She realized her legs were shaking, wobbling like poorly set jelly.

The men cheered.

"Th-thank you, g-g-gentlemen," she said, her chin quivering.

To her relief, Dagger nudged aside the men's helping hands and practically carried her into the classroom. His body felt wonderfully warm against hers. The heat of the schoolhouse hit her like a blow and she staggered.

"Here, here, sit down, now, before you fall." His deep voice backed by iron-hard arms eased the trembling she couldn't seem to control. He set her down gently into her chair. Murmuring voices, concern, questions, faded in and out. Blinking back the fuzziness, she looked up to see her students and the men gathered around her.

Anne's father was holding the girl, his face tight with emotion.

"School's out for the day," Dagger announced. "Your teacher's too cold to teach."

They ignored him and pushed up against her, giving her hugs, patting her shoulders and her hair with their little hands. Even Pike squeezed her hand and nodded. She had to blink hard to keep from crying.

"All right, young 'uns, she'll be fine. Now head out." Dagger held the door open for the departing students and men. Ben, Billy, Anne and her father remained behind.

Dagger knelt in front of Janet, taking her cold hands and turning them palm up. The skin was blistered and bleeding, but she couldn't feel the pain. "Rubbed all the skin off, looks like," he said. "We'll stop by Doc Matson's house and get some salve."

She tried to pull her hands away, but a kitten would have been stronger. "I'm fine. But how is Anne?"

"Thanks to you, miss, she'll be fine," her father answered, then frowned. "Or she will be when she can sit down again."

Anne buried her head in his shoulder.

"How did it happen that you were on the roof, Anne?" Dagger asked.

"I climbed the ladder. Billy and Ben helped me lift it up."

Dagger turned questioningly to Janet.

She nodded. "Mr. Haws left it here. I told the children to stay away from it and they told me they wouldn't touch it."

A sense of betrayal and anger surged through her, and she glared at them. "They lied to me."

Dagger's mouth turned up in a quirk and he nodded solemnly. "That's very bad."

He turned to the three children. "Well, you'd best be off for now. We'll deal with you later."

Their eyes widened at the implicit threat and they ran out of the classroom, Anne pulling her father behind her.

"C'mon, schoolmarm," Dagger said, tugging her to her feet. "Let's get you home."

* * *

"Here you are," Dagger announced, stopping in front of Janet's room. He set her on her feet and steadied her.

She blinked, rousing from the half-dream she'd been in. How in heaven's name had she gotten up the stairway without noticing? And Dagger was . . . a man on the woman's side of the boardinghouse. Mrs. Malvern would have hysterics.

"I—well, thank you," she murmured.

When he started to pull his supporting arm from her waist, her knees wavered, and she clutched his arm.

"Ah! Now I know you care," he said with a grin.

"Poppycock. You flatter yourself."

"Do I?" he said in a soft voice. He touched her cheek with the back of his fingers. In spite of the cold outside, his hand felt warm as the sun's rays against her frozen cheek. Her eyes opened wider, belatedly realizing how close he was to her.

"I was worried about you, you know. You could easily have fallen, even died today." His arms enfolded her, pulled her against his chest in an all-enveloping hug. "I'm glad you didn't."

His chest was so hard and muscular, his arms like iron bars around her, and she was imprisoned within yet safe. Letting her head drop onto his shoulder, she savored the feeling of being held and comforted.

He smelled wonderful, leather and man, and a hint of familiar gun oil. "I'm a bit relieved myself," she said, trying for a calm voice, but it came out sounding winded. Lifting her head, she saw his rugged face only a few inches away.

Lines of laughter and sadness crinkled the skin around his eyes, his firm jaw held a trace of whiskers, dirt streaked one cheek and yet he looked as appetizing as Mrs. Chappell's pastries. She licked her dry lips. What in the world was wrong with her?

His hand touched her cheek again, leaving fiery longing in its wake, as well as an ache she'd never felt before. "Dagger," she whispered.

He gave a low groan and rested his forehead against hers. "You could drive a saint to sin with those eyes of yours. But this is not the time."

He rubbed his cheek against hers and pulled her tighter into his embrace. "I'll see you tomorrow at the recital. Save me a dance?"

Dance? She didn't know how to dance. "Well, I'm not sure—"

His fingers pushed her chin upward, and his lips came down over hers. Warm, firm, velvety and oh, so appealing. His mouth was like a pine forest in the summer, full of heady spice and mysterious shadows. She felt sheltered in his arms, yet stronger herself.

After a time he pulled away, reluctantly, slowly. His eyes were gray, serious. "Save me a dance?"

"Yes . . . I will."

Head spinning, she entered her room. The coldness had disappeared from her bones, melted by the heat of that kiss. Oh, that man could kiss.

Not that she'd had much experience. And wouldn't that have looked funny if she'd tried—some man kissing her bearded face. But surely Dagger's kisses would win a prize among the kissers of the world.

Dropping onto the bed, she snickered at the thought of starting a new contest for the Independence Day festivities. A kissing contest, held right after the pie-eating contest and just before the sharpshooting prizes. By jiminy, if she introduced it, she'd have to be allowed to judge it, right?

She pulled off her boots and rolled down her thick stockings. Her lips still tingled and she licked them thoughtfully. A dance. She'd promised the man a dance. How was she going to manage that without looking like a fool?

Maybe Hannah would be able to teach her a few steps.

Clothes dropped onto the floor, she stepped over to the washbasin. The water was cold, but adequate to remove the blood from the scrapes on her arms.

She examined her forearms. Nothing needed stitches, thank goodness. But she'd be darned sore tomorrow. A fingernail was broken back to the quick. Probably from the time she lost her footing and only saved herself from sliding off the roof with a quick grab.

Shaking her head, she wondered how many lives she'd be down if she were a cat. And how strange the world could be. She had almost died when the marshal had put a bullet into her, and today Dagger had saved her life, and Anne's as well.

A lawman coming to the rescue. The thought left funny quivers in her stomach, but so had Dagger's kiss. And his arms around her. She realized with a jolt that just the sight of him riding up had calmed her; she had known he'd take care of her.

What kind of fool did that make her?

And yet he had.

Cleaned up, she dropped the washcloth back into the basin and shrugged on her robe. She still needed to figure out what to do about Billy, Ben and Anne. Billy and Ben had lied to her; Anne, too.

Her lips twisted at the thought. She had trusted them, hadn't doubted their word at all, but they'd managed to look her in the eye, even knowing they had been doing what they'd been told not to. What kind of a per—she stopped short and shook her head.

Hell, her kind of person would do that. She'd been lying all her life to anyone except family. Pa had beaten that lesson into them: you don't lie to family. But everyone else was fair game.

So by her own rules, people could lie to her and so could the children. That fact sat like a chunk of wood in her stomach. How could she trust anyone? She was surrounded by people who weren't family.

It was only fair that they could lie to her—after all, she was lying to them. Especially the marshal.

Regret filtered through her veins, the wish that she really was exactly who she claimed to be. Then she could—he could . . . She pressed her lips together with a sigh. She had never had a lover and he certainly couldn't be to her what she wished he might be.

If she told the townspeople the truth, they would fire her, then hand her over to the county sheriff. And Dagger . . . what would Dagger do?

She bit her lip, a feeling of loss flooding her. A loss that she had no right to feel. Whatever she felt for the lawman, she'd best just keep it shut up tight.

Chapter Fourteen

"Yoo-hoo, Janet, we're here!"

In front of the looking glass, Janet spun around when the door of her room crashed open. Susanna and Hannah waltzed in, their arms filled with paper-wrapped packages.

"What the he—...hello, Sus, Hannah. What brings you—" She caught the soft package tossed at her.

"We've been shopping," Hannah announced, flopping onto the bed and letting her purchases fall around her like autumn leaves. "And we're going to help you dress for the party."

"Help me—"

Susanna gave one of her wide smiles. "I remember my first party—Hannah was a godsend. And I don't think you've had much more experience than I had then."

The package felt like material. What could be in it? Janet suppressed the urge to rip it open like an eager child. "Listen, you two . . ."

"Was that what you were planning to wear?" Susanna frowned at Janet's brown dress. "You wear that every day in class."

"I don't have anything else." She couldn't afford fancy clothes yet.

"See! I told you she wouldn't have party clothes," Susanna crowed to Hannah. She slipped an arm around Janet. "Don't be embarrassed; neither did I when I got here. I brought a couple of frocks, and we've got just enough time to take one in. Pick one."

Hannah opened one of the bundles, displaying a soft pink gown, then another of pale blue. A quiver of pure feminine delight shot through Janet. "They're lovely. I couldn't—"

"Don't be a silly goose, of course you could." Eyes narrowed, Susanna ran her gaze over Janet's body. "You're a lot shorter, but our figures aren't too different. Which one do you want to wear tonight?"

Oh, what a cruel decision. "The pink—no, the blu-pink—uh, hell!" Her hands clapped over her mouth.

Hannah fell backward, snickering. "Look what you've done, Sus. If her students could hear her now!"

"Miss Prim-and-proper, always the correct behavior. Wouldn't they be shocked," Susanna agreed.

Was that how people saw her? Janet tore her eyes from the dresses long enough to smirk at her friends. Damned if she hadn't done a fine job of playing the schoolmarm. She ignored the small, cold question of just how much was playacting and how much was real.

"We'll do the pink," Susanna decided. "More partylike, and it'll show off your blond hair to a treat. Do you have something to wear under it? It will show a bit of bosom, more than your teacher clothes."

Janet grinned and opened the dresser drawer to

show off her new booty. Olivia Harris had delivered the first of the whitework two days earlier.

"Oh, look at that chemise," Susanna cooed, plucking the garment from Janet's fingers. "Just think how Bowie would—" She turned a lovely pink color and Hannah snickered.

"Ahem." Susanna handed the chemise to Janet. "Who does this fine work?"

"Olivia Harris. She's a widow and could use more work," Janet murmured. Men liked women in fancy unmentionables? Then if Dagger saw—she shook her head to eradicate the thought. What did she care what the marshal thought of her clothes? And he certainly wouldn't get a peek at her new frilly petticoats, let alone the chemise. Yet just the thought of him seeing her unclad made a tingle go through her stomach.

"What are you two wearing?" she asked hastily.

Susanna nodded to the long garment bag she'd carried in. "Our gowns and shoes are in there. Not that I will be dancing much." She patted her stomach and grinned. "Junior here wears me out quickly. Hannah will probably be up all night, though, especially since Blade will be there," she teased.

Hannah tossed a pillow at her, smacking her in the head.

"Blade?" Janet's hands clenched. The man she'd shot. Crippled.

"He's back from school. They closed for a break before the next session." Susanna pulled out a pincushion from her bag. "Put on the gown and let's get started."

"Blade and Hannah?" Janet started to pull off her blouse, then hesitated. Her scar . . . but her camisole should hide that. She'd just have to be careful changing.

Hannah scowled at Susanna. "Sus is funning. The man doesn't even know I exist. He's too buried in his medical studies."

Susanna gave a small smile. "For now, not forever, I'm sure." She sat on the floor with a grunt. "Hannah, get out your curling iron. You do her hair; I'll start pinning up the hem."

Janet surveyed her two friends, warmth spreading through her. "Which of you two is going to teach me to dance?"

Excitement increased the speed of Janet's footsteps as she flitted back and forth in the schoolroom. Outside, the evening was clear and cold, perfect weather for the dance.

Inside, the room was filling slowly with people. First the churchwomen arrived with banners and bouquets to decorate the room, then more women with heavenly smelling desserts. A giant crystal bowl brimmed with lemonade. The men hauled the long school tables outside and pushed benches against the walls to make room in the center of the floor for dancing.

Janet kept glancing at the door, telling herself she was only watching to be sure all the children arrived, but the lie was exposed the minute Dagger walked in. The disconcerting leap of her heart let her know he was the one she'd been watching for. His flashing smile when their eyes met made her glow inside. Then his gaze skimmed down her body, taking in how she looked, and his eyes widened in a way that made her preen with satisfaction. All that primping was well worth the effort to see him look at her like this.

"Miss Danner," Mrs. Wilson called. "It's seven o'clock. Let's start the program."

Janet took a deep breath and lifted her chin. So this was how the children felt when she made them recite in front of the class. Like the whole world was watching to see if they made a mistake.

She clapped her hands, and the bubbling children surrounded her. "All right, let's show your parents how much you've learned. Line up the way I taught you."

Like little soldiers, the students formed a line, and the recitations began. Laura read Dickens. Ben Perkins made everyone shiver with his rendition of the popular Poe, "Nevermore." Tears stung Janet's eyes at the sound of her mother's favorite poem.

Rosie Wilson won the children's spelling bee. To no one's surprise, Arnie, the bookstore owner, won the adult spelling bee; he'd held the title for the past two years.

They sang favorite mining songs, both children and grown-ups. Janet grinned at Susanna's sour face when Dagger boomed out "Oh, Susanna." They finished with Stephen Foster's "My Old Kentucky Home," and with a breath of relief, Janet realized the chattering and arguing were signs that everyone was having a good time.

"Good job, teacher."

Janet jumped at the low voice near her ear. Dagger leaned in farther, and she caught the tantalizing scent of pine soap and leather. "You've kept everything moving, and the kids are doing great. Used to be people fell asleep at these recitals. Not today."

Oh, what a lovely compliment. She beamed at him before stepping up to the front. "That concludes the school's recital. I hope you enjoyed yourselves. The children worked hard on this program, and I want you to know how proud I am to be teaching your wonderful children."

She felt the heat rushing into her cheeks as the crowd broke into applause. Giving the little curtsy she'd practiced, she slipped back to where Dagger waited, surprised at how many people reached out to pat her on the back, tell her how pleased they were with her work.

"Looks like you've made yourself a place here," Dagger commented.

She couldn't get the smile off her face. It had gone so well! "Wasn't it wonderful? Didn't Anne do well with her solo?"

She got an answering grin in return. "You look like you could dance on the roof."

Shudder. "No roofs today, thank you." She tilted her head, frowned. "Look, there's Thomas."

The child slipped into the room, shivering. Couldn't that father of his find the boy something warmer to wear? And couldn't he have brought Thomas on time, so he could recite? He'd worked so hard on his piece. Janet bit her lip, then pushed her way through the crowd to the child's side.

"Thomas, I'm so glad you're here. There's still enough time to recite." She glanced around, wondering if Boudreaux had stopped off at the wagon outside. "Is your father inside?"

"Pa's . . . he's not coming."

"You walked here? At night?"

Before the child could answer, Dagger appeared and hoisted him to his shoulder. His loud shout silenced the room. "We have a late young 'un here to give his piece. Let's hear him recite."

Red-faced and beaming, Thomas was set onto the recital bench. He gulped once, then settled down and gave a fine, stirring speech from Shakespeare's *Henry V*.

"I've always liked Agincourt myself," Dagger whispered in her ear before leading the crowd in a cheer as Thomas finished.

Janet tapped her fingers to her lips. Would the children be able to perform a play, Shakespeare perhaps, next year? Wouldn't that be something?

"Janet! Over here!"

Janet looked up to see Hannah in her modest but lovely green frock, standing beside a tall young man.

"Well, I'll be. He came," Dagger exclaimed. "Let me introduce you." He took her hand and led her over to Hannah.

"Miss Danner, may I present my brother, Blade Blackthorne? And Blade, this is Janet Danner, the schoolmarm we're so pleased with."

Her lips numb, her stomach churning, Janet managed to greet the crippled victim of the Garret gang. Younger, slimmer and taller than Dagger, he was dressed in a white dress shirt with a dark red vest. The lines in his face deepened each time he shifted his weight between his leg and the cane he used.

A cane. Janet's gaze skittered away from the symbol of her devastating effect on his life and focused instead on the bright humor in his blue eyes.

"I've heard a lot about you," he said, taking her cold hand. "The children are full of stories about their pretty, feisty schoolmarm. Why weren't you teaching when I was in school?"

Hannah nudged him in the side. "Probably because she'd have been at the desk beside yours, silly."

Dagger smiled. "And the way your mouth always ran on, she'd probably have had you in the corner for most of the day anyway."

To Janet's shock, he pulled her hand out of Blade's grasp and appropriated it for his own. Why did Dagger's hand feel different than Blade's? How could just holding his hand make her skin feel so sensitive?

When Blade raised his eyebrows at Dagger, then exchanged grins with Hannah, Janet frowned. Had she missed something?

"Y'all go dance now," Hannah said, making shooing motions. "Blade and I are going to get something to drink."

"You don't have to stay with me," Blade protested. "I know how you love to dance. Just—"

Dragged away by an obstinate Hannah, Blade moved out of earshot. Janet gazed after them, feeling the regret even more deeply now that she'd met the man whose life she'd ruined.

Dagger interrupted her thoughts. "You look so sad, darlin'."

"Your brother. His cane."

"I know, just doesn't seem right. He can't go back into the military now, not with that bum leg." Dagger rubbed his face, as if rubbing away nightmares. "Before that, he'd attended medical school thinking he'd pick up enough to use with his troops. Now he'll be making it a career. Doctor Blackthorne instead of captain."

"I'm sorry."

"Not your fault. It was mine—and—" He shook his head. "May I have this dance, Miss Danner?"

186

Janet hesitated.

"Please?"

Trying to appear nonchalant, Janet placed her hand in his—damn, his fingers were hard and strong—and smiled. "I'd be delighted, Marshal."

As they stepped away from the chairs, the bouncy polka sequed into a slower tune, and she glanced up toward the front of the room. Arnie and Ernie Short were playing fiddles and, to her surprise, she saw Blade strumming a guitar. Blade winked at her and led his fellow musicians into a slow waltz.

"Well, now." Smiling in satisfaction, Dagger pulled her into his arms.

Tensely, Janet counted in her head, one-two-three, one-two-three, until Dagger's arm tightened and she found herself caught up in the music, her feet having no will of their own. She laughed, delighted with herself, the day, her partner.

"Fun, isn't it?"

Damn right. "My, yes." The occasional contact with his rock-hard thighs set her stomach to tingling. Looking up at him, she felt too vulnerable, so she stared straight ahead—at a corded, muscular neck. The black silk vest he wore accented his broad shoulders. She glanced around and frowned. Other men wore vests, but their shoulders weren't as wide as Dagger's, and their chests were less muscular.

Bowie swung by with Susanna in his arms. He was bigger than Dagger but lacked that deadly grace, a bull rather than a panther.

"You're deep in thought," Dagger commented, his breath warm against her ear.

Tingles ran down her spine. If she turned her head, just so, her lips would touch his and—

187

And they'd toss her right out of the school. She stiffened and he resumed the proper distance. "I was just admiring the way everyone looks all fancied up."

"Amazing, isn't it? First time I've seen Abraham duded up since his wife died."

She smiled over at the stocky owner of the freight office, pleased with his starched shirt and brightly colored vest. "Maybe he's ready to find David a new mother."

"Maybe. But Bethie would be a hard woman to replace. She had so much spunk, was so caring." His eyes crinkled at her. "Much like a teacher I know."

She stared up at him, mesmerized by the look in his eyes, the caress in his voice.

Pulling her gaze away, she glanced at the musicians. Eyes half-shut, Blade strummed his guitar, adding depth to the music.

She spotted his cane, the ghastly symbol of her crime—or her *sins*, the preacher would say. Her fingers tightened on Dagger's hand at the rush of sorrow for Blade, for the life he had lost. Her eyes stung with hot tears. What had she done?

Watching him from over Dagger's shoulder, she saw Blade glance toward the floor, obviously checking on them. His gaze snagged hers, hesitated. Embarrassed, she hurriedly blinked away the tears that sheened her eyes.

Still watching her, his brows drew together. He straightened abruptly, twanged a sour note on the guitar. Although his fingers regained the beat, a strange, almost haunted look appeared on his face.

She couldn't seem to look away as Blade frowned at her, shook his head, then stared at her again. A chill chased down her spine.

Surely he couldn't have recognized her.

When he finally turned his face away from the dance floor, Janet took a small breath and relaxed. He hadn't pulled a pistol and shot her, hadn't yelled for an arrest, hadn't pointed his finger at her, calling her an outlaw. Her guilty conscience had made her over-wrought.

His face had drawn into grim lines, his mouth tight. He was tired, that's all, tired and hurting.

The music slowed, bringing the waltz to an end. With a stroke of his fingers on her hand, Dagger released her, reluctantly it seemed to her.

"May I get you some punch?" he asked.

As he stepped farther away, she smiled, casting her worries to the winds. Her first party, her first dance. "Yes, let's get a drink."

Pity schoolmarms couldn't visit the wagon parked outside where the whiskey was being dispensed. She curled her fingers around his arm, delighting in the feel of rippling muscles.

Dagger gave her a startled look, then placed his hand on top of hers. "All right, then."

At the punch bowl, Jenny Perkins beamed at them. "Don't you look lovely, Miss Danner."

"Thank you," Janet said. "Didn't the ladies do a fine job of decorating the room? It looks so different."

Dagger stood beside the schoolmarm, listening quietly, the feeling of belonging slowly dissipating. As they'd whirled around the room, one couple in a mass of other spinning people, he'd felt like one of the town, a member of this society. But now . . . listening to the women chatter . . .

189

"Don't you agree, Marshal?" Janet asked him, her blue eyes lightened as if by sunlight.

Hell, what had he agreed to? Stupidly, he answered, "Sure."

Jenny's eyes widened. "Well, I never thought you'd say yes, but this is wonderful. The next school board meeting is Thursday. I'll look forward to it immensely."

Janet was bouncing up and down. "It's not as if we're asking anything so unreasonable. I'll be donating my time. We just need use of the schoolhouse."

Use of the schoolhouse for what? Images of hanging parties, sewing circles, spun through his head.

"I'm so glad you're on our side, Dagger," Janet said. She patted his arm. "The women in this town shouldn't go through life ignorant. I know everyone will be better for it if they learn to read."

He gave Jenny a half-smile as he was dragged away by the little whirlwind called a schoolteacher. Pieces of the conversation were coming back to him. So, he'd just agreed to get the council to permit using the schoolhouse for teaching women to read. Well, all right; that did make a kind of sense.

They wandered around the edge of the room. Damned if the woman didn't seem to know just about everyone in town after only the few months she'd been here. Janet kissed one woman's cheek—a seamstress—with compliments on her work that turned her cheeks fiery red. Dagger found himself pulling out his money roll and peeling off a few bills in response to Janet's interest in the church's orphan society. She volunteered him for a barn-raising and to help hunt down a poaching mountain lion. Told everyone he could be bribed with sweets.

Whatever distance he'd felt from the town had disappeared by the time Arnie grabbed her for a polka.

Dagger's eyes widened at the glimpse of intriguing ruffles under her skirts as she whirled away. He moved back and leaned against the wall next to Bowie. "How's Susanna holding up?" he asked.

Bowie nodded toward the other side of the room. "She's trying to convince Tucker to carry plants—seedlings—this spring. Herb plants and such." He gave Dagger a wry glance. "Woman never stops. She'll make us rich in spite of ourselves."

Dagger laughed. "Having a few young 'uns might slow her down."

"Doubt it." Bowie nodded at the floor. "Your little schoolmarm seems to be having a fine time."

Dagger hadn't been able to stop watching her. She'd been laughing or smiling the entire time. Like a beam of sunlight on the water, she never stopped sparkling. "Woman's got more energy than's good for her."

"You look dazed. Did she wear the good marshal out?"

"The good marshal," Dagger drawled, "has been volunteered for more activities than he knew existed in this town."

He'd forgotten how Bowie's laugh could make the windows shake.

Chapter Fifteen

"There. It's locked up tight." Dagger rattled the door handle.

"Very good." She gave him an arch look. "I haven't forgotten how you forgot to lock it one day."

The hell he had. His frown faded at the sight of her face. Trying not to smile made every dimple she had appear. "You are going to tease the wrong man someday and get into trouble."

Her smile disappeared, as if wiped away with a blackboard wash rag, and her frightened gaze took him by surprise. "I know."

What had he said that disturbed her like that? "What . . ." But she wasn't going to confide in him. She'd already turned away. "Let's get you home."

She walked beside him through town, uncommonly sedate for the first block, until the bounce reappeared in her step. Pleased to see her happy again, he smiled down at her.

"Did you enjoy the dance?" she asked.

"Best I've ever gone to," he said. But the reason was

her presence, not the decorations or the music. Wherever she was, the air seemed lighter, like a warm wind whipping away the clouds.

As they neared the boardinghouse, Dagger stopped. Deep barking came from his house. "Sounds like Tanner has found some trouble."

He started to walk her to her house, then paused, impressed by the urgency of the barking. "Can you wait just a moment while I check this out? Then I'll get you home."

"Heavens, Dagger, I can walk down the street by myself."

He scowled. "No, you can't. Not in my town."

She huffed. "Oh, all right. Let's go see what Tanner has caught."

The big hound had caught himself a pregnant cat. Very pregnant, and just delivering her third kitten in Dagger's bedroom.

"Oh, aren't they sweet?" Janet dropped down beside the heap of clothing and kittens in the corner.

Dagger grunted. Sweet, his ass. They looked like bald mice, and that was his pile of clothing being used for a birthing place.

He squatted on his heels beside the schoolmarm, used a finger to push the new kitten closer to the mother's head.

"Doesn't she need—shouldn't we be helping or something?" She reached out with a timid hand and then pulled back.

"Never seen kittens being born?"

She shook her head and imitated his laconic speech. "Never seen anything born. This is so wonderful. Look, another one. And they're so little!"

Her face glowed, even more excited than she'd been

at the dance, and Dagger's heart gave a lurch, like an old river log that had been snagged up suddenly coming loose and sliding back into the current.

She imitated his action, moving the new kitten closer for the mama cat to tend, then stroked her hand over the cat's head. Gently. Tenderly. Oh, yeah, the current looked to be strong and fast.

With an effort, he glanced away from her, from those hands, sweetly feminine yet capable of so much. He cleared his throat. "Mmm, how about a drink? We can't leave her until she's done." Of course, from the look of her, the cat was several years old and had probably had a litter every year. Still . . .

"Uh, sure." She didn't even look up. "Oh, another one's coming."

"Lemonade? Water?" No answer, so he added jokingly, "Whiskey?"

"Whiskey'll be good," she murmured, not reacting to his sputter. She picked up one of the first kittens. "Here little one, how about trying for some milk?"

Whiskey? Hell, she'd asked, hadn't she? Dagger grinned all the way to the kitchen, visualizing the way she'd look when she had her first taste.

To his shock, she tossed it back like a bottle-a-day miner and set the glass down on the wood floor without a comment.

Dagger glanced at the bottle he held—yup, 'twas whiskey all right—and closed his mouth before flies wandered in. "More?"

"Sure." She glanced up at him, her eyes glowing. "I think she's about through. Her stomach seems soft and she doesn't have that hurting look in her eyes."

Dagger shook his head and poured himself a healthy slosh, then filled her glass.

She picked it up and took a drink. "Don't you think you should start a fire? We don't want her to get cold—she's had a rough time."

He glanced at the cat. Scarred fur, chewed-on ears, broken tail. A survivor. The cat could probably kill any dog in town. "I'll make a fire."

Janet pushed herself to her feet and sat down on the edge of his bed to watch the new family. *On his bed.* Her golden hair had begun to fall out of the high knot, little tendrils springing loose, touching her soft pink cheeks. She looked slightly mussed, like she'd just woken up after a long night of loving. *On his bed.*

He was so hard that kneeling in front of the fireplace was damned uncomfortable.

Janet let the whiskey swirl around in her mouth before it burned down to her gut. What a fantastic night! Dressing up fancy, dancing and now—kittens! She could just burst with delight. Giving a little bounce, she grinned at Dagger. "How many kittens have you watched being born? You seem pretty easy about it all."

The fire took off as he rose to his feet, all lean lines and broad shoulders. Made her stomach quiver, seeing him move like a cat himself.

"Well, I grew up on a ranch. Lots of barn cats. They had a few litters every spring." He settled on the bed beside her, his thigh warm against hers, his shoulder bumping against her.

Another splash of whiskey and her glass was full. Her brows pulled together. She really shouldn't be drinking with him. Still, it'd been a long time since she'd had a whiskey, let alone one so fine as this. Went down smooth as silk.

"To kittens, even if they are being born in the

wrong season." He touched his glass to hers with a clink.

"Christmas presents, I guess." She giggled, dammit. Pa always made her stop drinking at one glass, since two made her giggle. Beards and giggles didn't mix.

"You have the cutest laugh." He leaned forward, his eyes silver gray, like the metal they were hauling out of the Comstock in Colorado. Valuable metal.

"And you have the cutest—" Feeling very daring, she reached around and patted his seat.

"Ah, well, then." The silver in his eyes darkened as he touched his lips to hers.

Oh, and his lips were soft, a heady contrast with the callused hands running down her neck. Her skin burned where he touched.

He nibbled on the side of her mouth, teasing little bites, soft gentle kisses, until she opened her mouth and he took full possession. Was this allowed?

She stiffened, then her arms tightened behind his head and she kissed him back, fully, wonderfully.

He felt her tremble when his hand slid down her arm, brushed against the fullness of her breast. Just the slightest sound, a moan, and he had to hear it again, needed it to the depth of his soul, and his hand slid upward over her ribs to rest just below her breast.

Slowly, he unbuttoned her dress and found a treat beneath. Silky lace and smooth skin. His breath came hard as his fingers caressed the tender skin just above the corset. Her breasts made plump mounds over the stiff fabric, the valley between a shadowy place begging for his lips. And he complied.

Oh, the scent of her, gloriously female, like sunshine and roses. He felt alive in every part of his being.

Each touch of his lips elicited a soft moan, a shiver, until she shook like a leaf in his arms.

She needed . . . needed something, but she didn't know what. She pulled him closer, reveling in the touch of his lips on her bosom, feeling her breasts tighten into hard buds. And as if he read her mind, he loosened the corset, opening it like unwrapping a birthday package, and then his hot breath seared across her tender skin. When he took one nipple into his mouth and sucked gently, she arched uncontrollably.

"Please," she whimpered. And somehow her dress slid off her hips—his clothes disappeared. Had she helped him? She wasn't sure, too pleased with the way his naked skin felt on hers. She tangled her fingers in the silky hair on his chest, followed the line down to— her fingers curled around him and he was so big!

"Dagger, I don't know—" She'd seen her brothers a time or two by accident, and seen animals. There was no possible way that he and she would fit.

He nuzzled under her breast and heard her breath catch. If her fingers slid around him again, he'd be on the downward slide off a cliff. Her flowery aroma dazzled him, and he nuzzled her again, licked the soft skin.

She was like a flower herself, maybe one of those poppies Susanna had shown him. Growing wild along the roadside, taking drought and poor soil, yet flourishing with a wild beauty. In the sunlight a poppy glowed a magnificent gold, and in any light Janet glowed.

He slid down her body, nipping here, kissing there, until he reached his destination.

"Dagger?" Her voice shook and he grinned, then

breathed gently out, fluffing the curly hair.

Like a flower indeed, with the softest, most fragrant petals of all—he devoted attention to each petal and the tiny bud hidden within until the smooth muscles of her thigh tightened and she cried out, arching upward like a stem in a high wind, then wilted, soft and limp.

Oh, he'd never felt so alive as when he moved back up her body, feeling the tiny tremors still coursing under her skin.

"Janet?" he whispered.

Her eyes opened, a swimmingly satisfied blue color he'd never seen before and would remember until he died. And when he slid inside, she purred like the cat below.

"Oh, yes."

He moved, slowly at first, she was so tight, there had been this hesitation, she was—

He froze. "You were—you hadn't—"

Her lips were puffy from his kisses as they curved into a satisfied smile. "But I have now, haven't I?"

He buried his head in her neck as she rocked upward beneath him and his tightly held control frayed like a hard-used lariat. Seemed like she'd kept all that energy in check before, because when she loosened the reins, there was no stopping her.

Her hips moved side to side, and he groaned, grasping her to stop her. "Listen, darling, you—"

She arched upward against him, rubbed those magnificent breasts against his chest. He could feel the hard nubs, and he tightened again, moving uncontrollably until he launched himself over the peak and fell into a valley of flowers.

When his heart slowed and he could put two words

together, he cleared his throat. "Hmmm, am I too heavy for you?" He pushed over to her side, levering himself up on an elbow.

Her arms resisted the movement, tightening around his back. "No, I like the way you feel."

He smiled down at her. Her cheeks were flushed rosy pink and her eyes were sparkling. He'd never seen anyone more lovely in all his life. He stroked a hand up her arm, across a shoulder, and watched her lips curve. "Are you sore at all?"

That brought more of a flush. "I'm fine. Really." She struggled to sit up. "I should be going."

He nuzzled her neck, nibbled on an ear. "Stay. For a while."

She shouldn't and she knew it, but he felt so good against her. Her body felt lush, pampered . . . satisfied; even the slight soreness was wonderful.

"We could . . ." She kissed him, felt him respond, and knowing she could do that to him thrilled her.

A long, satisfying kiss, then he growled, "No, we couldn't. You wouldn't be able to walk for a week— and I doubt the rest of the school board would be as understanding as I am."

"Hmph." She pouted, delighted when he kissed her again.

Rolling onto his back, he tucked her against his side, her head on his shoulder. "Just cuddle with me a bit. I'm not ready to let you go."

She heard his heart under her ear, under the hand she placed flat against his chest. His breathing rocked her like a boat on a gentle sea, and the lub-dub of his heart slowed, his breathing deepening as he fell asleep. His hold on her never loosened.

She could see the side of his face, his strong jaw

with the shadow of a beard making his face appear rougher. The fleeting smile she could draw from him was gone as he slept; he looked so serious. He was a serious man, but he smiled for her, and that in itself made her lips curve up as she followed him into sleep.

The little schoolmarm was smiling in her dreams when Dagger woke and he watched her contently. She had a right to be exhausted.

The trials of the day—and he had to admit, she'd done herself proud with the recital—and then the whiskey and the late night had done her in. She slept like a kitten, soft, sweet, irresistible. The firelight danced over the flawless skin, the slope of a breast, the curve of her shoulder. She was so damned beautiful, she could steal a man's heart before he knew it.

Dagger felt the ache of it now, like someone sawing on the reins of his isolation with a rusty knife. He'd never felt like this with a woman before, not even Moon on Still Waters. When she looked at him, he felt strong, smart . . . needed. Part of the community, filling a place that no one else could fill.

He played with her fingers gently, kissed them. She needed him. He knew that. She needed someone to keep her safe, keep her out of trouble. Someone to enjoy that fast mouth of hers, that rebellious sense of humor that went so poorly with the schoolmarm half of her.

"No," she whispered, and he smiled.

"But yes." He leaned forward, ready to start all over, then stopped. Her face had tightened into a mask of terror. Eyes closed, she still slept, but her fingers tightened around his, her body gone stiff. She breathed in shallow pants.

"No, don't lock . . . they left me . . . no, no." Her

head tossed from side to side, and when he looked down, her hands were pulled together at the wrists, like they were roped together. What was she dreaming about?

He shook her shoulder, kissed her cheek, and she wrenched aside. "My clothes! ... Bastard ... don't touch ... no!" With a scream, she sat up, her eyes wide open. "Oh, God, oh God, dammit," she half-sobbed, hugging herself.

"Janet."

He saw when she came back to herself, realized she wasn't alone, he was there. "I—"

"Just a dream, honey; you had a dream."

She shivered. "I know, same dream."

"Want to tell me?"

A long sigh. "It's nothing important, really. Just a silly fear."

This woman had shot a snake into tiny bits and punched Boudreaux without a qualm, yet a lousy nightmare rendered her white and shaking. Not a *silly fear*, he was thinking. "Tell me," he ordered, holding her gaze with his own.

"I, um, got locked up once in a little room, almost as small as a closet." Her eyes dropped to her hands, wouldn't meet his gaze. "It was something of a mess, and the ... person who put me there was mean. It was a while before my father arrived and got me out. I was dreaming about being in a ... small room."

He had a feeling there was more to it, but he wasn't going to get more out of her tonight. "I wish I'd been there to help you."

Her lips tightened in a way he couldn't read. When he reached out to touch her, she winced away, then stopped. Her eyes finally met his again, and she heaved a deep breath, her muscles visibly relaxing.

"Sometimes I forget what a nice person you are," she whispered. Slowly she stroked her hand up his arm, across his chest. Snuggling like a milk-fed puppy, she pressed against his side. "You are very nice and warm," she announced, as if discovering a student could suddenly spell.

Resting on his shoulder, her face tilted up to him, and he saw mischief sparking in her eyes. "Guess you'd best warm me up, too."

Her fingers touched his stomach, slid lower . . . "Guess that would be the gentlemanly thing to do," he agreed hoarsely.

Later, much later, when the window showed the first streaks of light, she was feeling nicely warm.

"It's morning, Dagger," she whispered.

He muttered, then pulled her head against his and kissed her.

Reluctantly, she pulled her lips from his. "I must go."

His eyes opened and he raised up on one elbow. "I know."

He pressed a kiss into her palm and closed her fingers over it. "A kiss for . . . luck, my mother always said."

As she entered the boardinghouse on silent feet, Janet realized her fingers were still closed around Dagger's kiss.

When she walked to school the following day, Janet couldn't help watching the streets for a tall, lean, broad-shouldered figure. One that moved like a panther on the prowl.

And there he was, down the street a ways. Her knees

turned quivery. Shoot, she felt so aflutter, she'd probably not even be able to hold her gun steady. God,
she was hopeless, bad as Harry when he'd fallen for
some barmaid. Mooned around that tavern for
months. She straightened her face into what she hoped
looked aloof—damned if *she* wanted to look moony-
eyed. Maybe he wouldn't ask why she was a half block
from the school street.

"What are you doing?" It was a good, very casual
question, even if her voice sounded high. One that
deserved an answer, she realized, as his activity fully
registered.

He looked up from where he was kneeling by the
door of Miner's Bakery. Running his fingers over the
edge of the door, he scowled. "Trying to figure out
how the bas—the robber got in."

A jolt of fear shot through her. "Mrs. Chappell's
been robbed?" Looking into the bakery, she saw the
plump woman seated at a table, her shoulders
slumped. The sweet woman was always handing out
treats to the children, had shared many of her receipts
with Janet. Her voice raised in shock. "Who would do
something like that?"

"Well, now, that's the question, isn't it?"

His slow drawl brought her back to just who she
was speaking with, and she inched a little closer. "Do
you think you can find him?" Inane question. She just
wanted to keep talking, wanted to run her hands
through the thick black hair touching his shoulders.

"You look mighty pretty today, Miss Schoolmarm,"
Dagger said softly.

The heat rose in her face like a fire out of control.
"Why, thank you, sir." She cast about for something

to say . . . then her eyes narrowed. "There's dirt on the floor."

"Yes, well, that's what happens to floors in a town." Dagger rose to his feet, close enough that she could feel the heat of his body before she stepped back. He tilted his head. "Doesn't it?"

"Normally, but this is Mrs. Chappell's bakery, and she doesn't allow dirt on her floor. Any dirt here had to come from the robber." A lifetime of covering tracks, wiping out trails, had made Janet aware of the smallest details, but she suddenly wondered if the marshal would question her observation. The dirt had been so evident, surely he wouldn't notice anything more than just an interested woman.

Dagger stepped inside the store and bent over, brushing his fingers through a clump of dirt on the floor. Specks of dirt and mud were scattered across the entire room. "I hadn't been inside yet, so the mud isn't from me. And Dorothy came in the back door."

"She'd have wiped her feet very well anyway. And I know she sweeps the floor before she leaves every night."

He picked up the dirt, brushed at the pine needles wedged into it.

Janet followed him in and sat down next to the baker. The woman's pink cheeks were damp with tears, and Janet took her hands. "Mrs. Chappell, I'm so sorry."

"What kind of man would steal? I would give money if someone needed it. But this . . ." She gestured helplessly toward the broken lockbox. "And so much damage—he tore my flour sacks open, the sugar."

A rush of relief stunned Janet. Shoot, she hadn't

really suspected Clint, but he'd never be so sloppy. They'd been brought up right—clean robberies, take the money and get out. Only the bookstore had ever had anything else stolen.

"Flour, huh." She patted Mrs. Chappell's hand again and rose to her feet. "Marshal—"

Dagger was in the baking area. "He got in here," he commented over his shoulder, showing Janet the gouged doorjamb. "Used a crowbar, looks like."

"Mrs. Chappell said he'd been into her flour and sugar. I'd think that would mean it's someone who— Dagger, look!"

Dagger walked over to the table, his gaze on where her finger pointed. "Interesting pattern."

A round circle had been pressed into the sugar, the wavery scalloplike edge so familiar. "I've seen that before, I know." Janet walked to the other side of the table. "He put something down here, maybe used it to carry the sugar? Like a bucket or pail; oh, hell!"

Dagger's lips twitched upward at the profanity. "What?"

Her mouth was dry, a rock weighing down her guts. "Thomas, little Thomas Boudreaux. His lunch pail— he got creative one day and hammered the bottom edge into scallops."

"Ah." Dagger leaned back against the counter. "Seems like I've heard Boudreaux isn't having a good winter. His mine came up dry. He's been in the Golden Nugget drinking and gambling every night."

"Losing?"

Dagger snorted. "The man's too dumb to pour piss out of a boot when he's sober. Drunk?" He shrugged, then pushed himself upright. "Looks like I need to pay a visit to the Boudreauxs."

She remembered Boudreaux, his knife, his mean-
ness, and the full meaning of Dagger's words took her
breath. "Dagger . . . be careful."

The smile he gave her sent her stomach into her
throat. "I do like the sound of my name on your lips."
He took her hand. "And thank you. You have sharp
eyes, woman."

Bending like a San Francisco gent, he pressed a soft
kiss to the back of her hand, sending goose bumps all
the way up her arm to her heart.

Lord, the man had a way about him, was all she could
think as he walked out of the pastry shop. She felt
tingly all over, very alive, awake as if she hadn't spent
the entire night wrestling in his bed.

She watched him stride down the street, so very
masculine, so confident. What would it have been like
to have grown up knowing that you belonged somewhere, living where everyone knew you and who you
were?

"He's a good man," Mrs. Chappell said. She wiped
her eyes with her apron and pushed herself to her feet.
"A woman could do much worse."

Do worse? The meaning of the cook's words washed
over Janet like a hot blast from a stick of dynamite.
"No, he isn't, I didn't . . ." She could tell from the
amused look she got that her protests weren't worth
spit.

"He's been watching you since you arrived."

And Janet knew she was pretty far gone when instead of wanting to catch up her mare and make a run
for it, the idea of the lawman's interest only roused
warmth in her. What was happening to her? A soft
smile curved her lips. She'd been caught by a lawman
and put into a jail of her own making.

"You are good for him, you know."

Janet started. Shoot, she'd totally forgotten where she was, just standing here leaning on the door frame, dreaming away. Building castles in the air, her mama would have said.

She frowned at Mrs. Chappell. "Why do you think I could be good for him?"

"He laughs when he's with you, talks to everyone, he's . . . he doesn't scare people as much." Mrs. Chappell began to clean up the mess on her counter, and Janet moved to help.

"Why would he scare people?"

"Well, you are the one person who never seems to find his appearance or his manner frightening. He even made me nervous until I realized he has a sweet tooth and a gentle heart to go with it." A glint of humor shone in Mrs. Chappell's nut-brown eyes. "I decided as long as I could cook, I was safe."

Janet gave a snort of laughter. "He wouldn't hurt the hand that feeds him cookies, is that it?"

Dorothy Chappell chortled. "Exactly. Why don't you bring that broom from the back room and we'll sweep up the floor?" Her eyes twinkled as she added, "And we'll discuss the way to a man's heart."

Chapter Sixteen

Dagger stepped up onto the boardwalk in front of the Miner's Saloon. "Hank," he said, suppressing a grin.

The rail-thin drunk was dressed as a doctor today, complete with black bag and top hat. Doc Matson wouldn't be pleased with the impersonation. Hank scratched his fuzzy whiskers and squinted. "Hey, Blackthorne. How's that leg of yours? Want me to look at it?"

Dagger flinched. "That's my brother, Blade, with the hurt leg. I'm fine, uh, Doc."

The drunk beamed at the designation. "Lookin' for someone, Marshal?"

"Yup. Is Boudreaux in there?"

"That the Frenchie miner? Mean drunk?"

"That's the one."

Hank belched, and the ripe fumes of rotgut whiskey engulfed Dagger. "He's at the back table playing cards. Losin', I think."

"Thanks, Hank."

" 'Betcha. Come back and see me if'n you catch some lead."

Dagger didn't deign to answer that horrifying suggestion. Once he'd finished this business with Boudreaux, he'd better get old Hank into another guise before he conned some tenderfoot into letting him doctor him. He'd been much safer dressing up as a priest, although Father Sean had threatened to excommunicate him.

Pushing open the swinging doors, Dagger stepped inside. The aroma of sweat, cigar smoke and dirty spittoons fought with the whores' flowery perfumes. The sporting ladies greeted him with waves and high-pitched cries. Men at the bar turned, a few nodding before returning to their conversations.

Dagger settled his hat more firmly on his head and strolled across the room to the back table. Boudreaux was playing poker with the bartender and two disgruntled men who'd already folded. Playing with the money he'd stolen.

Dagger's teeth ground together. Damn, he hated thieves even more than murderers. At least a killer usually had a reason. Thieves, though, just too lazy to put in an honest day's work, had to destroy other people's lives to make their own easier.

"Hey, Marshal." Pierson Sprague nodded at him, then lay down his hand. "Beat that, Frenchie."

Boudreaux glared at the cards on the table, then tossed his into the pot. "*Merde.* You have all the luck."

Murmurs of agreement came from the other two men.

"And the money," Pierson chortled, raking in the pile of paper and silver. "Wal, I best get back to my bar before them floozies steal me blind." Pocketing his haul, he snapped his garish suspenders and stood. "What's your poison, Blackthorne?"

"Nothing, thanks. I'm just here to talk with Boudreaux."

Sprague hesitated.

Dagger jerked his head sideways, and the bartender obediently lumbered away. A frown set the other two men heading off also. Dagger pulled out a chair and settled himself.

Boudreaux eyed him uneasily. "Wat you want wit me?"

"Been to your house, Frenchie. Took a look inside."

The red swam up into Boudreaux's neck, making it appear to swell. "You got no right to be in my house."

"You got no right to be stealing from honest shopkeepers." At the words and the memory of Mrs. Chappell's tears, outrage tightened his jaw. Pounding on the bastard seemed like a fine idea.

"Not me! I done nothing."

"I found pastries, flour, sugar and her special cakes in your cabin. You're under arrest for robbery."

Dagger rose, grabbed Boudreaux's collar and yanked him half across the table. "You can come with me quiet or not. Doesn't matter much to me."

Boudreaux came up swinging and bellowing.

Dodging the first swing, Dagger grinned. Looked like he'd get his wish, even though he'd had to prod the miner just a tad. He plowed a fist into a hard stomach and stopped the man dead. A right cross landed squarely on Frenchie's cheekbone and Dagger felt skin split under his knuckles. Blood splattered as Boudreaux stumbled backward, arms windmilling. When he flattened a table, Dagger winced. Pierson would make him buy a new one.

Boudreaux rolled over onto his belly, pushed up onto his hands and knees and shook his head like a dog. Dagger stepped back to give him room.

"Dammit, Marsh—Look out!" the bartender hollered.

Boudreaux came to his feet with a lunge and a wickedly sharp knife. It sliced clean across Dagger's shoulder like a burning brand and suddenly the fight wasn't a game anymore.

Dagger stumbled back against the men behind him. Off balance, he frantically twisted to avoid Boudreaux's next lunge. The knife slashed a piece of his shirt. Grabbing an arm, Dagger yanked the man backward and gave him a hard shove into the center of the room.

Hands steadied Dagger as he staggered from the effort. He spun to meet the next charge, but it never came. Flat out on the floor, Boudreaux wasn't moving.

"Huh, knocked out," Dagger said, but a cold feeling dampened his anger like the first step into an icy stream.

"Boudreaux, Boudreaux!" He knelt beside Frenchie and shook his shoulder, then yanked him roughly over onto his back. The breath left Dagger's lungs with a rush.

"Well, hell," Pierson swore. He squatted beside Dagger and closed Boudreaux's staring eyes. "Poor bastard landed right on his own knife."

The jail was quiet with no prisoners in the cells. Outside, the town was subdued, except for the minor bustle that accompanies a death.

Dagger knew that the undertaker was probably hitching his wagon right now to pick up the body from Pierson's office. The Methodist Ladies Sewing Circle would be starting on a shroud, their contribution to the town's needs.

He leaned forward in his chair, elbows on the desk, and dropped his head into his hands. His head pounded and his stomach was threatening to upchuck. He swallowed uneasily.

What was his contribution to the town? He, the wonderful lawman of Shasta. What was his job?

Well, now, that would be killing off thieves and saving the county all sorts of money. No judge, jury, jail or court costs. There you go.

Dagger Blackthorne, marshal and executioner all in one. Ah, there, almost forgot. He'd also saved the taxpayers the hangman's fee.

He shook his head, trying to get the morbid thoughts out of his mind. He'd killed men before, with the Indians, in the army, as a scout, later as a marshal, but never, never like this. Each man whose life he'd taken—after a time they'd come back to haunt him. He'd see their faces, the shock in their eyes. They'd appear in his dreams, or sometimes in the flames in the fireplace. Looking at him, asking him why.

He'd never been able to answer.

But Boudreaux . . . the haunting had already started. Over and over again, he lived those last few minutes. If only he'd just dodged, not grabbed an arm, not swung him away. If only he'd gone about the whole arrest differently. Why had he—

"Dagger?" The door swung open and daylight blazed in. "Are you in here?"

Janet stopped in the doorway and frowned. Why

didn't he answer? Why hadn't he come to find her? She'd been worried about him all day, and now there were rumors running all over town. At the livery, Pike and Albert had told her that someone had been killed, but they weren't sure who. They'd been waiting to check out the undertaker's wagon.

Finally she'd taken matters in her own hands and come to see the marshal herself. But he wasn't acting at all like himself.

Janet tilted her head and took a step forward into the office—the jail. God, she hated jails, but she needed to see him, needed to know he was all right. She had to resist the urge to go over to him, run her hands up and down his body, check for bullet holes, knife holes.

What in the world had happened? His face was gray, his eyes haunted. "You look terrible. Are you ill?"

"I—it's hard to explain," he said. His voice sounded like a freight wagon had rolled over it and crushed it into the gravel. "Boudreaux, the man who robbed Mrs. Chappell—"

"Thomas's father—"

To her amazement, he flinched.

"Has something happened to Thomas?"

"No, not Thomas." He drew a breath. "Boudreaux; he's been killed. No—I killed him."

Dead? Thomas's pa was dead? The star on Dagger's chest glinted as he straightened in his chair, and abruptly she remembered who she was talking to: a marshal.

Goddamn lawmen! She took a step away from him, the star on his chest seeming to grow to encompass his entire shirt. "For being a thief, you killed him?"

"No. Yes. Hell, I don't know." He dropped his head back into his hands.

What the hell kind of answer was that? She spun on her heel and walked to the door, shoved it open, then hesitated, staring blindly at a freight wagon rattling by. He was a lawman, yet this lawman was Dagger, the keeper of stray animals, the children's best friend . . . her lover.

She let the door close again softly. Leaning back against the doorjamb, she crossed her arms and studied him.

The slumped shoulders didn't make him look like a man happy with what had happened to a thief. No gleam of victory had shone in his eyes; rather, the reverse.

"Dagger," she said quietly, "tell me what happened."

He sighed and rubbed his face, as if to erase the memory. "I went to arrest him in the Miner's. He'd been playing cards, undoubtedly with the stolen goods, Dorothy's money. I lost my temper. I *goaded* him into a fight, God help me, and when we fought, he fell on his knife."

She chewed on her lip for a minute, listening absentmindedly to the rattle of wagons outside, the profane shouting of the mule skinners. Dagger had blood on his shoulder; a rip in his shirt gaped open. "So you didn't stab him—he just fell on it?"

"Yeah, but I might as well have shoved it into him myself. I went to arrest him, not be judge, jury and executioner, dammit. That's not my job. I-I let my anger push me into behaving as badly as a criminal—and I cost a man his life, and a boy his father."

"Oh, Dagger." A funny feeling ran over her, a

giddy, bittersweet emotion. She pressed her hands over her chest as she figured out what had caused it, and the shock shook her like a cottonwood in the wind.

He was a lawman, yet he'd stolen something. Right there in front of her, he'd taken her heart. She'd have to do something, but she wasn't sure what. The future was too difficult to think of right now, not when her lawman was hurting.

The way back to him seemed much shorter than the distance away. She leaned over and hugged him, relieved when his arms came around her waist and pulled her tightly against him. "You didn't kill him. Knowing you, you didn't even pull your knife."

"No, but there wouldn't have been a fight if I hadn't pushed him."

She snorted. "You can't possibly be that stupid."

He looked up at her, black brows drawn into a frown. "I'm not—"

"Stupid. And you are. Not even a saint could have brought that man in without a fight. He'd probably have tried to knife you if you'd asked him to church, let alone jail."

The knotted muscles in his shoulders loosened slightly. "That may be—"

She lay her cheek on top of his head and murmured, "It is. Maybe you were wrong to be angry for what happened to Mrs. Chappell, but the fight would have happened either way. You aren't to blame for his death."

She closed her eyes, wondering at how her world had flipped so topsy-turvy that she could be comforting a lawman for killing a thief, that she could be losing her heart to a lawman.

And what would happen when he found out that she was a thief, too?

"Here he is, Marshal." Arnie Fromm gently nudged the small boy into the schoolhouse.

Dagger's hand tightened on Janet's fingers. She turned to smile at him and squeezed his hand before moving toward the boy.

Thomas'd never spoken of any other family. She hoped the others gathered in the schoolhouse had some ideas for the child's future.

Arnie nodded at Janet. "Miss Danner."

The hubbub in the schoolhouse quieted as Thomas Boudreaux halted at the sight of the four grown-ups. Jenny Perkins made a small, sympathetic noise silenced by Maude Tucker's frown. Gus and Dagger stood along the side, quietly waiting.

"Miss Danner?" Thomas looked terrified. "Is something wrong?"

"Arnie—didn't you . . . ?" Mrs. Tucker scowled.

The bookstore owner looked down. "Couldn't do it. He's so—"

"That's my job anyway." Dagger walked to a corner of the room and motioned for Thomas to join him. Sadness moved through Janet as Thomas joined him without any sign of hesitation. Poor baby didn't have any idea what Dagger was going to tell him. The others moved away from the corner over to the woodstove, distancing themselves from facing death.

Janet sat down on the long recital bench, alternately gazing out at the gray winter day and watching Thomas. When the young face crumbled into tears, her heart pained her in sympathy. She had a good idea how he felt. Pa, Daniel, Harry, Mama—she'd lost

216

them all. Although the pain lessened in time, the sorrow never went away.

Dagger looked like a panther with a paw caught in a trap, desperate, hurt. After a minute, both of them turned toward her, and Thomas came running.

"Miss Danner, is it true?" She heard a forlorn hope in his voice that maybe the marshal had got it wrong, that his pa wasn't gone.

She killed that hope dead as his pa. "I'm sorry, Thomas. Your father is dead." She opened her arms and accepted a bundle of boy, remembering the fears that always eased with Mama's hugs. And now she knew what Mama had received in return. Lordy, it eased a body to be able to help, even in this small way.

She rocked him back and forth, murmuring softly and gentling him like a wild pony. Dagger straddled the bench beside her, ran his big hand over the boy's shaggy black hair, almost a match for his own.

The regret in his eyes hurt her, and she touched his cheek with the back of her fingers and received a half-smile, half-grimace in return. The man was as deep as a dry country well. He had so much hidden pain in him, pain she wanted to ease.

"So, does Boudreaux have any kin in the area?" Maude marched closer and plumped herself down on the student bench.

"Don't know. We didn't get that far." Dagger sighed. "Thomas, lad, do you know if your pa had any brothers or sisters?"

Thomas shook his head and burrowed deeper against Janet.

When Dagger raised an eyebrow, Janet nodded. Her turn. She took Thomas by the shoulders and moved him far enough away to see his face. "Thomas, we need to know. Do you have any kinfolk around here?"

His breath hitched, but he managed to answer. "No'm. Pa said we got some folk back in Louisiana, around New Orleans, but he's the only one got gold fever."

"Louisiana. That's a far ways," Jenny exclaimed. "It'll be a while before we can get an answer back. What do we do in the meantime?"

"Huh. I think Walsh down at the horse market was wanting a stall boy," Arnie said. "But I'd hate—"

She'd be damned if Pike's father or Pike got a chance at this boy. "Dagger'll take him."

Dagger'd just opened his mouth to protest Walsh as a choice when his pretty schoolmarm volunteered him for Pa-duty. "I—what?"

"The marshal?" Gus asked. "I don't know if that would be—"

"He'd be good for the boy," Janet said firmly, "and it's part of his job, isn't it? Taking in strays?"

Dagger had trouble getting past the fact that she thought he'd be good for Thomas. "Listen—"

They trampled over his words like a stampede.

Jenny plucked at her lips, then smiled. "He may scare the adults spitless, but I've noticed the children don't feel the same way. My Ben and Sally are always trailing after him."

Maude tilted her head. "Jenny, I think you're right." She nodded, then looked around at the others. "So, are we in agreement? The marshal takes the boy until the family is contacted."

Dagger saw the smiles and nods like nails in his coffin. It wasn't as if he didn't like Thomas, but—"I have duties. There are times—"

218

"I can take Thomas during the day when you're working," Janet offered, dimpling the way she did when she won an argument. Had he just been conned? "And in the evening if you're called out, Thomas can go to Jenny's or Maude's house; isn't that right, ladies?"

They agreed, and his only chance of escape was cut off at the pass. Caretaker, temporary father to a—

"How old are you anyway, Thomas?"

Thomas's dark blue eyes evaluated him carefully, warily, old bruises from his pa's fists marring unfreckled cheeks. "Six, sir. I'm six."

Dagger endeavored a smile and saw the boy's eyes lighten, hope clearing away the clouds, and knew he was doomed.

That night, Dagger stepped out onto his porch and sat down in the porch swing with a heavy sigh. The chains holding the swing creaked in chorus with his sore muscles. He was getting old, old and tired.

In the back bedroom, Thomas lay sleeping. Hopefully.

The child had cried when Dagger tucked him into bed, and the memory made Dagger's chest tighten. Funny how a child or a dog could take abuse and still mourn the abuser.

At least no one would be hurting Thomas again. His fists tightened at the thought, and he almost wished someone would try, would give him some way to show Thomas how sorry he was.

He wasn't sure how this taking care of a boy would work out, but he had to admit somehow the house felt warmer with Thomas in it. Janet had the same effect, he'd noticed. Lighting up a room. Everyone seemed to move faster, smile more when she entered a room.

Across the street, he could see her room. The drapes were closed, with just a narrow opening giving him tantalizing glimpses of her as she moved about in the soft candlelight. She was wearing just a chemise, he noticed, and smiled again at the lacy stuff on it. What she wore was like those special cakes Mrs. Chappell made, plain on the outside with fancy filling inside. The schoolmarm was full of surprises.

He rocked for a while, enjoying the cold night air, the distant tinny piano from the Golden Nugget, the rumble of a late freight wagon heading out. Normal sounds for Shasta.

He thought again of Thomas, now without family. How could a child grow to be a good man without a family? Dagger had been blessed with good parents, and then, when they were killed, Bowie had taken over as best he could. They had all grown up fast that year, turning into men before they could shave. But he'd had family around him always, others to knock the sense into him, to be disappointed when he let them down, to back him up when he got in over his head.

Casey trotted up the porch steps, his nails making ticking noises on the steps. With a shiver of delight, he jumped up onto the swing, setting it rocking as he turned three circles before settling down next to Dagger's thigh. He gave a long sigh, turning dark brown eyes hopefully up at his owner.

"Fool," Dagger muttered, then gave in as always. Casey's eyes closed blissfully as Dagger scratched his ears, ruffled his coarse fur.

"So, how are you liking having a boy around?" Dagger asked.

Casey tilted his head.

"Yeah, I haven't decided either. He's a good one, though, don't you think?"

The terrier blinked.

"We can't raise a child by ourselves. The lad needs a mother." Dagger's gaze was drawn again to the window across the road. "Someone who'd love him whether he was hers or not."

Casey cocked one ear forward.

"I'm not sure yet. Don't push me, all right?" She surely did look fine in a chemise, but a man couldn't marry—

His thoughts stopped right there.

Marry? Was he considering marrying the little schoolmarm?

The sense of warmth rising in him had nothing to do with Casey's small body snuggled up to him and everything to do with Miss Janet. He'd been planning on marrying her all along, now hadn't he? He wasn't the type of man to lie with a good woman; he'd never done such a thing in his life.

Down deep, he'd always known he'd be marrying her if he took her to his bed. And oddly enough, the thought didn't bother him. In fact, he couldn't imagine life without her.

The world had been dark without her in it.

Besides, she needed him, whether she knew it or not, and he'd just have to show her that. Time for some serious courting.

Chapter Seventeen

Janet checked the oven again and stirred the coals below. The cake looked just about right. She turned and tripped over Shep, Thomas's rescued puppy. The dog had sprouted into a gangly half-grown animal and never seemed more than a few inches from her shoes.

"Lord a mercy," she muttered, and smiled. She'd been practicing using no profanity. After all, a schoolmarm shouldn't be coming out with phrases that a mule skinner might use, no matter how much more satisfying they were.

Stepping over Shep's lazy carcass, she hurried to the parlor and looked out the front window. The early winter sun sat low on the horizon. Dagger had dragged Thomas along on one of his town tours, but there was no sign of her men returning. She'd have a few more minutes to whip up the glazing.

The cake was on the kitchen table, glistening with frosting, when Dagger and Thomas walked into the house. Waked from a sound sleep, Shep barked shrilly, then recognized Thomas and dashed over to welcome him.

Thomas giggled, the most appealing sound Janet had ever heard, and dropped to the floor to wrestle. Stepping carefully around the tussling, Dagger grinned over at Janet. "I'm putting my money on the dog."

She laughed. "I wouldn't take that bet." She raised an eyebrow as Shep knocked Thomas flat and proceeded to clean his face. "Shep's got the fastest tongue in the West."

Dagger glanced around the newly cleaned parlor and sniffed at the air. "Not that I'm complaining or anything . . . but were we expecting you?"

She hooked an arm in his and pulled him toward the kitchen. "No," she murmured, "but I found out something during school today, and I just had to do something about it."

"Sounds ominous."

"No, not that. It's just that Thomas let drop that today's his birthday."

"Well, da-darn." Dagger ran his hands through his hair. "I wish I'd known—I'd have gotten—"

Janet grinned, delight bubbling inside her. "You did."

"I did? Did I get him something good?"

He looked so sweet, so concerned, she pressed a soft kiss on his lips. "You are—"

His arms wrapped around her and pulled her hard against his body. "I am, indeed." He took her lips in a thorough kiss that left her breathless and clinging to him. "And you are so soft," he growled against her lips.

223

When he bent for another kiss, she pushed against his chest, laughing. "Marshal Blackthorne," she scolded, "I'm trying to have a conversation here."

"Oh . . . right. What did we get for Thomas?"

"You got him new trousers and a belt. I got him a new red shirt and some candy."

"Sounds about right—those britches get any thinner and I'd have to haul him in for indecency. He's too young to start bein' an outlaw."

Janet suppressed a wince. She hadn't been much older when she'd gone with Pa the first time, and the law they broke hadn't been for having a hole in her trousers.

Dagger stepped over to the kitchen table. "Cake!" She nudged him away before he had a chance to mess with her work. "You and Thomas wash up and we'll have a party. I made a beef roast."

Dagger glanced longingly back at the cake before disappearing into the parlor. The giggles were broken off abruptly by a squeal and more barking. Dagger reappeared with Thomas lying across one shoulder, the child laughing so hard Janet was afraid he'd be sick to his stomach.

"Dagger, be careful, you wretch!"

He let the boy down slowly. Scooping warm water from the stove reservoir, he poured it over Thomas's hands and then his own. They dried off on the scrap of cloth that Dagger called his kitchen towel.

"We're clean, Miss Janet," Thomas announced. He sniffed the air. "Something sure smells good. Did *you* cook?" he asked hopefully.

"Scamp," Dagger said gruffly. "You saying I'm not a good cook?"

"Uh . . ." Thomas eased a step away, his eyes warily

watching Dagger's hands, and Janet's heart broke at the look of realization, then anger, in Dagger's eyes. She knew exactly what he was feeling, anger at himself for raising memories in the boy's mind, and anger at the child's father, who had put those memories there in the first place.

She saw Dagger force a smile, his chin raised. "All right, you insulted me, so I'd say a punishment is in order."

"Dagger!" she started.

"Maybe an extra long bath?"

Thomas blinked. He loved bathing, making bubbles in the tin washbasin.

"No, that's too easy. Maybe having to listen to two stories tonight?"

The fear disappeared from Thomas's eyes, and he bounced on his toes. "You should be really mean and make me listen to three stories. I could say you're a really, really bad cook."

Dagger sent Janet a wry look. "He's too smart for his own good. All right, three stories. After all, you're a year older today."

Blue eyes widened. "How did you know?"

Janet had backed over to the kitchen counter and now pulled out the presents. "Happy birthday, Thomas!"

The joy on his face was almost shocking. "For me?" Hands trembled as they reached for the packages. "You bought presents for me? My birthday?"

Janet set the presents into two piles and then pulled out a chair. "Sit, boy. These are from me and these are from Dagger."

She jammed a hip into Dagger's leg and shoved him toward a chair. "You sit, too. Just let me get the cake."

Thomas bounced out of the chair like a startled jackrabbit. "A cake? I have a birthday cake?"

She set it on the table, pleased with the look against the red calico tablecloth. Very festive. "Just a little piece now. You can have more after supper."

The glow in Thomas's eyes made all the rushing around more than worth it, and the warmth in Dagger's eyes made her insides twist like Olivia's fancy lacework. He sat beside her as Thomas ripped open wrappings, exclaiming and shouting.

A warm hand curled around her fingers on the tabletop. "You are a very special lady," he said softly in her ear.

"And you're not a complete cad either."

The bruise marks had faded from Thomas's face and the small shadowy remainders were eliminated by the sparkling smile on his face. He absolutely glowed.

"You are the bestest moth—lady," he told Janet.

She wrapped him in a hug, burying her face in the soft neck. "You're the bestest boy," she whispered, her heart trading the word *son*, just as he had. Blinking back silly tears, she squeezed him hard, then tickled his ribs until he shouted with laughter, erasing the sentiment. "There, that will keep you quiet, heh, boy?"

"I'm quiet . . . I'm quiet."

She let go and frowned at him suspiciously. He stepped back and then raised his voice, "I'm loud!"

"Hah!" Snatching him back, she tickled him into submission again, until he whispered, "I'm quiet," between giggles.

"What do you think, Marshal? I think we've got us a nuisance here."

Dagger rubbed his jaw and squinted at Thomas.

"There's only one sentence we hand out to nuisances."

Thomas crawled away backward on his hands like a crab. "No, no, please, Marshal, don't sentence me." His pleadings were choked with giggles.

"Sorry, son. It's to the jail with you." Dagger slung Thomas over one shoulder. "Where's the washbasin?"

Janet motioned to where she'd set the tin tub up next to the woodstove and ignored the shriek as Dagger yanked off his boots and dumped Thomas in, clothes and all.

When the marshal straightened up, he glanced worriedly at Janet. "Children don't die from laughing too hard, do they?"

A couple of hours later, Janet finished cleaning up in the kitchen. She stopped to poke at the fire in the parlor, then dropped down beside Dagger on the sofa with a sigh of pure contentment. "How many stories did he con you out of?"

"He fell asleep halfway through the third. How many pieces of cake did he wheedle from you?"

"Three. We're spoiling him, aren't we?"

Dagger slung an arm around her and pulled her closer. "Nah. We're just trying to balance out the past a little. . . . Damn, you smell good."

His lips grazed under her ear and nibbled down her neck, nuzzled her collarbone. "Now, Dag—"

When he took her hands and eased them under his shirt, she couldn't help running her fingers through the soft mat of hair hiding the hard planes of his chest. Oh, he was all man.

She saw the need building in his eyes as her hand stroked lower, down onto his stomach, felt the need

227

building in her, tightening her insides with an ache that only he could satisfy.

And she knew just what to do about it. Pulling herself away, she stood, then dropped down onto his lap, her skirts and petticoats hitching up around her legs.

He froze in surprise, and she took full advantage. Running her fingers through his hair, she tightened her grip and pulled him right into a do-or-die kiss. She tilted her head, took him deeper, launching a full-scale assault.

What had he done to earn this? Dagger wondered as the schoolmarm swarmed over him like hot lava. His fingers slid under ruffling petticoats, across intoxicating thighs, and found his reward accompanied by her gasp of pleasure. She was slick, hot, wonderful, and he'd never been taken like this in all his life.

When she pushed him back on the couch and stole his shirt right off his back, he could only laugh.

Her eyes glinted evilly in the firelight. "What do you think you're laughing about, Marshal?" She bit his shoulder and his laughter turned into a gasp. He was so hard his britches were becoming acutely uncomfortable, and she'd positioned herself right over him.

Each squirming move she made brought him closer to losing control.

Janet rained tiny kisses up and down Dagger's neck, his cheeks, his eyes, then recaptured his lips in a hot kiss, wanting to experience again that thing he did with his tongue.

And then his lips were on her breasts, teasing bites and nibbles and licks as he loosened each corset string. When he took a nipple and sucked gently, she moaned, whimpered, "Please, please."

Her hands worked at his trousers, fumbling at the buttons until he shoved her fingers aside and undid them himself. She felt smothered by all the petticoats, too hot, wanting to feel his skin against hers, and she jumped to her feet only to be grabbed.

"Oh, no, darlin', allow me," he murmured. Her corset dropped to one side, then the skirt, accompanied by a kiss to her stomach that made the muscles quiver. The outer petticoat fell next with another kiss, even lower. His hands on her waist were all that kept her upright.

The next petticoat, and the next, as each one slid down, his mouth following, but never quite where she wanted him to go.

"Dagger, you have to . . ."

He stood suddenly, picked her up and laid her on the sofa in one smooth, powerful move. There she lay, spread out for his pleasure, and she couldn't feel an ounce of embarrassment. He knelt beside her and circled one nipple with a callused finger, the rasp erotic against her sensitive skin.

His face was rough against her stomach, his hair tantalizingly brushed her inner thighs, his mouth, so hot, sucked, licked, stroked, and she came to pieces in his arms.

God, he loved this woman, was his only thought when she looked up at him with those clear blue eyes, her lips puffy from his kisses. Instead of her fiery sunshine, now she glowed like moonlight, all woman.

She reached, slid her hand down his stomach. Her lips curved into a smile when her fingers curled around him. "Well, I knew there must be something like this down there. Do you need a sheath for your weapon, Dagger?"

He rubbed his beard-roughened jaw against her breast in revenge and heard her gasp. "Have you a sheath to offer, madam?"

"I might"—she pouted at him—"but it might be too small."

His voice sounded hoarse even to his own ears as the last remnants of his control disappeared. "Let's find out."

She tried to tease him further, but with a roar, he buried his weapon inside her sheath and, although her eyes widened, the fit was perfect.

When the moonlight through the bedroom window fell across Dagger's face, he wakened and glanced down to be sure Janet was still asleep. She was, her long lashes like feathers on her pink cheeks. She lay on her back, her breasts high and adorned with the pinkest, prettiest nipples he'd ever seen. In fact, that had been the reason for the delay by the fire before they managed to get up the stairs into the bedroom.

And when they'd flung themselves into the bed, the cold covers had made snuggling a necessity, which led to other necessities. Dagger rubbed his chest where a set of scratches burned. She didn't take kindly to teasing in bed—for a moment there, he'd been afraid she'd have shot him if she'd had a gun.

He gathered her into his arms, still wondering at the way they fit so well together. Her softness against his hard body, she snuggled into him as if they'd always been together. Rolling over, he tucked her up against his side, her cheek on his shoulder, and savored the feeling. His own little piece of heaven, right here, right now.

What would happen if he kept her? Married her?

* * *

Clint's note had said he'd be camping up around Hightown. Urging Brownie onto the Hightown road, Janet frowned at the mud slowing down the mare's gait. The sticky dirt clung to the horse's hooves like her past was clinging to her. And like Clint was clinging to her.

Dam—darn it. She loved him so much, but shouldn't he be moving on? Starting to do something worthwhile with his life?

Then she shook her head. She wasn't being fair to him. He hadn't had the experience of going straight, finding out what else there was in the world beside the outlaw life. Truly, she'd already become a little disillusioned with the excitement even before Pa's death. Having no home, no friends, having to pretend to be a man. She'd looked ahead sometimes and seen nothing wonderful for herself.

But Clint wasn't seeing that. He enjoyed the thrills of being a robber, outwitting the citizens, the lawmen.

Somehow she needed to get him thinking about going straight, at least trying it.

Annoyed by the mud, Brownie shook her head, making the reins jingle. Janet directed the horse onto rockier ground. The rain that had started last night as she sneaked back to her room had finally let up an hour ago. The mountain air smelled fresh and clean, with a piney tang.

She squinted up the road, then checked the sun again. She'd be getting back after dark again, and she bit her lip. How long could she fool Dagger with made-up stories? He certainly wasn't a stupid man, and she doubted there were many schoolmarms who took midnight rides.

231

Her lips curled then as a thrill of pure lust slipped up and down her spine. Could be she'd be able to divert him from thinking too much. She had a sweet vision of pulling him into his room by his—

A low-hanging branch forced her to duck hastily. She settled back into the saddle. How she loved touching Dagger, running her hands over that smooth skin rippling with hard muscles underneath. His stomach actually had little ridges running across it where the muscles bunched up. And his bottom was so different from hers, so tight.

Yanking her thoughts back, she scolded herself. Getting all aroused way up here on the mountain; that made a lot of sense.

She spotted Clint's sign high up on a tree, bark cut out, angling toward where she should leave the road.

Now how was she going to introduce the subject of going straight to her little brother? And how could she tell him that his sister was planning to remain a schoolteacher.

An hour later, Janet shoved her hat farther back onto her head and glared at Clint's back. "Listen up, Clint."

Nudging Brownie in the sides, she rode up along-side the clabber-headed, mutton-brained fool who called himself her brother. "I don't want to rob High-town, or anywhere else for that matter. I'm making a perfectly decent living now. I've quit riding on the wrong side of the law."

Clint scowled. "And exactly what am I supposed to do? I can't pull this off by myself, sis." He ducked under a low branch and turned onto the road leading toward Hightown.

232

"Why do you need to rob anything? Get a job like I did."

"Geez, Janet. I'm not a townie, a sheep, waiting for a wolf to come along and take everything I've got. I'm a wolf—and so are you!"

"Not anymore." She remembered Dagger's silvery eyes, the look of caring on his face, and her voice firmed. "I won't help you, so we might as well turn around right now."

Clint pulled up at a break in the trees and dismounted. Janet slid off her horse and joined him. The low mountain looked down on the small town of Hightown. "There's the express office, right there"— he pointed—"and there's the way we'll leave."

Janet squatted down on her heels. "No."

"It's the last job I'll ask of you. It'll get me enough money to start up somewhere else, put together a few men."

"Clint, you're too young to get anyone to join you."

"Then I'll join someone else. I just need to get a rep going."

"Dammit, I'm not going to steal anymore. I'm part of these people now."

"This isn't even your town."

"They're all the same. Now I know how people feel when they're robbed, and it doesn't make me happy to know that I stole. Thank God they don't know what I used to do."

"You're turning into a yellow-belly."

She shoved him hard enough to almost toss him over the cliff, then pulled him back from the edge by his belt. "Watch it, little brother."

His mouth pulled into an ugly sneer. "Maybe I'll just let those wonderful townies of yours in on the secret. How much would they like you then?"

At the thought of Dagger's reaction, her gut tightened, ice forming at the bottom. "You wouldn't." She loved Clint; he wouldn't betray her like this.

"Oh, yes, I would." He kicked a dirt clod, watched it fall over the cliff. "You'd leave me without any family, any gang? Just dump me on my own like a worn-out pair of boots? Why wouldn't I tell? Don't you want to go straight? Better start out clean, eh?"

"Clint—" Her heart was hammering. Dagger—what would he say . . . do? He'd go crazy. And her job . . . her friends . . . Thomas. "Please, don't do this."

He leaned back against a tree, tucked a blade of grass in his mouth. "I won't, sis—if you help me out here. Just this once."

She closed her eyes, despair fighting with anger. "And you'll leave me be? Stay away from Shasta?"

"You got my word."

Even as she nodded, she wondered what good was the word of an outlaw?

Clint's plan had been a good one, Janet conceded. The burglary had gone down just as he had laid it out. Her little brother was fully as smart as Pa had always boasted. And for the first time she felt the regret of that, the waste of intelligence being used for something so destructive.

She loaded the last of the money bags stenciled with HIGHTOWN BANK onto the packhorse, then poked her head through the back door of the bank. "Are you coming?" she hissed. "It's starting to get light."

"Yeah. I just wanted to leave my mark." Clint emerged from the bank, a triumphant grin on his face.

They mounted and sedately walked their horses out

of town. *Look like you're running and you soon will be*, Pa had always said. As soon as they turned off onto the trail toward Shasta, Janet leaned forward. "What did you mean by your *mark?*"

"You'd have loved it. I carved our name into the bank counter, right at the teller's window."

Horror gagged her for a minute. "You did *what?*"

"Yup. They'll have to pass money over the *Garret gang* until they sand it out."

She closed her eyes and tried to draw a breath. He couldn't have known how much she wanted the notorious Garret gang to die a quiet death. Or how badly a marshal was wanting to find them. But he had known that she was living in the town next door. Fury welled up inside her.

She edged her horse sideways and backhanded him right off his horse.

"What the hell!" He came to his feet in a rush. "Janet, I outa—"

After sliding off her horse, she untied the packhorse's reins from Clint's saddle. "You ought to quit. I'm going to."

"What are you doing?" He tried to grab the packhorse's reins as she knotted them to her own saddle.

"I'm taking the money back."

His grip was hard on her shoulder as he spun her around to face him. He was a man, she had to acknowledge, no longer a kid brother. And it was time he grew up. Her heart hurt at the thought.

"Janet . . . we already had this discussion."

"Tell you what, we're going to have it again. You pointed the finger at the Garret gang. That wasn't in the deal, now was it? You wanted to force me to move on, to come back with you. It'd be so hot here I'd have no choice."

She read the truth in his eyes. "Well, it's not going to work, *brother*. This time around, the Garret gang will be doing a good deed—giving back to the robbed."

She still held the reins of the packhorse. He closed his hand over hers and squeezed hard, trying to make her drop them. Her free hand fisted and she nailed him with a hard right to the jaw, staggering him backward.

"Dammit, Janet," he howled and rubbed his chin. "You're not going anywhere with my money." He lunged forward, reaching for the reins.

Both horses sidestepped nervously, yanking Janet with them. Off balance, she couldn't defend herself against Clint's buffet to her head. Da-darn, that hurt! She kicked his shin with her hard boot and earned a bellow of pain. And then it got downright dirty.

A right hook, a head in the stomach, a fall and tussle, but she sprang free by nailing him in the privates, then kicked him solidly in the ribs. She stood panting while he tried to recover.

He groaned and rolled onto his side. "I think you busted my ribs."

"Hell, you split my lip. How am I supposed to show up in class looking like this?"

"Don't go back."

She dropped down beside him and licked the blood from her lip. Clint's face looked young again. Woeful. Lonely. As the excitement left her veins, guilt took its place.

"Clint, I don't want to ride the trail anymore. I like

what I'm doing, who I am now. Can't you understand that?"

Silence, then he muttered, "If I say that I understand, can I keep the money?"

She nudged his ribs with her boot and enjoyed the way his eyes squinted shut. "No."

He opened his eyes and glared at her. "You won . . . this time. But you're a Garret, and the Garrets are outlaws, sis. We're outlaws."

"Not anymore. I'm a teacher." The words sounded good to her.

An hour later, disguised in her woolly beard and dirt-streaked face, she stopped a peddler on his way into town. Handing him the reins, she told him to take the packhorse to the sheriff. "And don't try to pull nothin' foolish, cuz my brothers will be watching you."

From the top of the ridge, she watched the jubilation as Hightown discovered the return of their money. One woman waltzed down the street with the banker. Janet's lips twisted wryly. She could have used that money, gotten some new clothes, fixed up her room . . . then again, she might have gotten herself sent to jail, and who needs clothes when they're behind bars?

The thought brought a shiver of fear. She'd been arrested only once, but the nightmares of that day had never disappeared. The tiny cell with no room to move, to dodge. He'd beaten her savagely, then discovered she wasn't a boy. She shivered against the feel of the brutal hands tearing her clothes, touching her— if Pa hadn't arrived . . . as it was, she hadn't been able to walk for a week.

She was a teacher, not an outlaw. She would be an

honest citizen from now on. The sense of relief, of a burden lifted made her feel light as a feather.

She rose and eased herself into the saddle, and the featherlike feeling disappeared. Every knock and blow she'd taken woke up and complained. "Got hard fists on him now, doesn't he, Brownie?" She fingered her lip and winced at the pain.

Pain from the cut and, she discovered, the pain of knowing Clint wouldn't be there for her anymore. Their fight had the feeling of something final. She sighed. Maybe someday he'd get over being angry and find her.

But even if he did, he'd still be an outlaw.

If her dreams came true and she managed to have a family—children—then what would happen if a brother with a price on his head came to find her?

But if he didn't, he'd die somewhere, robbing some bank, and she might never know.

She was torn; she couldn't lift the reins to get Brownie moving. She wanted to go back, kneel beside Clint and tell him she'd always be with him, be his family.

Heart aching, she pulled in a breath. She'd made a decision up there today, and Pa always said to move forward.

Maybe she could have dinner with Dagger and Thomas.

"Let's head home, horse."

"Got a letter for you, Marshal," Ernie Short shouted from inside the express office as Dagger passed the door.

Dagger halted and entered the building. "How's it going, Ernie?"

"Good, Marshal," the young man said. "This works out great, working in here during the winter and being a mule skinner in the summer."

He ducked under the counter, then emerged holding a letter. "From Stockton, looks like."

Dagger took the note. Maple Street School. Looks like he'd heard from Janet's old school. He shook the letter in annoyance. You'd think a school could respond in a timelier manner.

He saluted Ernie with the letter, stepped outside and leaned against a boardwalk post. The letter was short and to the point.

Maple Street School was a boys' school and they'd never heard of Miss Janet Danner.

"Huh." He stared down at the letter again, trying to make sense of the words. But the gist was plain.

She'd lied to him.

Crumpling the missive in his hand, he strode down Main Street, his jaw working as if to spit out the foul taste inside.

Lucas Wilson waved him down from the other side of the street, and Dagger crossed over to join him.

"Marshal, can I talk with you a minute?" Wilson took off his spectacles and polished them carefully. "We've been having a problem recently."

A problem. Hell, that's all he needed. But he tipped his head. "What sort of problem, Lucas?"

"Seems we've been missing money from the till. The count's not coming out right of an evening."

"Happened more than once?"

Lucas glanced toward the door and lowered his voice. "It's happened four times now—four times in the last week, and we've never come out wrong before."

"How much is missing?"

"That's just it, Marshal. I'm only coming up short by a few bits each time. Maybe a dollar once. Seems if a body was going to steal, they'd take more than that."

"Ahuh." When Lucas checked the door again, Dagger had the glimmering of a thought. "Mrs. Wilson know about this?"

"No."

Dagger crossed his arms and fixed Wilson with a stare. "Seems like that piddly amount would only be of interest to a child. A boy, maybe?"

The shopkeeper heaved a relieved sigh. "I didn't want to be the one to say it. Mrs. Wilson would take my head off for even thinking that Richard might take money that wasn't his."

"You think he's been doing that?"

"It's possible. The store's always teeming with the boys once school's out for the day. And Richard, Ben, Billy and your Thomas are usually around."

"Want me to talk to them?"

"I'd appreciate it, Dagger. I couldn't think of a way to haul Richard off without the missus finding out, and she'd never believe he'd do such a thing."

Dagger nodded understandingly. Mrs. Wilson was a formidable woman and ran her family, and her husband, with an iron fist. "I'll take care of it—maybe Miss Danner knows something about what's going on." He grinned. "If they give me any trouble, I'll haul them down to jail."

Lucas blanched, then gave him a sour grin. "And wouldn't there be hell to pay then. Try not to get me killed by the wife, all right?"

* * *

"You think the children are stealing?" Janet put her hand to her throat, feeling like it had dried up and closed on her.

School was out for the day, and Dagger had shown up to walk her home. She wouldn't have been nearly so pleased if she'd known this was the reason he wanted to talk to her.

"Lucas has been losing money from the till. And—" He frowned at her, then took her chin in his big hand. "What did you do to yourself? If I didn't know better, I'd say someone punched you."

His fingers were gentle on her split and puffy lip. She pulled back. "It's nothing. I tripped over the rag rug in my room and went face first into the table." Her heart aching with the lie, she blinked innocently at him. "It surely did hurt."

He touched his lips gently to hers as if to take the pain away. "I'll bet it did, honey."

She frowned at him. They were too close to Main Street for him to be making up to her like this. "Behave, Marshal. You were saying that Lucas has lost money?"

"So has Tucker at the general store, and Jenny at the diner. All their boys are in this together . . . and so, it appears, is Thomas."

"Our Thomas? I mean—"

Dagger gave her a grin. "Yup, *our* Thomas. And I'm wondering if he's finding a way to come up with money also. I keep my money tucked away somewhere safe and nothing's missing. However, you've been visiting fairly often."

She felt the color draining from her face. "You think he might have been stealing from me?" She reached down to jiggle her reticule and frowned. It did seem rather light. In the old days, she would have noticed that immediately.

After opening the string top, she spilled out the coins inside. "I'm short two dollars."

Dagger's mouth tightened. "Stealing, and from a woman to boot. I'll—"

"No."

"Janet, we need—"

The fear that had gripped her at the thought of a lawman arresting her Thomas loosened. This was Dagger. Still . . . "It's me he stole from, and it's me who will handle it."

That stubborn chin of his lifted, his silvery eyes narrowed, but then he nodded. "All right. You can have first crack, but if it continues, he'll be talking to me." The threat made a shiver run down her spine, but she had to agree to the fairness.

"It won't continue."

As the door slammed behind the boy, Janet sank down onto the front steps of Dagger's house and groaned. That hadn't gone well at all.

From his hollow beside the porch, Tanner rose to his feet, ambled over and laid his big, bony head in her lap in sympathy.

"How in the world do people raise children?" she asked him.

He looked at her with knowing brown eyes and wisely offered no reply.

"He can't keep on snitching money out of my reticule." She shook her head. Dagger wouldn't want a thief around—and come to think of it, neither would she. Leaning back against the porch rail, she played with Tanner's ears. It had hurt to have Thomas steal money from her; the sense of betrayal was worse than the loss of the money.

Her stomach still churned from his lies, lies he'd insisted upon even though she'd seen him take the money when she'd deliberately left the purse on the table. She'd figured on catching him in the act, not realizing how painful the sight would be.

What would she do now?

How did a person raise someone to be honest? Especially someone who wasn't honest herself.

Regret rose up in her. She'd give everything she had to be able to face Thomas with a guilt-free conscience, but she couldn't. Here she was, scolding him for taking two bits, and she'd robbed banks, stages, purses—anything she could lay her hands on.

But . . . she wanted him to be better than she was; shoot, she wanted to be better herself.

Realization dawned slowly and lightened her heart. She was already better. She'd changed a lot; she hadn't stolen anything in months, and would never do so again.

Giving a snort of laughter, she pressed a kiss to Tanner's head and heard the slap of his tail against the dirt in answer. "I've been straight since I started this job, for months, and I didn't even realize it. What do you think of that, Tanner?"

The tail wag increased.

"But what about all the lies I've built this life upon?" Sometimes she felt she was living out that strange story of someone who had a tiger by the tail. How did you let go and still live? Yet how could she continue like this? Dagger . . . Dagger had come to mean everything to her. And Thomas, too. What would they think if somehow they found out about her past? How could she dream of building a life with Dagger knowing it was based on a lie? Could she actually take vows with him, have his children, knowing she could be arrested, jailed, if the truth came out?

She tilted back her head and watched the clouds overhead in the darkening sky. The wind held a hint of rain, a touch of snow, and the blackness in the western sky had completely blotted out the setting sun. Even if she knew she'd never be found out . . . could she continue living this lie with Dagger, having to elaborate on each lie, continue to build on this entire false childhood, false family, false past jobs? She could barely keep all the stories straight now. How could she elaborate on them for the next twenty years? She just couldn't do it. She *wouldn't* do it.

Even now when she had to tell Dagger an untruth, her stomach churned. The lies that had come so easily at first now left her mouth twisted and her soul feeling soiled.

But how could she quit? What would happen if she tried to tell him the truth? She winced, envisioning his—

"Miz Janet?"

She turned so suddenly that she thumped her head against the porch post and dislodged Tanner. The dog rose and padded over to lick Thomas's hands. The boy's face was damp, his eyes swollen from the tears he'd shed, and her heart wrenched to see him so miserable.

"Oh, Thomas." She patted the step beside her. "Come sit and we'll talk."

He didn't move, his chin raised obstinately in spite of the slight wobble it gave. "I stole your money. Not only today, but two days ago, too."

"Oh . . ."

Dropping several coins in her lap, he stood, obviously prepared to run, to dodge a blow. Touching the money in her lap, she gave a heartfelt sigh. "Well, sweetheart—"

She couldn't think of what to say, what the proper response would be. After a moment he asked, a quiver in his voice, "Do you hate me now?"

The response came easily after that.

Later that night she paced the floor in her room. Back and forth. Across the street, she saw the glow of light from Dagger's window. He must be reading one of those mysteries he loved.

She looked again at the coins Thomas had returned to her. Arranged on the dresser, they made a tiny stack of wealth. She felt wealthy when she looked at them, these coins that represented Thomas's honesty.

And her forgiveness.

She hadn't found it at all hard to hug him and tell him she'd forgiven him. And that they'd start afresh.

He'd promised to be good, to be honest, and she believed he would.

Would Dagger believe her? Forgive her? Her crimes were so much bigger than stealing a few coins.

Chapter Eighteen

With the skill of years of practice, she silently eased up the window in her room and slipped out over the sill. Swinging down from the front tree, she landed on the damp ground outside the boardinghouse. She paused just long enough to scuff out her tracks, then stole across the street to Dagger's house.

Lantern light glowed through a window; he was still up. Moving to the unlocked back door, she let herself in, laughing at the enthusiastic greeting of the three dogs, who acted as if they hadn't seen her for months rather than since just that afternoon.

"Nicest burglar I've had in a long time." Dagger leaned against the doorjamb of the kitchen, a glass of spirits in his hand.

Concealing a wince at the term, she tilted her head. "Thank you. I thought it must be my turn to . . . um, take the first step. Uh, so to speak." She felt her cheeks heat and shrugged. "I invited myself over."

"Well, now, I won't argue about anything that

brings me so lovely a lady. Can I get you something to drink?"

She eyed the bottle of whiskey still sitting on the counter but shook her head. Better she stay clear-headed for this. The resolve weakened in her, but she firmed it right back up. She could do this. "I'll settle for a warm bed. It's downright chilly out there; the storm's almost here."

The slow smile that creased his cheek weakened her knees. Damn, it was unfair how handsome he looked, the way the black lashes darkened his gray eyes, the firm jut of his chin. He held out his hand and she couldn't have said no if he'd been leading her to the scaffold.

Sinking down on the bed, he gave her a slow smile. "Since you're feeling so needful of taking turns, I'll let you take a turn at undressing me."

She looked at him through her lashes, laying there so indolently on the bed, and her smile widened. "Well, I guess I could bestir myself a bit further to-night."

First maybe she'd see how well he would bestir himself. His trousers already looked a bit tight. The first few buttons of her bodice loosened easily; but then, under that silvery gaze, her fingers fumbled. Her skin felt sensitive, like his look was burning into her. Her top came loose, the corset undone, and her breasts spilled free under the silky chemise Olivia had made for her. The harsh intake of Dagger's breath was her reward.

He started to sit up and she shot him a chiding look and used her best schoolmarm's voice. "You'll get your turn, Master Blackthorne. You've not been instructed to move yet."

A wry look on his face answered her, but he lay back again, this time with an obvious strain on his trousers.

The skirts, petticoats, drawers dropped one by one. Clad in only her chemise, she moved toward the bed. Dagger's eyes seemed fixed on the bottom of the chemise, and she knew she was giving him wanton glimpses. Just for fun she stretched, pressing her bosom out against the chemise, then raising her arms up like a sleepy cat. She could feel the cloth inch up past her bottom, then lower again.

"Come here." His voice sounded rusty, harsh, and she could hear his breathing over the rapid pant of her own. Who would have thought that teasing a man would also excite her? But she wanted him so badly she was taut with the feeling.

"You can't touch me," she admonished, and stepped back when he reached for her.

"Dear God, you're killing me."

"Oh, I think you have a strong heart. Let me check." She drew closer, knelt on the side of the bed beside him and slid her hand between the buttons of his shirt. The crisp hair tantalized her fingers as she slid them across the hard planes of his chest. "You are so strong. . . ." she marveled, unaware of speaking aloud until he answered.

"And you're soft." His fingers touched her leg, caressed up past her knee, settled on top of her thigh, and she shivered.

Settling to her task, feeling almost . . . urgent about it, she managed to get the buttons of his shirt open. Oh, he had a magnificent chest, and she kissed her way across the broad expanse.

His hands found the end of her chemise and took all sorts of liberties. Her legs were trembling by the time she had his trousers undone, and he helped her at the end by pushing them off. Straddling him, she settled down, just above . . . but he'd reached his limit.

His fingers fastened on her hips and he pushed her down as he raised his hips up. So big, so hard, she cried out with overwhelming pleasure and buried her face in the crook of his neck.

He moved inside her so fast and hard, and his fingers were active on her so cleverly that—she convulsed on top of him. A moment later, his body tightened and he gave a cry, one she found more satisfying than any robbery she'd ever committed.

Dagger smiled to himself as his heart quieted. She snuggled against his side, her head on his shoulder, a soft bundle of warmth. Trapped a sunbeam, he had. Stroking her shoulder, he savored the feel of the velvety skin, so smooth over the firm muscles underneath. On a slow slide to her breast, his fingers encountered an area of puckered skin that had a different feel to it. "What's this?"

Her breath caught, and he felt the tightening of those lovely muscles against his body. "A scar."

"I know that. What happened?"

"Dagger." She raised herself up on one elbow, her blond hair falling tantalizingly down over a breast. She caught his hand before he could continue his explorations and frowned at him. "I need to talk to you."

"Can we talk later?" He could see the nipple peeking out at him, like a challenge.

"No. It has to be now, while I'm . . . we're talking now."

Hell. Women had the damnedest timing. How was

he supposed to listen when all the blood in his body was centered between his legs? Then he looked at her again. So worried, a frown between her brows, biting at that soft lower lip. Any other woman looking like that would be wringing her hands, but not his tough little schoolmarm.

With a sigh, he pulled back and tucked both hands safely beneath his head. "All right; what are we talking about?"

"M-my scar and . . . my past, and—" She swallowed.

"I know you weren't as experienced as you led the school board to believe," he stated, trying to gentle her down. It gave him a warm feeling to know that she wanted honesty between them, was going to come clean about the inexperience he'd figured out. She hadn't taught at a boy's school; perhaps he wouldn't tell he already knew that.

She gave a little snort, almost laughing. "Well . . . good. But there's more, and you're going to find it— well, can you just listen, Dagger?" The pleading in her voice startled him.

"Just remember that I'm really, really sorry about—" Her hand touched his shoulder and shied away.

The worry trickling down his spine shoved him up in bed to lean against the headboard. This sounded far more serious than what he'd figured. "Just spit it out, girl. Let's hear it." He gave her a wry marshal smile. "What'd you do, kill someone?"

Pain, vivid and undeniable, flashed through her eyes. "Almost," she whispered. "I crippled a man. Dagger, I'm the one who shot your brother . . . and you." Unerringly, she reached out and laid her fingers on his chest where the bullet of last spring had left its mark.

His mouth was dry. "I was shot by a Garret—a man."

"A woman. In a very bushy beard. Me."

"No." Head spinning, he grabbed her chin, turned her face to one side, then the other. She let him, like a flaccid doll in his hands. Those eyes—he knew he'd seen those eyes before. "Dammit! You're a Garret!"

A tear traced its way from under closed eyes and she nodded. "They're my family, they were—only my brother is—"

Horror turned his fingers icy cold, his brain to red rage. "Brother—don't talk to me of brothers. Mine can't walk right . . . because of you." The memory of Blade's face when he stumbled, when he had to pick up a cane, filled him, shoving aside all rational thought. He pushed her away from him, out of his bed.

She fell to her knees on the floor, her lips tightening against the pain that even in his anger he noticed.

He yanked on his trousers, feeling exposed before her wounded gaze. She opened her mouth.

"Don't." That wasn't his voice, so hoarse. "Don't say anything. Just . . . leave."

"Dag—" she started, and unable to bear more, he turned and left the room, walked down the stairs and out into the stormy night.

As the bedroom door swung closed behind Dagger, Janet dropped her hands to her knees, feeling as if all the stuffing had been knocked out of her. In shock, she saw her hands trembling like aspen leaves—she couldn't have held a gun if her life depended on it.

He wasn't supposed to be this way—he was supposed to forgive her, like she had forgiven Thomas. Slowly she pushed herself to her feet, her breath coming in little jerks. Sure, she knew it would be hard for him to accept her past, the fact that she'd shot him and his brother, but, hell, he'd shot her, too, and she wasn't holding that against him.

Dammit, he was a lawman; he was supposed to have a better character than she did, wasn't he? She jerked her gown on roughly, ignoring the petticoats. No buttonhook for her shoes; she left them undone.

Her chemise, her corset; where were they? She found them thrown down at the bottom of the bed she tried not to look at. As if pulled, her gaze rose to the pillows, the scattered covers, the place where she'd been made a woman, made love to a man. To Dagger.

And the tears came.

"Oh, Pa, why did you leave me?" she whispered, her knees giving out. She laid her head on Dagger's pillow. His scent clung to the fabric, and her body wrenched with the hard sobs of a woman unused to crying.

Her dreams of settling in Shasta, marrying Dagger, maybe even having children, all her hopes spilled onto the bed with her tears, disappearing as if they'd never been. And that was the bitterest portion of all, that her hopes had died so quickly, before they'd ever had a chance to be.

When her sobs had faded to small choking sounds, she lifted her head and peered around the room, eyes half-swollen shut. The candle he'd lit was half-burned. How long had she been sitting here weeping? Oh, God, she needed to get out of here before Dagger returned.

Tripping over her unfastened shoes, she snatched up her petticoats and pushed the door open. Clumsily moving down the stairs, she emerged onto the dark porch. A spatter of icy rain struck her in the face and took her breath away.

She set off across the muddy street, desperate to be back in her own room. A lone light burned in her window of the boardinghouse across the street, and she frowned. She hadn't left a candle burning; she'd never be so careless. Dagger? The rush of hope sped her footsteps and hurried her over the windowsill.

"Dagger?" she whispered as she stepped down into the room. She looked around eagerly. A shadowy form seated by the window over the street moved, stood, entered the light thrown by the candle in the corner.

"Clint!"

He grabbed her chin, pushed her face up to the candlelight, and his eyes narrowed. For a moment she didn't understand, then she knew why he was studying her, what he was seeing: puffy lips, beard-reddened skin, marks on her neck. Defiantly, she pushed her wet hair away from her face just in time to receive a stinging slap from his big hand.

"You whore! I know whose house that is—the marshal's." He shook her roughly and she let him. "Having a good time tonight, rolling in bed with the man who shot me? A bastard lawman?" He shook her again, then pushed her away from him.

"Listen, Clint, it's not—"

"No. I don't want to hear anything you have to say." He picked up his coat from the bed and shrugged it on. "I came here to say I was sorry for the fight, that we were family, but ... God, how could you do this to me?"

"I love him," she whispered, holding out her hands. Her little brother—surely she could make him understand.

"Ah-uh." He sneered at her, his face twisted into an unrecognizable mask of hate. "Well, let's hope he loves you too, Miss *Garret*, cuz he's all the family you got left now. You're none of mine."

As he slid out the window into the storm, despair dropped her to her knees and she buried her head in her hands. What had she done?

Chapter Nineteen

She dressed carefully the next morning, thankful it was Saturday and she wouldn't have to face a classroom of students. Her head ached, and her body felt drained of all energy. The night had yielded no answers, no hope.

Dagger hadn't appeared, Clint hadn't returned. Thomas was lost to her. Everyone she loved . . .

And she had yet to decide what to do, where to go, for leave she must. Dagger wouldn't let her continue to teach school now that he knew who she was. Or would he?

A glimmer of hope flickered, her pulse sped up. Could she perhaps persuade him to let her finish out the year? He had no proof that she'd been one of the Garret gang, other than her own confession. No one would recognize her, and they'd laugh at him if he tried to convince someone she'd been disguised as a man. Men didn't believe a woman could do anything, after all.

Her fingers quickened as she buttoned her shoes.

Patting her hair into a proper bun, she nodded at herself in the looking glass. No one would believe that she'd been anything but a fine, upstanding woman all her life, now would they?

She ran down the steps, hoping to catch Dagger before he commenced his morning round of the town. Turning the corner, she breathed in the cold, clean scent of the air. Glimmers of fragmented sunlight shone in the dark puddles and her lips trembled. The little glints seemed too much like her dreams, fallen and broken into a dark morass.

She turned the corner onto Main Street. Mrs. Chappell waved at her, Tucker touched his hat, Arnie called out that he had a new book he thought she'd like. Familiar greetings, bittersweet this morning.

A small part of her knew that her hope of continuing in town was futile, but it gave her an excuse to see Dagger again, to confront him and—

Shots rang out from down the street, and her heart jolted. Dagger! Where there was shooting, there would be the marshal. Lifting her skirts, she broke into a run.

The express office door hung at a broken angle, gaping open. On the boardwalk in front, Ernie Short sat, hands tied in front of him. And Clint stood behind him, two heavy bags thrown over his shoulder. As his pistol covered the crowd, he presented a formidable sight, and Janet had a momentary pang at seeing her little brother so grown up. So much a man.

So in danger. What the hell was he thinking, launching a robbery after first light? But she knew—his anger at her had made him careless, foolish. This was her fault, and fear tightened her hands into fists. "Go," she whispered. "Get moving, you fool."

Gun still at the ready, he swung one-handed up into the saddle, so damned slowly, then glanced around. His eyes met hers, and she saw the angry taunt in them. He opened his mouth, and her lips thinned, waiting for him to tell the town what and who she was, but he stopped, then touched his hat with mocking fingers. He wouldn't tell.

That much he'd—

A shot blasted behind her and blood spattered from Clint's arm. He shouted, slapped the horse on the rump and headed down the street at a gallop.

Janet spun. Behind her, Dagger stood, pistol aimed at Clint's back.

"No! He's my brother," she shouted, and barreled into him. The pistol fired, deafening her. Splinters from the boardwalk roof showered over them.

The marshal shoved her away, tried another shot at the now distant figure, and missed, thank God.

"Dammit, I almost had the bastard!" Dagger turned, his face reddened with fury.

"Congratulations, Miss Garret," he yelled. "Your brother is to hell and gone now, along with all the miner's money for their winter supplies. I'm sure they'll think of you when they're starving or dying of scurvy."

Her mouth opened, but she didn't know what to say, what to do. Clint needed time to get away. The shot had hit his arm, so he'd probably be all right, but not with this master tracker behind him. Stall. "Listen, Dagger—"

She saw a muscle twitch in his jaw as he stared at the road where Clint had disappeared. A long second passed before he turned his eyes to her and cold lawman's eyes raked over her. Undoubtedly he could see on her face the remnant of tears, the dark circles under her eyes, and his face softened for a second.

She raised her chin, unsettled at having him see her so vulnerable. She was no stray pup to be pitied.

At her action, his jaw tightened. He opened his mouth and she braced herself. Now he'd tell the town everything.

But he didn't.

Instead, he spit on the sidewalk as if he'd tasted something foul. Holding up a hand, he forestalled the words she was struggling to find. "Don't talk to me, don't come near me. Stay away from me."

Under all his anger, she could see a hint of hurt, of the damage she'd done with her lies, and her heart squeezed a little tighter. Janet took a step forward, but he turned away. In spite of his anger, he hadn't been able to bring himself to arrest her.

But he'd said enough and so had she, from the expressions of shock and wrath forming on the faces around her. The express office was in the center of town, and people had been in the nearby shops. Surprise still evident on her face, Maude, a shopping bag over her arm, looked at her, tightened her lips and stepped away, crossing the street to avoid her.

"Miss Danner . . . Garret . . . whatever your name is—"

Janet turned at the haughty woman's voice. "Mrs. Wilson, I—"

"Consider yourself fired. And stay away from our children." Pulling her skirts back as if afraid to be infested with vermin, Mrs. Wilson averted her face and stalked past.

Janet took a breath and then another. They always

said you imagine worse fates than would come to pass.

They were wrong.

That night, after a silent supper, Janet walked down the stairs of the boardinghouse. She needed to figure out what to do, but her brain seemed to have halted completely. A long walk in the cold night air might help.

"Miss Danner." Her boarding lady's strident voice stopped her halfway down the steps.

"Mrs. Malvern."

The stout woman's lips pursed, as if she'd eaten a rancid piece of meat. "I have received word that you are no longer employed as a schoolteacher. Of course, you understand that the room you inhabit is reserved for our instructor."

Oh, hell. She hadn't even stopped to consider that. "Of course I realized that."

"I believe a day should be sufficient to allow you to remove your belongings?"

Janet's hands closed into fists, the urge to loosen the woman's teeth overwhelming, but she fought it down. With an acknowledging inclination of her head, she moved past Mrs. Malvern and out onto the street. But the victory cost her. Her knees sagged as she reached the front gate and she clung to the post for a moment.

All right. First she needed to fetch her coat and reticule from Dagger—the marshal's house. Then get Brownie from the livery and load up what she could. She'd be traveling light again.

The thought of leaving all her new finery hit her with a pang of regret that seemed funny after a moment. Here was her life in complete chaos and she was missing a few ruffles.

She knocked on the marshal's door, hoping no one was home. But light footsteps pattered toward the door.

Thomas's brown eyes peered around the door. "Miz Janet!"

"Hello, Thomas. I . . . left my coat over here yesterday."

His face flushed and his eyes shifted sideways, but he opened the door wider.

She stepped inside and picked up her things from the sofa. "There; I'll just take these and be out of your—" Tilting her head, she weighed her reticule in her hand. Too light. She could judge the contents of a purse to within a couple of bits, and she'd had more coins last night than were here today. She frowned and looked at her pupil. "Thomas?"

His mouth twisted into a mulish expression. "What?"

"You stole money from my purse again. Give it back." She'd need every penny to get herself set up someplace else.

"No." He put his hands in his pockets and glared at her. "I don't have to give anything to a dirty, rotten *thief*. You probably stole that money from somebody else anyway."

A clean blow to the heart, his words sliced deep and true. "Oh, Thomas—"

He gave her a look full of hatred and loathing and heartrending pain before running into the kitchen and out the back door.

Her hand fell back to her side, useless as any words she might offer. Her head bowed—something no amount of blows or whippings had ever accomplished. Turning, she left the lawman's house, closing the door quietly behind her.

Out at Bowie's ranch, Dagger pulled up his horse and dismounted. His shoulders tightened as he looked around at the wet pasture. Under a cold, gray sky, sheep huddled in miserable patches. Susanna's beloved garden was barren, with only stubble left.

On the wide front porch, Blade sat in a rocker watching. He lifted a mug in welcome. Dagger nodded back and suppressed a pang of loss. Would Blade even be talking with him when this was over? Would he lose family as well as a woman? He shivered and pulled his coat closer. Seemed like the world had turned colder in the last few days.

Firming his lips, Dagger stepped up onto the porch. He owed Blade the truth, and damned if he'd sidestep it.

" 'Bout time you got out here; I was beginning to think you were avoiding me since the dance."

"You could have come in to see me rather than sit on your butt out here."

"I had some pondering to do first." Blade took a sip of steaming coffee. "Want some?"

"No. I need to talk with you."

"Don't you look serious now, even for you. I mean, you being the serious Blackthorne and all that. How's that pretty schoolteacher of yours—"

"Stop!"

Blade halted, and his wry smile slowly faded to a frown. "Who died?"

Dagger dropped into a chair and leaned forward.

"No deaths—not yet anyway. I . . . got a lead on the Garret gang."

"Well, what are you doing sitting here and jawing, get after them." Blade made a flicking motion with his hand, but his eyes stayed steady on Dagger's face.

Dagger rubbed his brow, futilely wishing the ache in his head would ease up. "It's not that simple. The gang—you remember they're down to just two members now?"

"Uh-huh. The old man's dead, so that leaves the two sons."

Dagger wanted to gag every time he thought of what he'd been doing with Janet. "Not sons; not both of them."

"Dagger, just spit it out and stop all the fancy prancing. What're you trying to say?"

"One of those sons was a woman, and that woman is the schoolteacher." The words felt like they'd been ripped out of him. He'd been associating—hell, he'd been warming the sheets with a Garret.

The silence stretched further than a person could tolerate. When Blade turned his face away, looking to the western mountains where the shadows stretched dark and cold, Dagger felt like a low-down coyote.

"Blade, I'm sorry. I was—I did—"

"You bedded her, didn't you?"

Dagger nodded.

"Ah. I could tell you were inclined that way." Blade's gaze dropped to his bum leg, and all Dagger could do was sit and wait for the words that would destroy their family forever.

After a moment, Blade stirred, shook his head and then took a slow breath. The deep lines that pain had wrought lightened as a smile quirked his lips. "Some lawman, aren't you? Hunting all over the county for them and one was in your bed the whole time."

When Dagger winced, Blade gave a bitter laugh, then a more natural one. Choked out a snicker. A minute later, he was leaning back in his chair, pointing a shaking finger and roaring with laughter.

"It's not funny." Dagger pushed himself to his feet and stomped to the other side of the porch, trying to ignore the full-bodied laughter behind him. Bastard brother'd always had a sense of humor like a bent horseshoe.

After a while the noise died down except for an occasional snort.

"Dagger, come on over here."

With a sigh, Dagger turned and walked back, still waiting for his brother's anger to take hold. Didn't Blade realize how Dagger had betrayed him? He slumped into the chair.

"You're feeling guilty because you were taken in?" Blade asked, his eyes level.

"I got you shot and then I didn't even see what was plain in front of my face. I could have clapped her in irons—" But his throat closed over the thought.

"Bullshit." Blade set the coffee down on the table beside his chair. "I got something to confess, too."

"Yeah?"

"Your pretty schoolmarm? I recognized her at the dance. She was the bearded one."

Dagger straightened.

"Yeah. She was staring at me over your shoulder— her face hidden except those big eyes filled with tears. Just like she'd looked with her face covered with that beard and hi—her eyes all shiny from watching old Garrett die."

263

"Why didn't you tell me?"

"Well, now." Blade scratched his jaw. "I thought about whipping out my knife and gutting her right there, but—hellfire, Dagger, she's a woman!

"Then I figured I'd let you arrest her, only those big eyes kept popping up in front of my face. You know, she was crying when she looked at me, there, at the dance. Just like she did for her pa."

"You're too softhearted." Blade had always been the peacemaker, always arguing for mercy rather than vengeance. Damned if there'd be any mercy this time.

"Maybe. Seems like she was just doing what anybody would if they were cornered."

"She's probably been laughing at us all this time. She shot you, dammit."

"As I recall, you shot her back."

Dagger tried not to cringe at the thought, tried to tell himself that she'd only got what she deserved, but the memory of the blood on her shoulder—the way it had hung limp—sickened him every time he thought of it.

"So, are you sure she thinks this is a joke? How'd you find out about her anyway?"

"She told me."

"No fooling? Did she laugh? Gloat?" Blade asked with all the callousness of a brother.

Dagger could see her face, so white in the candlelight, the first time he'd ever seen her falter. Gloat? He suddenly realized she'd been crying when he left.

When he swallowed, the spit stuck like a rock in his throat. "No," he said hoarsely, "she wasn't laughing."

Blade tipped his head back, staring at a vulture black against the sky. "You know, Bowie was up in Hightown yesterday delivering a bunch of yearlings. Said their bank had been robbed by the Garrets."

Dagger was out of the chair in a flash. "I knew they were—"

"They gave the money back."

"What?" He sat a lot more slowly than he'd risen. "Gave it back?"

"Yup. The one with the big beard gave the pack-horse to a tinker, told him to take the animal to the sheriff. The tinker said the man was pretty beat up— split lip, bruised cheek. Maybe there's a division in the gang."

Dagger stood and frowned down at Blade. He remembered that day at the school when she'd had a puffy lip. Fell into a table, had she—more likely her brother's fist. If he'd had a gun, he'd have shot the bastard again.

"And she gave the money back," Dagger said in bemusement.

Blade tried to cover his smirk with one hand. "Uh-huh. Now what do you plan to do?"

She stuffed the last bit of finery into her saddlebag, her fingers lingering on the soft-as-kitten's-fur lace that edged the neckline. That had been an altogether satisfactory bargain she'd made with Olivia Harris; maybe even lopsided on her part, since she'd had the satisfaction of hearing Olivia read. How proud she'd been! They'd both cried when she finished her first book.

With a sigh, Janet fastened the straps on the saddle-bag and glanced around the room. The basket of pretty rocks the children had given her still rested in one corner, the painting of Tanner that Thomas had drawn hung on one wall, the massive rock veined with gold ore weighted down one end of her table and the small hooked rug Jenny Perkins had made for her lay beside the bed. She was leaving parts of her life behind, little bits of herself.

Giving a shake of her head, she scolded herself. Time to get moving before Dagger returned and decided to haul her in. Of course, he'd have a hard time proving anything unless she confessed again, and it'd be a cold day in hell before she did that.

She leaned her head against the window frame and watched the quiet activity in the street below. Mrs. Malvern, all starch and proper, marching back from her shopping trip. Tanner, raising a howl in Dagger's yard. Flossie playing jacks down in the yard with Sally Perkins. Phoebe Patterson stood beside a peddler examining peacock feathers, undoubtedly for her hat shop. A surge of loss swung through her again. She'd planned to buy a new hat soon; now she wouldn't. She'd be gone.

And, oh, she was going to miss this town.

But even if she'd never told Dagger about her past, she wasn't sure if she could have continued. The sense of relief at being found out had been shocking in a way. The increasing guilt at lying to her new friends, of acting differently than she really was—she doubted she could have held up much longer.

And now . . . now she'd move on. But if she didn't go back to being a robber, what could she do? Sure, she could teach school, but her past would trail her, much the way a Pinkerton agent would follow a train robber, never giving up.

Her breath came ragged for a moment at so dismal a future.

On the street below, Priscilla Malvern stopped to

greet a rider on the street, pointed to the boarding-house. He glanced at the house, and Janet stepped back at the sight of the badge on his shoulder. A sheriff.

Priscilla waved her hands toward the house, and Janet could guess at the conversation. *Sheriff, we have a criminal in the house, a woman who's a member of the Garret gang.*

The sheriff said something with a sneer. *What kind of fool thinks a woman would be in the most notorious outlaw band?* Priscilla's back stiffened, as if someone had tightened her corset strings with a crowbar.

Snickering, Janet sat back down on the bed, then sobered abruptly. What if the sheriff had believed Priscilla? What if she'd been arrested, led away in cuffs? Her breath came hard at the thought, but on the tail of it came a glimpse of something else. She'd serve time, yes, but at the end of that time she'd be a free woman. Not checking over her shoulder, not worried about someone finding out about her past. Free to marry—she thrust the thought of Dagger away—marry someone, to have children.

But she'd have to turn herself in, confess and be locked away. She wrapped her arms around herself as she shivered. She glanced at the window; it was closed.

The cold was from pure terror.

Chapter Twenty

The sheriff had dead eyes, like a lizard. Unblinking and hateful. She stared at his face, unwilling to look down as he snapped the cuffs around her wrists.

He hadn't needed to do that, she thought. Wasn't as if a person who'd come up and turned herself in was gonna run away again. But she figured he just liked the feeling of having someone at his mercy. He had that kind of eyes.

The handcuffs stung like ice around her wrists. Heavy.

"All right, missy, let's put you where you belong." He shoved her, and she stumbled enough that he had to catch her. His hand on her arm clamped brutally tight, and when he rubbed the back of his fingers against her breast, she closed her eyes. She'd been here before.

But she'd been younger then; she was a woman now, and she had chosen this. She lifted her hand-cuffed hands to get moving room and rammed her elbow into his gut.

As he swore, she stepped away from him, waited out the snickers from the people gathered on the boardwalk.

"Listen, you little bitch—"

She lifted her eyebrows and gave him her best prissy teacher look. "No gentleman would manhandle a woman, whether she's a criminal or not."

"Dammit, you—" He stopped at the realization that he had an audience.

"That's right."

"She doesn't deserve that."

"We won't have women abused."

"Beat her up good."

The majority of the onlookers appeared to agree with her and Janet took a small breath. For now, for the moment only, she was safe. What happened in the jailhouse, or wherever she was imprisoned—well, she'd worry about that when it happened.

She took a few steps toward the jailhouse, then stopped and looked back. Head held high, she pursed her lips and gave the sheriff a reproving look. "Well, are you coming or not?"

The crowd laughed.

The milling of raucous people in front of the Miner's Saloon drew Dagger's attention as he rode into town. He tied up his horse and crossed the street to see what was up. Probably a drunk Sprague had pitched out into the mud.

What he saw stopped him dead in the center of Main Street.

Janet, chin held high, back straight as Mrs. Wilson's, strode down the street followed by a sheriff— damned if it wasn't that bastard Victor Cluny. He'd been a bounty hunter before some idiot in Sacramento

appointed him sheriff. He'd been known for his bru-
tality as a bounty hunter, and his reputation as sheriff
hadn't changed. Most of his prisoners were brought
in bleeding or dead.

Dagger narrowed his eyes and stepped forward,
then stopped. She'd chosen that life, as an outlaw. She
deserved what she—

"Damned bitch," a voice said beside him. Grover
Walsh. Hands in his pockets, he rocked back and
forth. His face flushed red as he licked his lips. "She'll
get what's coming to her if I know Cluny. Wish he'd
give me a piece. 'Course, being an outlaw, she'll probably enjoy the hell out—"

Fury was a red emotion. Dagger'd never realized it
before, but the color was darker than the blood that
gushed out of Walsh's busted snout. He split his
knuckles and savored the pain as he followed the right
hook with a left cross that sent the bastard backward
with a broken cheekbone. Walsh landed with a satisfying thud on the ground.

Cursing foully, Grover raised himself up on one elbow. "What the hell—"

"Don't talk about Miss Danner like that."

"You bastard, she's a damned Garret and she stole
all our money."

"She wasn't involved," Dagger said, realizing down
to his gut it was true. "All she did was keep me from
gunning down her brother, and it'd be a piss-poor sister that didn't do that."

Dagger looked down at his bleeding left hand. He'd
gotten soft.

Barely resisting the urge to plant a boot in Walsh's
ribs, he turned and headed for the jail.

Slamming open the door of the building, he stepped inside.

"Cluny." The sight of the sheriff solidly planted behind Dagger's desk set his teeth on edge. "Heard you got yourself a prisoner."

Cluny set down a quill pen and sneered. "Seems you had yourself a Garret right under your nose all this time. If she'd a been a snake, she'd have bit you."

"Who turned her in?" Dagger asked mildly. He'd string the Judas up like a—

"She did."

"She what?" Dagger took two steps forward. "You're lyin', you bastard."

"Nope. She came right up to me and told me who she was. Truth be told, I didn't believe her at first, but she knew facts that only a Garret would know. Still doesn't seem right, a Garret being a woman."

Dagger leaned against the door frame, his jaw tight. Why the hell would she turn herself in? What had possessed the woman? Didn't she know how they'd treat—of course she did, he told himself. She wasn't stupid.

"Mind if I speak with your prisoner?"

"Be my guest." Cluny scratched his chest. "Just remember she's *my* sweetmeat. Hands off."

The idea of Cluny touching her had Dagger reaching for his knife. But gutting Cluny wouldn't solve anything. He forced his hand back down and nodded at the man. "Appreciate it."

He moved past the desk to the door that led to the three cells. Janet was in the far cell that overlooked the alley off Main Street. He shook his head when he realized he'd been considering breaking her out, pulling out the window bars in an extravagant escape. What the hell was he thinking of?

But any thoughts he might have been entertaining were forgotten when he saw the pretty schoolmarm sitting on the edge of the cell's single cot. "You . . . you turned yourself in."

When she tried to smile at him, he saw the terror in her eyes, the carefully controlled way she clasped her hands at her waist, her knuckles white. "It seemed like the right thing to do."

"You . . . could have talked with me first." He'd have persuaded her out of this foolish idea in a heartbeat.

"You weren't speaking to me, remember?"

"Well." He moved up to the bars. "I'm sorry for that. Why did you surrender? No one could prove you were a Garret without your confession. Being the sister of an outlaw isn't a crime."

She tore her gaze away from his strong face, wishing futilely that he'd been away for all this. How could she answer his question, she who'd never been burdened with the truth in her life? How could she explain the need to be free of all the lies, the need to start again?

"I . . . I want to be a respectable person, an honest member of society."

"You were already that."

"No, I wasn't. I was living a lie. How could I teach Thomas about honesty when I wasn't telling him the truth? Or you?"

His eyes darkened and he took a step back. She knew her feelings for him must be sitting right there on her face like a trail marked in mud, one even a blind man could follow. As his jaw tightened, his face became unreadable.

272

He didn't want her love—or her. She looked down at her hands, down at her gown already marked by the filth in the cell. A jailbird; that's what she was now.

She was going to cry; she could feel the stinging in her eyes, the hitch in her breathing. Da-darned if she'd cry in front of him.

"It's time for you to be going." She motioned with her chin toward the door.

"Listen, Janet—"

"So long, Marshal. Been a pleasure knowing you." She turned her back on him, listened as he took a step forward, hesitated. Then the soft pad of his footsteps retreated. The door creaked as it closed with finality behind him.

Dagger paced back and forth in his living room. His audience of two dogs and three cats sat along the sofa and floor.

"She doesn't understand what she's in for," he explained to Tanner, the most understanding of the group. "She won't survive the state prison; I've been there. Prisoners die."

The thought of Janet hurt, dying, alone in the prison, stole the breath from his lungs. "Why didn't she wait? I wouldn't have stayed angry forever."

But wouldn't he? Blade'd teased him that he could stay mad like no other, till the sun went cold. Would he have even thought about forgiving her?

He groaned and dropped onto the sofa beside Casey and the black cat. Blackie kneaded his thigh while Casey snuggled closer and licked his hand. His useless hand that couldn't keep the woman he lo—what had he just thought? He loved her? A robber? An outlaw queen?

But she wasn't that, just a girl whose father had pulled her onto the wrong trail. Shoot, she had more honor than most people he knew.

Look at the way she'd taken over the teaching job— with firmness and kindness, putting in extra time. And confronting the parents to get the best for their children.

She did care for them; that wasn't something the children could be fooled about.

Pulling Casey into his lonely arms, Dagger rested his chin on the small head and suffered a lick to his neck. "So what are we going to do about this mess?" he asked the crew. "Just let her go to prison and rot?"

Tanner shook his head and sent Dagger the type of mournful look only a hound dog can generate. Blackie kneaded harder, using claws now.

"Ouch, all right. I get the point." He stroked the cat. "I take it we've got to get her out of this mess then."

Tanner gave a hearty woof and Casey trembled with excitement against him.

"Easy for you to say," Dagger commented. "I can't break her out of jail. That wouldn't do us any good." He paused for a moment to savor the satisfaction he'd get from stealing Cluny's prisoner out from under his nose.

"So, it's gotta be legal." He scratched Casey under the jaw. "She gave the money back to Hightown, you know. They're pretty happy with her right now. I wonder if I can't use that to my advantage somehow."

Two days later, high up in the mountains, the air was cold and thin. Firelight glimmered through breaks in the pine forest, a beacon pulling Dagger toward it. He studied the boot track in front of him, a notch marring the left heel. The pretty barmaid had been right about where Clint Garret was holed up.

Ducking a low-hanging branch, Dagger worked his way silently down the stream bank toward the outlaw's camp. Garret had chosen well, with the rocky outcropping behind him and the bank in front. 'Twould be difficult to approach without being seen.

Difficult, but not impossible—not for someone raised by the Indians and trained to stalk. Before approaching, he'd exchanged his riding boots for soft leather moccasins, removed any metal that might clank. The one mistake Garret had made was camping so close to a stream. Although the water provided a good place to spot someone, it also concealed any small noises.

Almost there.

Garret sat staring into the fire—another mistake—and morosely sipping from a tin cup. His horse, tethered under a nearby oak, patiently cropped at a patch of thin grass. A screech owl hooted once and was answered by another across the creek. Some small animal in the brush rustled away.

Dagger drew his pistol and gave a mirthless smile. All this time hunting for Garrets in the past, and now that he'd given up revenge, they were dropping into his clutches like flies in a room full of spiders.

Dagger stepped out into the small clearing, into the light of the fire. "Evening, Garret."

"Shit!" Garret lunged on his belly for the rifle that leaned against a tree.

Idiot. Dagger smoothly planted a bullet in front of the man's fingers, sending dirt and pine needles splattering over the outlaw.

Garret went still, breathing hard. After a minute he rolled up onto his elbow, raising the other hand. "You got me, damn your eyes."

"Good, glad you realize that."

Garret sat up, his eyes steady, and Dagger's heart jumped at the resemblance to Janet. The same icy blue eyes and blond hair. He was finding it hard to hate this . . . this boy. "How old are you, anyway?"

Garret looked as if he'd been slapped. "Old enough."

Dagger raised an eyebrow, subtly tilted his pistol.

"Seventeen," the kid said sullenly.

Dagger frowned. He and Blade'd been jumped by a young woman and her kid brother, a kid barely old enough to shave. This just kept getting better and better.

Keeping a keen eye on his opponent, Dagger shoved a stump closer to the fire and took a seat. He studied the boy-man, taking in the worried eyes, the lack of lines or scars. He'd been that young once.

Dagger nodded at the rabbit skewered over the fire. The aroma of the roasting meat made his stomach growl. "You mind?"

Garret huffed out a laugh. "Go ahead, Marshal. Can't stop you, can I?"

"Nope." Dagger gingerly wrenched off a leg and set it beside him to cool. "What's your name, anyway."

"Garret. Clint Garret."

"So, Clint Garret, when's the last time you saw your sister?"

"You should know." Garret leaned forward, glaring, and with one hand swept ashes from the fire into Dagger's face.

"Dammit!" Blinded, Dagger swiped at his eyes, saw

a shape in front of him, but he couldn't pull the trigger. Couldn't kill Janet's kin.

Garret slammed into him, knocking him backward off the stump and landing on top. "You bastard, you think you could get away with humping my sister like she was some slut? I'll kill you."

Eyes streaming tears, Dagger blocked one fist, but the other got through, sending stars flashing through his brain. Bringing up his legs, he hooked his boots around the kid's head and sent him flying onto his shoulder. He shouted in pain, and Dagger remembered with a touch of pleasure that he'd planted a bullet in that arm during the kid's fiasco of a robbery.

Dagger rolled over and dove into Garret, flattening him onto his stomach with a satisfying crunch.

The kid grunted as Dagger dropped onto his back. "My turn, kid."

Garret tried to buck, but Dagger smacked him on the head. "We're still talking."

"Get the hell off me."

"Nope. I asked when was the last time you saw your sister."

Silence. Then a muttered, "When she kept you from plugging me with lead."

"Ah. Did you know she's in jail?"

The kid rolled so fast and hard, like an unbroken horse, that Dagger went sprawling. He regained his feet before the kid, barely, but fast enough to plant a solid kick to the boy's gut.

Air escaped Garret's lips, sounding like a newfangled train whistle. The young man sank to his knees, bent over his stomach.

It took some time to get that air back, Dagger knew

from experience. Always figured you'd never breathe again. He waited patiently.

After a minute the words came in a half-whisper. "You low-down bastard, you arrested her!"

Relief surged through Dagger's veins. The kid hadn't known she was in jail, obviously cared for her. His mission wasn't hopeless after all. "Actually, I didn't; wasn't going to, either. There wasn't any proof she'd been riding with the gang. Go sit down, would you, so I can eat."

Glaring, Clint pushed himself to his feet and took his seat on the log across the fire. "If you didn't arrest her, then why's she in jail?"

"Would you believe she turned herself in?"

"No." Clint's reaction was fast and certain. "She'd never do that."

"She did. Confessed to Sheriff Cluny. I must admit, that came as a shock to me, too."

"Why, cuz you didn't manage to arrest her first?"

Dagger's jaw tightened. "I could have arrested her. I didn't."

"Why not? She's just another whore to you, right?"

"Call her that again and I'll give you the whipping you deserve."

The kid scowled, then his eyes narrowed. "You got feelings for her, don't you?"

"That's right . . . and now she's in jail."

Garret shook his head, picked up his spilled cup and poured more from the coffee pot sitting on the coals. "Doesn't make sense to me. She . . . she has nightmares about being arrested. Scares her silly."

Dagger remembered the way she'd woken one night, trembling, covered with cold sweat, and refused to discuss it. Scared, hell, she'd been terrified. "But—"

"She was arrested once. Damn banker came in early to work and shot at us when we were riding out. Nailed her horse and it pinned her under it."

"I can see how that might—"

"No, it was the marshal who arrested her. He figured out she was a girl, had his hands all over her when we broke into the jail."

Dagger frowned. He thought the Garret gang had never killed anyone.

"Pa kept me and Dan from killing him." Clint scowled. "I still think he was wrong." He took a sip of coffee. "Instead Pa yanked out his knife and cut off the marshal's trigger finger. Pa told him if we ever saw him again, he'd finish the job, one piece at a time, finish up with his dick."

"Sounds pretty effective."

"The bastard headed East on the next stage."

"And Janet has nightmares."

They sat in silence, staring at the fire. Dagger didn't know what Clint was seeing in the flames, but he knew what he saw. A young girl, bright-eyed and eager, following an outlaw pa into a life she couldn't escape. A life where men could jeer at her, put their hands on her. His jaw gritted tight.

"Why'd she turn herself in?" Garret asked softly. "Something to do with you?"

After a moment Dagger put the pistol down beside him. "Probably. I think she wants more from life than to follow the outlaw trail."

"Yeah, that's what she said. But to turn herself in . . . she'll serve time."

"Well, I have an idea. . . ."

* * *

Janet paced the small cell, back and forth, three strides one way, three strides back. The tiny barred window let a thin stream of light into the cell, enough to avoid banging into the chamber pot or tripping over the cot. Damn this was boring.

When she'd walked two hundred times across the cell, she gave up and leaned against the cold brick wall to stare out the window.

The window looked out over the alley and provided a view of wagons being loaded and unloaded behind the grocery. Tidbits of conversation floated up to her window: prices of eggs and salt pork, the last of the produce from Susanna Blackthorne, how many miners were left up in the hills for the winter and, occasionally, gossip about the infamous lady outlaw housed in the jail.

Janet wasn't sure whether to be complimented or insulted by the rumors about her. Depending on the person, she was either a misguided angel or a demon in disguise.

"Haven't seen the marshal for a few days," Leroy Kimball remarked, and Janet pressed closer to the window. Is that why she hadn't seen him, hadn't heard his voice in the jail? She'd felt so empty when he walked out.

"Said he'd be gone for a bit, had some business up in the hills."

"Wonder what he's up to. Seemed like he was getting pretty close to the Garret wench."

A pause. "I thought they looked good together. He smiled more when she was with him. Hard to believe she's a thief."

The other man spat out a thin brown stream. "Women, they can be damned sneaky."

"Ain't that the truth."

As the men moved away, Janet slid down to sit on the hard, hay-stuffed mattress, watched a cockroach scurry away and shuddered. Bugs were so different in jails than out in the woods. Bedbugs, lice, fleas, cockroaches. A longing for the clean air of the forest overwhelmed her.

How could she survive years of this, locked away from the sun, from people? She tightened her lips to keep from breaking down and bawling like an infant. Some infamous outlaw she was.

"What the hell have you up and done?" came an annoyed question from under the window. Susanna's voice.

Shock stunned her silent. Blinking rapidly, Janet stood and looked out. Susanna and Hannah stared up at her from the alley. "Uh . . . hello."

Susanna snorted and glanced at Hannah. " 'Hello,' she says, like she's greeting us in her parlor. The girl's addlepated." She pointed a finger at Janet. "We're coming in . . . just you stay right there."

Janet rolled her eyes. As if she could leave. Her lips twitched up into a smile.

God, it was good to see her friends.

After the sounds of a brisk bout of arguing, the door to the office slammed open and Susanna and Hannah marched in. Their color was high, their eyes flashing, and the stale air in the cell fled before them.

"Look at this filthy place," Susanna exclaimed. "Dagger should be ashamed."

Hannah rattled the cell door and yelled out into the jail office. "Get in here and open this door. I'm not going to stand out here and talk. My feet are aching."

Dagger's deputy, Horace Gates, slunk into the

room. "The sheriff would have my—" He flinched away from the women's glares.

"All right, all right." He grabbed the massive key ring off his belt and opened the cell door, then locked it behind them. "Just you shout when you're ready to leave."

He glanced back at them from the door. "And uh, thanks for the pie, Mrs. Blackthorne."

The smell of lavender and rosewater filled the small cell as Susanna and Hannah settled beside her on the bed. Janet raised her eyebrows. "Bribery, Mrs. Blackthorne?"

Susanna chuckled. " 'Twas Hannah's idea . . . and it worked like a charm."

"How are you doing?" Hannah asked.

Janet shook her head. "I've been better." Her eyes filled at their sympathetic murmurs and she blinked the tears back. "I knew this would be hard. I'm ready for it."

"Bullshit." Hannah jerked her head at Janet's shocked look. "Well, it is. Whatever possessed you to turn yourself in?"

"I wanted to start fresh, clean. I'm tired of living a lie." A small flame of anger lit inside her. "What are you two doing in here visiting now you know I'm a criminal?"

"We're friends," Hannah said simply.

"And it's not as if I didn't figure you had something in your past to hide," Susanna added. She flicked a bedbug away from her skirt. "Finding out you were a Garret—well, that came as a bit of a shock."

Janet stared down at her hands, her stomach whirling from more than the unpalatable glop she'd had for lunch. "How did Blade . . . did Blade say anything?"

Hannah gulped back a laugh. "Has anyone ever seen that man *not* saying anything?"

"He said Dagger had talked it over with him and that he wasn't inclined to hold a grudge."

"That's impossible." Janet gasped.

"Blade saw that Dagger has feelings for you." Susanna gave a soft smile. "Dagger's been alone, lonely, too long, but he's different since he met you. Blade figured hurting you might cripple Dagger, and that would hurt Blade much worse than a bum leg."

Hannah sighed. "Blade is so brave."

Susanna snickered. "Rude, too. He said something to the effect that if you corner a couple of wildcats you might expect a few scratches."

"Well!" Janet had to shake her head.

"He also pointed out—typical man—that they'd given you and your brother some scars, too."

Hannah's mouth dropped open. "Is that true? They shot you? A woman?"

"They didn't know I was a woman at the time," Janet pointed out dryly. "And yes, Dagger put a bullet into my shoulder."

"Damn. Can I see?" Hannah leaned forward.

Janet gave a cautious glance at the door, then unbuttoned her dress far enough to bare her shoulder. The puckered skin surrounding the dead white scar tissue still looked horrible to her eyes.

"Oooweee," Hannah breathed. "Bet that hurt."

Susanna shook her head, then shoved Hannah hard enough to have her flopping to the floor. "You're more curious than a cat at a gopher hole. Keep that up and you'll be more of a busybody than Mrs. Wilson."

Hannah picked herself up, disgustedly brushing the

283

filth off her skirt. "No need to be insulting. I just wanted to know."

She plopped back onto the bed, making the ancient cot creak in agony. "I still want to know why you turned yourself in. Seems like a bullet should have been enough punishment if you felt you needed some."

Janet shook her head. How could she explain to young Hannah all the tormented arguments she'd had with herself? "Just being punished wasn't enough . . . not if I didn't . . . if I was still hiding my past. I needed everything to come out in the open."

Hannah pursed her lips. "I think that's dumb. But if that's what you need to do—well, I can't stop you."

Susanna sent Janet a sympathetic look over Hannah's head that warmed Janet's heart.

"I worked very hard hiding a secret from Bowie," Susanna said softly. "Worrying, covering up . . . when I finally told him, the relief was so sweet that I cried. Not being able to be honest is more of a burden than people realize."

Janet tightened her lips against the tears that kept wanting to flow, but she felt them gleaming in her eyes as she nodded. How had she gone all her life without friends? How could she go on now?

"Well, all right," Hannah said, her practical nature taking over. "What happens now?"

"I'll be taken to Sacramento for a trial, then jail for a while, then a new life." Janet endeavored a smile. "Maybe the jail sentence will be over before I'm old and gray."

"No trial here?" Hannah asked.

Janet shook her head. "Cluny said we're going out of the area."

"So we won't even see your trial?"

Susanna nibbled on a fingernail. "And what about Dagger?"

The name was like a blow to her gut, chasing her wind away. Needing more space, Janet walked over to the cell door, fingered the lock. "That's over."

"You don't think he'll forgive you?" Hannah asked.

"I know he won't." She turned and leaned against the cold, hard bars. "He stopped in before he left town."

Scowling, Susanna jumped to her feet. "Why, that—"

"No, it's all right. I'm not doing this for him." Not entirely. "I'm doing it for me. So I can move on." And if Dagger knew she'd paid, maybe he could move on also. Not with her, but at least he wouldn't be tied to finding justice for his brother.

"Still, I'll talk with—"

"No." Janet held up a hand that shook only slightly. "I don't want you getting involved in this. Not this time. Dagger has a right to his anger. Just leave him be, Susanna."

Susanna gave her a level look, then sat back onto the bed, only slightly huffy. "Well, we brought you some food. Are you going to reject that, too?"

"Not a chance." Her heart lighter for the company of her friends, Janet dropped onto the bed and pulled the basket toward her. "Did you bring a pie for me, too?"

Later that day Janet heard the door to the cells rattle. She jumped up and hastily shoved the stinking chamber pot back into the corner. People should have to

285

knock before entering the cell area, she fumed. Thank goodness she'd finished.

After smoothing her skirt, she positioned herself on the bed and folded her hands in her lap. The door slammed open. Oh, spit, it was that Cluny bastard, back from wherever he'd been for two days.

Nattily attired in a dark gray suit with a purple waistcoat, he leaned against the wall across from her cell door. "So, Garret. Have you enjoyed the accommodations?"

Janet brushed a speck of lint from her bedraggled gown. "The amenities are a bit disappointing, but it serves."

"Does it? And you—do you serve as well?"

Was he implying what she thought? Her face burned hot, then cold. Surely he wouldn't—this was Dagger's jail. She'd felt almost safe here. "I'm certain I don't know what you mean."

"Oh, I think you do." His thick lips pulled into a leering grin. "I've been looking forward to *seeing* you for far too long." A step put him at her cell door and he opened it with the massive key.

She looked up from the bed—God, he was big—and stood to put them on more even ground. Her hands clenched into fists at her sides. She wasn't as young as she'd been last time. "I may have been a thief, but I'm not a whore, Sheriff. Keep your distance."

He didn't. She backed before his advance, an icy feeling in her stomach. The brick wall stopped her retreat and she realized her mistake as he put a hand on either side of her.

"You are a pretty little bit of calico, aren't you?" His face was so close she could feel his breath, smell the whiskey he'd imbibed. Her jaw tightened when his gaze dropped to her bosom.

Terror crept up her spine like a snake; no one else was in the jailhouse. She was alone with him here, just like the other time. Gritting her teeth, she put one hand on his big barrel chest and shoved him back. "Leave me alone."

He grinned. "I could arrange more comfortable quarters, good food. All you got to do is be nice to me."

"I'm quite comfortable here, thank you."

His watery blue eyes darkened. "Or I can make your life very difficult."

As if it wasn't difficult enough. She choked back a half-hysterical laugh. "Just leave me alone, Sheriff."

"No, I don't think so." He grabbed her hair, wrenched her head sideways, then bent and claimed her lips in a brutal kiss.

Her anger won over fear. Without thinking, she brought her knee up hard between his legs, pleased at the hoarse cry that came from him, even more pleased to be released. She spat on the floor to rid her mouth of his foul taste.

He was half bent over, his hands cupped around himself, and she just couldn't resist. Hauling back, she punched him, left, right, then hesitated. Two black eyes seemed barely adequate payment for that disgusting kiss.

His fist came out of nowhere, slamming her up alongside the jaw and sending her spinning backward into the hard brick wall. She pushed away, her shoulder aching from where it had made contact, and spun around, fists at the ready.

His eyes were already swelling and he squinted at

her. "You'll pay for that, you bitch. Oh, you'll pay and pay."

Not bothering to speak, she tilted up her chin. He only outweighed her by, oh, maybe a hundred pounds, had a bit of a reach on her and a few inches, maybe half a foot. Piece of cake, she assured herself, trying to make her eyes focus right.

She blocked his first punch, but the second got through and her teeth snapped together, her head slamming back against the wall and her legs, suddenly weak, dropping her down onto the cell floor.

She saw his hands reach for his trouser buttons, and kicked out with her feet. Weak, too weak. Oh, God, it was happening again, and there would be no Pa to rescue her.

One button, two.

Her breath jerked, and she curled her shaking hands into claws. It didn't take as much strength to scratch. She wouldn't give in—never.

"Sheriff, you in here?" A man's voice drifted back from the front of the jailhouse. She knew that voice. . . .

"I'll be out in a minute," Cluny yelled, frantically rebuttoning his trousers.

"So, there you are." Arnie, more welcome than rain in the desert, stood in front of the cell door. Janet blinked at him, felt her eyes sting with relieved tears.

He stroked his gray sideburns as he studied her with a frown. "Your prisoner seems to be a bit incapacitated, Sheriff," he said mildly.

Cluny huffed. "She went crazy when I tried to find out where her brother's hiding. Attacked me like a wildcat." He straightened his vest and stepped over to

288

the cell door. Walking a little bowlegged, Janet noted with pleasure.

The momentary pleasure died quickly when he turned back to send her a glare though puffy eyes that promised vengeance.

Chapter Twenty-one

Two days later Janet waited to be led to the jail wagon.
She washed as best she could and straightened her
gown. Darned if she would look like a tramp when
Cluny escorted her from town, even if she was going
in a jail wagon. She owed it to her students to give
them an example of dignity in the face of scorn.

Her smile was a rueful one, acknowledging the fool-
ishness of her pride. Really she felt like lying down
and crying her eyes out. Telling everyone she'd made
up her confession, begging someone to get her out of
this mess.

But she'd made the mistakes and now she would pay
for them. *Fair and square.* How she had changed this
winter. Pa always said fair and square was for fools.

Cluny marched into the cellblock and unlocked her
door. "C'mon, time to move you out. Trial's in two
days."

Good thing they had decided to hold her trial in
Sacramento rather than here. Here she'd probably get

lynched on the way to see the judge. Then again, some of the citizens—

Behind him, she saw Mrs. Perkins hovering near the door, and sent her a smile of gratitude. Ever since Arnie had stopped in, one townsperson or another had visited the sheriff, hanging around with questions, gossip, food. No one had come back to see her, which she'd understood. But they had kept Cluny from her, for which she would be forever grateful.

Unfortunately, her guardian angels would soon be behind her, and she'd be alone with him on the road to Sacramento. And she would fight again. A hopeless feeling ran through her at the knowledge that she might not survive this time.

He snapped the manacles shut around her wrists and yanked her forward. "Appears the town's come out to give you a send-off. They want to see the woman who stole their savings," he said with a grin. "Hope they don't have any rotten tomatoes."

Her head dropped, as did her heart. She so hoped they'd forgive her, that Dagger would forgive her. Instead they were here to send her off with curses.

As Cluny pushed her out onto the boardwalk, Janet took a deep breath of the bitterly cold air, then surveyed the gathered crowd. In the front, Maude Tucker stood, a bright red flash against the muted clothes behind. Beside her waited Mrs. Chappell, a basket dangling from one arm, but she wouldn't be giving Janet any pastries. Not anymore.

Arnie, arms crossed, stood between Doc Matson and Mr. Grotefend. Leaning against the ominous jail wagon, Bowie Blackthorne glared at the sheriff.

At the sight of the massive rancher, Cluny hesitated, pleasing Janet immensely.

Pulling her shawl around her more closely, she frowned. Almost the whole town was there, bunched together under the cold winter sun. No one smiled at her or greeted her, and she took a hurting breath. But at least they weren't throwing those rotten tomatoes Cluny had mentioned.

Across the street, a gawking mule skinner jerked back as a private coach barreled past. The buggy slowed in front of the jailhouse and stopped behind the jail wagon.

Richly appointed in gleaming brass and darkly painted trim, the coach was a sight to see. The driver jumped down and whipped open the door for a short man in a conservative suit. The passenger settled his top hat in place over a balding head and surveyed the crowd with a frown.

"It's the circuit judge." Maude's whisper was loud in the silence. "Judge Ripley. What's he doing here?"

The man's eyes fell on Janet and he looked her up and down. She raised her chin, pleased she'd taken the time to straighten up.

"This would be Miss Garret, I assume?" the judge asked Cluny.

"Uh, yessir. I was just getting ready to haul—uh, escort her to the capitol for her trial." Cluny set his jaw. "It was agreed that she'd be tried in Sacramento."

"Well, I arrived in time, then. I'm to be meeting the marsh—there he is now." The judge nodded his head toward the hotel and Janet turned. Her breath stopped.

What the heck had that lawman done now?

Dagger strolled across the street with his deceptively lazy gait, and beside him walked Clint.

Janet covered her mouth with both hands, stifling the impulse to scream at her little brother to run, run, run.

At her almost silent moan, Cluny glanced at her, then at Clint, and his eyes narrowed. "The young one looks a little like you, doesn't he?" he commented.

"Judge," the sheriff said, stepping forward and dragging Janet by the manacles. "That man—"

"This is Clint Garret," Dagger announced in a loud voice as the two men reached the boardwalk. "He's come to return the money he stole from Shasta. He's asking for mercy from the court for himself and his sister."

Return money? Ask for mercy? Janet gaped at her brother. Had the cold addled his brains?

Cluny's jaw dropped, the crowd gasped, then a murmur started up.

Tilting his head, the judge considered. "When you wired me, Dagger, I hadn't considered such an informal court, but I've conducted worse. Let's hear what the interested parties have to say."

"He can't get away with this," Cluny roared indignantly. "The Garret gang's been stealing for years. They've taken wagons of money."

Dagger stepped forward, jaw dangerously set. "The gang, yes. This boy here—don't be absurd. Does he look like a hard-bitten thief?"

The crowd turned to study Clint, and brief grins appeared. He looked like just what he was—a boy barely turned into a man, all skin and bones and scared spitless. Janet wanted to run over and give him a hug.

Cluny blustered for a moment until the judge frowned; then the sheriff turned and gave the manacles a savage jerk. "That's all very well for the boy, but what about this one? She's hardly a stripling."

"That's true." Dagger rubbed his face in thought. Putting one boot up onto a hitching rail, he faced the crowd. "When Bowie and I grew up, our mama and pa taught us right from wrong, raised us up to follow the same path they'd walked. I suspect the same is true for most of you."

Arnie nodded, and Janet saw others in the crowd do the same.

"So did Miss Janet here. Unfortunately, her pa, who I can say she loved with all her heart, set her feet on the wrong path. If the outlaw trail was how you were raised, all you knew, then how many of you would have had the courage to step off it and try to make a new life?"

Janet had trouble seeing through her teary eyes. He understood. He'd forgiven her. She could hear it in his voice, see it in the way he looked at her.

"When she came to us, she started to learn all the truths we teach our young'uns." A grin flashed across Dagger's face as his hand dropped onto Thomas's shoulder. "She even tried her hand at teaching a few morals herself."

Laughter blossomed at the grimace on Thomas's face.

"You all know how hard she worked for our youngsters, to make a place here. And it was probably harder for her than for any teacher we've had before."

Clint spoke then, his voice shaking a little. "I blackmailed her into robbing Hightown. She didn't want to do it. I'm ashamed of it now, but then I was just mad that she'd left me. She helped me rob the bank there—" that caused a grim murmur—"but then she insisted we give the money back."

More muttering. "She busted my nose to prove her point." Laughter.

Dagger folded his arms and waited. His gray eyes searched her face and seemed to caress her. Oh, she'd missed him.

Lucas Wilson stepped out from the crowd. "I say give her a chance, Judge. She saved my daughter's life. If she'd been only a meek little schoolmarm, my little girl would be dead."

"Yeah, give her a chance," shouted another voice.

Judge Ripley pulled at his lip, then looked at Clint. "Did you return all the money you stole here?"

Clint looked down, and Janet's heart sank.

"It's all here but . . . fifty dollars. I lost some money in a poker game the next day."

The judge's lips pulled down. "I'm afraid I can't dismiss the charges if the money's not all returned."

Not Clint. Janet stepped forward. "His half is returned. It's just my part that's short, so pardon him and sentence me to jail."

"Janet, no!" Clint cried, taking a step forward.

"That seems fair, being he's just a boy," the judge said. He waved his hand toward Cluny. "Why don't you put her back into her cell while we discuss this."

As Cluny dragged Janet back toward the jail, he whispered into her ear, "Looks like we'll be having a little party out on the trail tonight."

A cold chill went down her spine. The cell door clanged shut and Cluny stomped out, muttering.

Janet leaned against the cell door, the cold metal welcome against her hot face. What were they discussing out there? Cluny was a sneaky bastard. Judge

Ripley might still change his mind about Clint if Cluny worked on persuading him. She'd best be there to watch.

Pulling her lockpicks out of her hair, she let herself out of the cell. With a bitter smile, she paused long enough to open the manacles, too. They dropped with a metallic sound onto the floor and she kicked them into a corner.

The judge might be annoyed to see her loose, but what could they do to her—arrest her?

She slipped out of the jail and settled against the building next to Mr. Wilson. Not looking at her, he said, "I don't know; what do you think we should do? Hate locking her up like this."

"Oh." She choked back a giggle. "You could just let her go, I suppose."

He jerked away, looking at her for the first time. "You're out!"

Heads turned and Cluny saw her. "I locked the cell. Who let you out?" His bullet-shaped head swung from side to side.

"I let myself out, you idiot." She shook her head, thinking that lawmen seemed to get stupider every year. Then she saw Dagger's eyes crinkle in laughter. *There were a few exceptions, of course.*

The judge looked over at her. "I take it you could have left anytime?"

"Of course. But why would I leave? I *was* the one who turned myself in."

The judge frowned. "I do believe the sheriff reported that he tracked you down and took you prisoner up in the mountains."

The people who heard that laughed.

Puffed up with importance, Priscilla Malvern pushed

herself forward. "She turned herself in to him right here in town, and then she had to convince him that she was a Garret. He didn't want to believe her."

Other murmurs drifted up from the people. "That's right."

"I was there, too."

"I surely didn't like the way he manhandled her when he put the manacles on."

The short judge seemed to grow in inches as he stared down his long nose at the hapless Cluny. "You lied in your report."

In spite of the cold, a drop of sweat rolled down Cluny's face. "Listen, Judge, sir, I—"

"You're fired."

Judge Ripley was still frowning when he turned to Janet. "As for you, Miss Garret—"

Chin pushed out belligerently, Thomas stepped in front of him. "I got two dollars."

The child dropped several coins into the judge's hand. "I want Miss Janet back."

A stunned silence settled over the town, broken only by the whinny of an impatient horse down the street.

Then Gus Grotefend jerked at his vest and walked forward. "Here's five dollars."

Suddenly, everyone was jostling around the judge.

"We need a schoolteacher—here's another five."

"She got my girl off the roof."

"She taught my son not to be a bully."

"She brought my boy school lessons at home."

"She taught me to read."

Even the children came forward with their little amounts, and soon the judge had to ask for a sack to put the money in. "Stop," he announced. "The fifty dollars is all there."

He grinned and suddenly seemed like a human being. "Damned if I've ever been asked to conduct a trial in this fashion. You mountain people are as crazy as I've heard, but it's my pleasure to dismiss the charges against Clint and Janet Garret."

He gave them both stern looks. "You're free people now. Make your lives worthwhile."

Turning, the judge glanced at Dagger. "Blackthorne, you're as stubborn as a coon hound. I wasn't scheduled to visit Shasta for two more weeks."

Dagger slapped his shoulder and smiled. "All in a good cause, Judge. I've been needing a wife. Since you're here, you can perform the ceremony, too—if she agrees."

Dagger looked over at her, wicked humor and love mingling in his eyes. He opened his arms.

In one sneaky move, Janet shoved Cluny off the boardwalk into the watering trough and hurtled herself into Dagger's arms.

The crowd broke into laughter and cheers as Dagger pulled her tightly against him. Under her cheek, she could feel the hard, fast thud of his heart. He hadn't been nearly as calm as he looked.

He tipped up her chin and pressed a hard kiss against her lips, then murmured, "Miss Garret, will you marry me?"

She glanced at Susanna and Hannah, who were beaming like benevolent goddesses. Blade, beside them, nodded at her, his eyes gentle with forgiveness.

"Are you sure, Dagger?" she whispered. "I don't have a good—"

"I love you, woman," he growled. "Now say yes."

"Yes."

"She agrees," he announced, and then they were

surrounded by joyful people, patting her back, kissing her cheek, shaking Dagger's hand.

Janet smiled at everyone, her cheeks damp with tears. Her heart overflowed with emotions too big to encompass. A man who loved her, a town where she was wanted, a new life.

"You know, when Pa told you to go straight," Clint muttered in her ear, "he didn't tell you to marry the damn marshal."

She could only hold her lawman close and laugh.

Epilogue

Spring 1862

Like an irritable bear, the town of Shasta awoke in the spring.

The roads to the mountain mines were passable again; miners and supply wagons flowed into the area.

And the mail had come at last.

She studied the first letter.

Clint had written from Wyoming, a far piece from the Garrets' old stomping grounds. He was doing well, learning ranching, staying straight. He'd sent some money for the last fifty dollars, but she'd have to write him that she'd tried to pay already. No one would take her money. Apparently, people considered her freedom to be their wedding present to the marshal.

"C'mon, Janet, you're moving like molasses!" Thomas tugged at her hand.

As the sun glowed red over the western mountains, she followed the boy down the boardwalk past storekeepers closing up their stops and saloons that never closed.

She shoved open the door to the jailhouse, then tsked at the sight of the vacant room. "Well, shoot."

Thomas poked his head in. "He's not here."

She stepped back out and glanced around the busy street, impatiently tapping the second letter against her skirt. *Husbands. Seemed like they were never where you left them.*

"Hit him again!"

"Watch out!"

"Don't let Moose get you!" The noise of men shouting nearby grabbed her attention.

"Hear that, Thomas?" That exasperating man never could stay out of a fight. "I daresay that's where we'll find him."

They hurried across Main Street, ignoring greetings, dodging miners and drunks, pausing as mule trains and horses splashed past. Pushing through the raucous men gathered in front of the Miner's Saloon, Janet paused.

Up against three other men. Well, wasn't this just a fine to-do? Didn't he know how to count?

In the center of the crowd, Dagger sparred with a huge man who looked like some derelict just off the mountain. Two more stringy-haired, leather-wearing men attempted to land their own blows, but her marshal had no moss growing on him, she noticed with fond pride. He dodged them easily.

"They smell like something dead and rotted," Janet murmured.

Thomas wrinkled his nose in agreement and said, "That's big Moose. And his little brothers, Bull and Mule. They don't hit town much."

So far Dagger wasn't doing too badly. He kicked one man in the belly, punched the other and whirled back to engage the big one named Moose. Shouts of encouragement and enjoyment went up from the crowd.

Thomas eased a foot forward, balling up a small fist. "Can't we—"

"No, sugar. He told us last time that this was *his* job."

But then Mule grabbed a loose whiskey bottle and started to bring it down on Dagger's head.

Janet whipped out her derringer and fired.

The bottle shattered, glass spraying the combatants.

"That's *my* man," Janet instructed the shocked mountain men. "Don't damage him."

While the fools goggled at her, Dagger downed one, then another, before tossing a punch at the big one.

When Moose jumped back to avoid the blow, Thomas gleefully tripped him and Arnie thumped him with a board.

Standing alone, Dagger shook his head to clear his vision. Moose had landed a couple of hard ones early on in the fight, but if his addlepated wits were telling him right—

Looked like his lovely wife and the boy had lent a hand again. And now the entire town was helping out, too. He tried to ignore the warm feeling spreading through him as he watched the horrified mountain men try to contend with the populace of Shasta.

"Now just stay down." Arms crossed, Mrs. Perkins kicked at poor Bull. "If you get up, Mrs. Blackthorne will probably perforate your hide with that little gun of hers."

302

"Yeah," Ernie agreed. "She can be a mean one if you annoy the marshal."

Dagger snorted and took his mean wife by one arm. "Thought I told you to let me do my own work. Do I come and teach in your schoolhouse?"

She gave him the innocent look of an angel. "I am sorry, husband." She brushed at some dirt on his sleeve.

"Janet, I really—"

Ignoring him, she snatched the back of Thomas's coat and jerked the incautious boy away from an awakening Moose. "I have news and I didn't want to wait for you to finish your altercation."

"Want us to take 'em down to the jail, Marshal?" Ernie asked.

"Naw." Dagger glanced down. "I think they're done drinking for the day, right, men?"

Grumbling, Moose and Bull picked themselves out of the mud and hauled Mule to his feet. "What happened to having a little fun?" Bull asked. "Town's gone and got all civilized."

Dagger watched the trio stagger toward the livery.

With laughter, slaps on the back and congratulations to their marshal, Shasta's citizens scattered back to their businesses.

Shaking his head, Dagger turned to Janet. "You have news for me? What?"

Thomas bounced up and down at her side. He grabbed a bedraggled letter from her hand and handed it to Dagger. "Here! See what it says?"

Dagger didn't have time to read more than a word or two before Thomas blurted out, "No one wants me."

So the Louisiana relatives had finally written back.

A wave of anger tightened his muscles. Who wouldn't want this boy? But—"You sound mighty happy about your news."

When his dear wife suppressed a smile, Dagger frowned at her. "You look pleased, too. What have you two been hatching up?"

With an anxious look in his eyes, Thomas took Janet's hand. "Well, maybe . . . cuz no one wants me and I'm good at helping and—"

"We're keeping him," Janet announced.

Ah-hah. He studied her face, the soft lips compressed and firm, her eyes all sparkly, and a wave of love washed over him. How had he ever survived without her in his life?

Still . . . she might be the love of his life, but it wouldn't do to have her holding the reins. Not all the time. Dagger considered drawing this out, making the two of them work at convincing him, but then Thomas gave him such a beseeching look that the notion crumbled.

"Of course we'll keep him," Dagger stated. He ruffled Thomas's hair, recalling with pleasure the sight of him tripping Moose. Hell of a boy. "No question but he takes after us both. He's our boy, all right."

Thomas let out a high-pitched yell and hurtled into Dagger's arms, closely followed by Janet.

With a sigh of pure contentment, Dagger wrapped his arms around his family.

And as he hugged them, he felt the last lingering touch of loneliness waft off into the sunset forever.

Half Moon Ranch

Somewhere in the lush grasslands of the Texas hill country is a place where the sun once shone on love and prosperity, while the night hid murder and mistrust. There, three brothers and a sister fight to hold their family together, struggle to keep their ranch solvent, while they await the return of the one person who can shed light on the secrets of the past.

From the bestselling authors
who brought you the *Secret Fires* series comes . . .

___ *HUNTER'S MOON* by Bobbi Smith   7/03   5155-9 $6.99/$8.99

___ *RENEGADE MOON* by Elaine Barbieri   7/03   5178-8 $6.99/$8.99

___ *MOON RACER* by Constance O'Banyon   8/03   5188-5 $6.99/$8.99

___ *DARK OF THE MOON* by Evelyn Rogers   9/03   5214-8 $6.99/$8.99

Dorchester Publishing Co., Inc.
P.O. Box 6640
Wayne, PA 19087-8640
Please add $2.50 for shipping and handling for the first book and $.75 for each book thereafter. NY and PA residents, please add appropriate sales tax. No cash, stamps, or C.O.D.s. Prices and availability subject to change.
Canadian orders require $2.00 extra postage and must be paid in U.S. dollars through a U.S. banking facility.

Name_____
Address_____
City_____ State_____ Zip_____
E-mail_____
I have enclosed $_____ in payment for the checked book(s).
Payment <u>must</u> accompany all orders. ___ Check here for a free catalog.

CHECK OUT OUR WEBSITE! www.dorchesterpub.com

HANNAH'S VOW
PAM CROOKS

Four years in prison have made Quinn Landry a man who thinks nothing of using a young nun as a shield in a daring bid for freedom. But he has kidnapped no meek sister. Hannah Benning fashions a master key from her rosary with a skill of a common criminal, poses as his spouse with the poise of a con artist, and saves his life twice in as many days. Enthralled by his beautiful savior, the outlaw knows that captor has become captive. Quinn swears to protect Hannah no matter the cost—and to discover the secrets that lie beneath her habit. His eyes tell him he has found not a lady of the cloth, but a woman of the world; not a thief, but a lover. His heart tells him they have not a false marriage but the best of all unions—one built on love.

WYOMING
Wildfire

Leigh Greenwood

With the inheritance of half her uncle's Wyoming spread, Sybil Cameron feels she's gained her independence at last. Then she meeets her partner, Burch Randall—a man who believes a woman has no business running a ranch. She vows to keep her cool no matter what. Yet as Burch's muscular arms close around her, a deliciously hot feeling courses through her body.

To Burch, Sybil is a wild filly: spirited, headstrong, and in need of a man's brand. But he soon learns this is one woman not to be tamed. In fact, he finds he glories in her passionate abandon, revels in her raw courage, and wants only to take her and set the prairie ablaze in a Wyoming wildfire.

- -

CHASE THE WIND
CINDY HOLBY

From the moment he sets eyes on Faith, Ian Duncan knows she is the only girl for him. But her unbreakable betrothal to his employer's vicious son forces him to steal his love away on the very eve of her marriage. Faith and Ian are married clandestinely, their only possessions a magnificent horse, a family Bible, a wedding-ring quilt and their unshakable belief in each other. While their homestead waits to be carved out of the Iowa wilderness, Faith presents Ian with the most precious gift of all: a son and a daughter, born of the winter snows into the spring of their lives. The golden years are still ahead, their dream is coming true, but this is just the beginning. . . .

AFTER THE ASHES
CHERYL HOWE

A stagecoach robbery is the spark that sets fire to Lorelei Sullivan's plan for the future. She and her brother moved to New Mexico Territory to escape the past, to ranch, but Corey has destroyed all hope of that. Lawmen now want him—and Lorelei won't see the boy hang.

Yet defying the law places her between two men she can't trust: her sibling and Christopher Braddock, who is her brother's one shot at redemption—a hard, silent man who lights a fire inside her. And as his kiss fans the flames of desire, Lorelei wonders whether she will be consumed by this inferno or rise reborn from its ashes.

Bobbi Smith

SECRET FIRES

The Half Breed

In the midst of the vast, windswept Texas plains stands a ranch wrested from the wilderness with blood, sweat and tears. It is the shining legacy of Thomas McBride to his five living heirs. But along with the fertile acres and herds of cattle, each will inherit a history of scandal, lies and hidden lust that threatens to burn out of control.

Chase knows he has no legitimate claim to the Circle M. After all, his father made it painfully clear he wants nothing to do with his bastard son or the Comanche girl he once took to his bed. But Chase has his own reasons for answering Tom McBride's deathbed summons. He has a job to do as a Texas Ranger, and a woman to protect—a woman whose sweet innocence gives him new faith that love born in the darkest night can face the dawn of all his tomorrows.

___4853-1 $5.99 US/$6.99 CAN

Lionheart
Connie Mason

Lionheart has been ordered to take Cragdon Castle, but the slim young warrior on the pure white steed leads the defending forces with a skill and daring that challenges his own prowess. No man can defeat the renowned Lionheart; he will soon have the White Knight beneath his sword and at his mercy.

But storming through the portcullis, Lionheart finds no trace of his mysterious foe. Instead a beautiful maiden awaits him, and a different battle is joined. She will bathe him, she will bed him; he will take his fill of her. But his heart is taken hostage by an opponent with more power than any mere man can possess—the power of love.
